Lora Leigh

Marly's
CHOICE

ELLORA'S CAVE
ROMANTICA PUBLISHING

An Ellora's Cave Romantica Publication

www.ellorascave.com

Marly's Choice

ISBN 1843603314, 9781843606147
ALL RIGHTS RESERVED.
Marly's Choice Copyright © 2002 Lora Leigh
Cover art by Syneca

This book printed in the U.S.A. by Jasmine–Jade Enterprises, LLC.

Electronic book Publication 2002
Trade paperback Publication June 2003

Also by Lora Leigh

✌

About the Author

ာ

Lora Leigh is a wife and mother living in Kentucky. She dreams in bright, vivid images of the characters intent on taking over her writing life, and fights a constant battle to put them on the hard drive of her computer before they can disappear as fast as they appeared.

Lora's family and her writing life co-exist, if not in harmony, in relative peace with each other. An understanding husband is the key to late nights with difficult scenes, and stubborn characters. His insights into human nature and the workings of the male psyche provide her hours of laughter, and innumerable romantic ideas that she works tirelessly to put into effect.

Lora Leigh welcomes comments from readers. You can find her websites and email addresses on their author bio page at www.ellorascave.com.

Tell Us What You Think

We appreciate hearing reader opinions about our books. You can email us at Comments@EllorasCave.com.

MARLY'S CHOICE

ဆ

Chapter One

෨

Marly's eyes opened slowly, blinking in awareness that he watched her. Cade stood beside her bed, his body hard and aroused, his eyes nearly black as he stared at her naked body. Those eyes focused between her thighs, where her fingers moved slowly on her smooth flesh, the small bud of her clit clearly visible as she massaged it sensuously.

Her breath halted in her throat. He stood naked, his erection long and thick, one hand massaging it with slow, even strokes, his lashes lowered over the lust filled look in his eyes. Breathing harshly, Marly watched him lower himself beside her. She shook, recognizing the dream, but needing him so badly, she could only pray that this time, this time it was real.

He stretched out on his side, one arm going beneath her neck, bracing himself on his elbow, his other hand touching her cheek gently. His body was hot and vibrant, heating her blood, her passion.

"Do you know how beautiful you are, Marly?" he whispered, his voice low and rough, his head lowering to caress the corner of her lips with a soft, heated touch.

Marly could only whimper. She couldn't answer him. She didn't have the breath to.

Then she didn't have the chance. His lips moved over hers, parting them. His tongue licked sensually at her lips, sliding into her mouth, taking her in a kiss so heated it

Caused every nerve in her body to zing to life.

She arched against the hand that moved to her stomach. Hard and wide, warm and work-calloused, moving over her skin, sliding slow and sure to her heaving breasts. Her arms went to his shoulders as she turned to him. She wanted to rub against him. To luxuriate in the warmth and maleness pressed so intimately against her body. The *heated length of his shaft lay along her hip, searing her with the erotic touch of the silk-encased steel.*

"I've stayed away as long as I could," he growled against her lips, his hand palming her breast, his fingers rasping over her nipple, making her cry out at the pleasure. "As long as I could, Marly. I have to have you now."

His head lowered, his mouth covering the tip of a breast, drawing it into the heated warmth, suckling in strong, rhythmic motions at her swollen flesh. His tongue flayed the tender tip with slow, hot licks, his mouth drawing on her with all the sexually charged intent in his hard body.

"So beautiful." He moved over her, pushing her onto her back, his lips roaming from one breast to the next.

He licked and sucked. His hands pushed the mounds together, making the hard points quicker to access, making Marly arch desperately against him, needing more. She had known it would be like this. Mind destroying when he took her into his arms. Driving her crazy with the sensual demands he would make of her.

He moved lower…his lips sipping from the skin of her abdomen, his body moving further toward her aching center. Fiery need flayed her body, destroying her, rebuilding her. Her breathing harsh, her body humming, Marly watched Cade spread her legs, his eyes centered between her thighs, his lips sensually full. She whimpered. His hands, large and work roughened, ran along her thighs, his fingers moving slowly to her swollen, wet flesh. Her entire body ached, pulsed, begged for possession.

"I'm going to lick every drop of cream from your body, Marly," his voice, dark and rough, feathered over her. "Starting now."

His head lowered, and Marly cried out as his tongue swiped through her pouting flesh. She cried out moments later, feeling him circle her hard clit with torturously slow movements. Her hips arched to him, her thighs quivering with tension, the need to climax, to sate the hunger rising in her body, overwhelming her senses. His fingers moved to the soft lips, pulling them apart gently, his greedy tongue moving lower to catch the flood of juices spilling from her body. He lapped at her, his mouth sucked at her, his tongue licking her, *drawing the sweetness into his mouth, driving her to the brink of insanity.*

"I can't stand it," she whispered, her hands tangling in his hair. "Please, Cade, please take me."

"Not so fast, Marly." His hand pressed against her stomach, holding her to the bed. "I've only begun. You were warned. Weren't you warned about what I would want from you?"

His expression was tight and hard, his eyes nearly black when he raised his head, staring at her from between her splayed thighs. She shuddered, suddenly fearful. She had prepared herself, had made certain she could take what he would need, but now she wasn't so sure.

She felt his fingers spreading the thick essence around her vagina, running slowly, teasingly to the tight little hole, lower. She jerked as his finger dipped in, then retreated, spreading more of her lubrication, preparing her. With each pass, his finger would slip further inside her anus. Marly fought to relax against the building tension of her own out-of-control desires.

Her thighs tightened, her moans keening whimpers in the silence of the bedroom as he inserted first one, then two fingers into her. He moved slowly, stretching the small opening as his mouth continued to sip from her velvety inner lips, his tongue stroking her into an inferno of need while his fingers stretched her nether hole with deep, slow thrusts. Dipping out, drawing more of her natural lubrication as it pulsed from her cunt and spreading it to the tight little hole he was preparing with sensual, slow thrusts of his fingers.

"I want you to come for me." His voice sounded raw and sensual. He whispered the words against her straining clit, ignoring the grinding motions of her hips, the plea in her cries. "I want you to scream for me, Marly. Scream..."

His fingers thrust deep and hard, his tongue spearing into the gripping channel of her vagina. She was close, so close. She arched into him, her breathing suspended, her throat closed against the scream building.

"No scream, no climax." The dream shattered.

Marly's eyes flew open on a cry of protest, and silence greeted her. An empty room, an empty bed, an empty body. Her thighs quivered from her fight for release. Her breasts were swollen and throbbing, the nipples aching and hard. She whimpered in distress, turning into her pillow, her body curling into a tortured ball. She needed him. God help her, she needed him so bad she knew it would kill her.

Her body ached and pulsed in time to the harsh thump of her blood through her veins, her fingers curling into the mattress, her eyes closed tight on the building fever in her body. He was her dream, her only fantasy, and Marly knew she would never survive if he didn't touch her soon. Cade. Her Cade.

She had loved him forever. Since she was fourteen, thrown on him by her mother, his stepsister, in a desperate bid to hide Marly from her stepfather, Jack Jennings. He had been a deviant pervert intent on molesting her at every chance. When her mother, Annie, saw Jack's obsession with Marly, she had tried to leave, and to hide. But he kept finding her, and each time he had hurt Marly worse. Finally, Annie had given up. She had brought Marly to the only place she could think of where she would be safe, then Annie had disappeared, hoping to draw Jack away.

Marly missed her mother. It had been six years since she had seen her, and she wondered daily what had happened to her. But she had been right, bringing Marly to the ranch. Cade and his brothers protected her, even if their father hadn't.

But Joe was dead now. His burial the next day would end his reign of misery. The old bastard had lived to hurt anyone he could. He had finally died in his own bed, cursing Cade, and the miserable luck that had him tied to the small county of Madison, Texas.

She rolled over on the bed, burying her head in the pillows, trying to find sleep again. She wished she could sneak into Cade's bed, rub herself against him, feel him hard and hot as he made love to her. She suppressed her groan, thinking of the last two years of preparation, the lengths she had gone to, the acts she had committed.

Technically, she was still a virgin. The hymen was still present, but Marly knew technicalities didn't always count. She was determined to get Cade's attention, and keep it. She couldn't do that if she was as pure as snow. And she sure as hell wasn't pure anymore. Now, she was just horny and impatient, and very nearly out of control.

She was naked and willing. Her lips glistened with moisture, swollen and full from his kisses, her deep blue eyes were dark and glittering with need. Cade could feel his erection throbbing with need, pulsing with demand.

He watched, his breathing harsh, overly loud in the silence of the bedroom as she slowly went to her knees before him. Long, long black curls tangled in his hands as moist, heated lips closed over the head of his cock. He growled fiercely as lightning raced up the thick length of his flesh and seared his belly. His scrotum tightened painfully, his erection throbbed with the pent up need to spew itself into the tight, waiting depths of her mouth.

"Suck it," he whispered, his voice sounding demented even to his own ears. "Suck it deeper, Marly."

He was thrusting slowly into her mouth, groaning at the suckling sounds she made, at the tightening of his body. He wanted it to last forever. He wanted the pleasure to never end. It was incredible, her mouth so tight and hot, her tongue licking over him, a wash of searing, agonizing joy.

He looked down at her, watching as her mouth tightened on him, barely taking half his length, her mouth stretched over his flesh, her cheeks hollowing as she drew on him. She wanted it. She wanted him thrusting into her until he released every drop of his seed into her waiting mouth. She was hungry for it. Hungry for him.

He thrust harder, faster, feeling the moan that came from her throat, echoing along his shaft. It made his body shudder. Her hands were on his scrotum now, tightening, stroking him, her mouth suckling him until he was crazy to release.

"I'm going to come —" he thrust harder against her mouth, feeling the moist, heated motions increasing as her tongue flickered over his flesh. "I'm going to come, Marly."

He thrust harder, his breathing ragged, harsh. Then his hands tightened in her hair, dragging her mouth further over him, thrusting as far as the shallow depths of her mouth would allow before spewing his load down her throat. Spurt after spurt of hot sperm shot from the tip of his erection as she sucked harder, faster, determined to drain ever drop of his seed from his body…

Cade came awake with a ragged cry, his hand clenched over his bursting cock as he ejaculated harshly to his own stroking caress. Bitterness yawned inside him as the dream dissipated, and he realized she wasn't really there. Her hot mouth hadn't actually been stroking him, receiving his harsh thrusts as he shot his release into it. Her moans hadn't caressed his flesh; her body hadn't been naked and willing before him.

He cursed harshly, rising slowly from the bed and walking wearily to the bathroom. He washed his hands quickly, then his still-hard cock. When every last trace of his humiliating release was gone, he sighed deeply and stared into the mirror above the sink.

He looked the same as he always had. The same gray eyes, the same overly long black hair and tanned features. But he knew what lurked just beneath the surface. The monster he fought on a daily basis.

Cade knew he shouldn't have drunk the night before. Knew he shouldn't have sneaked into Marly's room and watched her sleeping. If he had left her alone, if he had just stayed away from her, he wouldn't be tormented now. But he had been unable to. He had slipped silently into the connecting bedroom, standing in shock at the foot of her bed, unable to believe what his eyes were seeing in the light of the low lamp she still refused to sleep without.

The blankets covered only her midriff. She had kicked them clear of her hips and thighs, and her full thrusting breasts. Her nipples had been hard, elongated and pointed, begging him to taste them. And between her thighs—he swallowed harshly. The flesh of her mound was waxed clean and bare. Not a wisp of a hair remained, and it had glistened.

Thick and rich, her juices had coated her flesh. He had been unable to resist, unable to stop himself. Drawing nearer he had leaned down, his fingers running through the sweet glaze of desire. Smothering a groan of need, he had brought his fingers to his mouth.

He could still taste her on his lips. Sweet, addicting. Like the lightest fruit, and he craved more. He didn't know how he forced himself away from her. Didn't know how he managed to keep from sinking his hard cock into her over and over again until they both screamed out in climax. But he had. He had retreated to his own room, his heart beating fiercely, his loins burning with need. He needed her. He needed her too damned much, and she was the one woman he couldn't have.

Shaking his head, he found he couldn't hold his own gaze in the mirror. He was as perverted as his father. As sexually deviant as the monster who had tried to take her when she was but a child. Not much better than the demon of his own

Nightmares. He had raised her, loved her, but he had always known she wasn't a blood relation. As she grew, that thought had always been in the back of his mind, and as she got older, it had tormented him more often.

God above, when had she begun waxing? Why had she? It was the one thing guaranteed to make him harder than anything else could. Guaranteed to make his mouth water, his need to taste her all the more imperative. Slick, wet flesh. Glistening with the dew of her desire. Her taste sweet and fresh. He was dying. Slowly, surely, a dead man expiring from need.

Chapter Two

ಬ

Grandpa Joe was finally dead. Marly stared out the limo window as they drove away from the cemetery, studying Cade's fiercely controlled expression in the glass. The savage features of his face, with its high cheekbones, brooding black-lashed eyes, and the sharp line of his nose. But his lips were softer when he wasn't pulling them tight like that. The lower curve just slightly fuller, and often smiling when he was with her. But he wasn't smiling today. He was distant, silent. He had been ever since Grandpa Joe's death. He didn't talk to anyone, least of all Marly. He had shut her and everyone else out.

Marly knew Grandpa Joe's death would affect him. She had left school as soon as she had learned of his death, but she hadn't expected this. Grandpa Joe hadn't exactly treated any of his children with love and affection. Marly especially had been exempt from his good will. But that had always suited her, because she had never cared much for him either.

Marly sighed, then turned her gaze to the others in the car with them. His brothers, Sam and Brock, were silent. They were twins and only two years younger than Cade, though they weren't nearly as hard as their older brother.

Sam and Brock had light blue eyes, and their hair was just as black and silky as Cade's. Their faces weren't as savagely hewn though. They were nearly as tall as their brother, with the same broad-shouldered, slim-hipped build that characterized the August males. They could have been triplets, their looks were so similar.

They were silent now, too, but more because Cade was quiet than out of reflection. Grandpa Joe had not been the nicest person in the world. Often, he was taunting, his tongue cutting like a knife. Cade seemed to be the only one capable of ignoring him. Marly had just stayed away from him as much as possible. It seemed her very presence was enough to set him off.

Sitting on the other side of the boys was her friend, Greg James. He had driven from Dallas with her the morning before to keep her company. Greg was nearly as tall as Cade's six feet four inches, but he wasn't nearly as comfortable with his height. He stooped his shoulders often to hide it, and complained regularly that he would be a string bean all his life. He wasn't a jock, and often bemoaned that fact.

Greg had thick, dark blond hair and hazel green eyes. He wore glasses in thin wire frames, and had more of an academic, rather than forceful male, demeanor. Marly thought he was the nicest guy she knew. He was quiet and considerate, and never made the crude advances that the other young men at school did. He was talkative once you got past the shyness, and had an amazing depth of loyalty. It was nearly as deep as that of Cade and his brothers. But, he was extremely uncomfortable right now. As though Cade's tension reached out across the seats and smothered him. As she thought about it, Marly didn't doubt it. Cade was more than intimidating, but usually the attitude didn't bleed over to her or to company. Until Grandpa Joe's death. Now he was hardly speaking to her. And that hurt Marly more than anything. In the eight years she had lived with him, Cade had never distanced himself from her this way.

Breathing deeply, Marly crossed her legs and went back to staring out the window. She smiled slightly as Sam made some comment to Brock. The sight of her straight, perfect teeth flashed in the image created in the window. It still amazed her how determined Cade had been that she not be ridiculed for her teeth when she was a child. It had been their first trip out of the house. The second had been for new clothes. Cade had always been there for her, no matter what. Fixing childhood aches, and soothing bitter tears.

Cade wasn't going to allow her to help him though, no matter how much he might need her now. But he was letting her sit next to him, crowding her against the door when there was plenty of seat for him to sit in. His thigh rubbed hers, and if she wanted, she could lay her head on his broad shoulder.

"Hey Munchkin, where did you get those legs?" Sam was looking at her legs as he spoke, acting as though he hadn't seen them before, shocking her from her thoughts.

His light blue gaze was curious, and frankly admiring as it traveled along her foot to where her thighs disappeared beneath the skirt.

Marly looked down frowning, wondering what was wrong. Surely she hadn't already snagged the new silk stockings?

"What's wrong with my legs?" she asked him, turning one this way and that to see what he was talking about.

"Hell, you finally grew some," he teased. "I hadn't noticed before. Damn fine ones too."

Marly looked up at him with the intention of blasting him, but seeing the near desperation in his eyes, she grinned instead. Cade's silences affected the other two men as well as they did her.

"You're as silly as ever, Sam." She shook her head. And he was. Sam was their prankster, and everyone loved him. Even at twenty-eight, he hadn't fully matured and stated often that he did not intend to ever do so.

"Marly has the prettiest legs in college." Greg spoke up earnestly then, as he cast Marly a shy look. His admiration only earned him one of Cade's fierce glares.

The look was darker than any Marly could remember seeing in a while. His eyes narrowed, his jaw jutting forward in a challenging motion. She was shocked. She had received compliments often in his presence over the years. Never before had he reacted so strongly to them.

"Marly's legs are not up for discussion," he informed them all darkly, the gray in his eyes darkening dangerously.

Sam gave Brock a knowing look. The other brother only shook his head as Marly looked on in confusion. She had no idea what kind of problem those two had.

Silence lapsed once again. An uncomfortable, heavy silence. You didn't mess with Cade when his voice got dangerous like that. Even Marly was extremely careful, for the most part. Shrugging, she crossed her legs, adjusting the hem of her short skirt as she did so to cover her thighs and staring out the window once again.

She saw him glance at her legs as his image reflected in the dark, tinted glass. His frown became darker. Then his gaze rose, taking in the long French braid of her hair, and her own refection as she stared back at him. Her eyes were wide, her lips parted, and Marly knew she looked as entranced by him as she always was. Cade's dark good looks, and muscular body had always taken her breath.

"That skirt is too short, Marly," he told her, his voice still dark and deadly. "I thought I just forwarded you enough money for new clothes?"

"This is new, Cade," she told him as she turned back to him, facing his wrath directly. "Shorter skirts are in style."

The thigh high, navy blue skirt, and matching jacket-style blouse was one of her favorites. Matching heels accompanied the outfit, and lifted her several inches taller than her normal five foot four inches.

"It barely covers your ass," he bit out.

Marly flushed as Greg's expression now reflected astonishment.

"Ignore him Greg, he never really bites. He just likes to bark a lot. Sort of like the junk yard dog you talk about all the time." Marly ignored the muffled laughs from the other two men, as well as the anger that lit Cade's eyes.

"Uh—umm—the dog bites too, Marly," Greg told her warningly as he glanced in apprehension at Cade. "Really hard."

"Well, Cade won't bite you, Greg. And if he dares try to bite me, then he just might find out I bite back." She shot him a fierce glare. "So stop trying to intimidate me and my friends, Cade."

Cade arched one black brow as the gray in his eyes shifted, like thunderclouds moving into alignment. It made her nervous when they did that, made her want to run and hide. But she was determined not to run any longer.

"I never try at anything, Marly," he reminded her darkly, his smile all teeth and no warmth. "You would do well to remember that. If I wanted to intimidate you, I would succeed."

"I didn't say you couldn't," she replied sweetly, "I'm merely telling you to stop."

He watched her curiously now, as though her newfound sass intrigued him.

"Damn, Marly's getting teeth," Sam murmured, earning him his own 'Cade' glare. "Sorry Cade." He shrugged, but Marly caught the careful control of his grin.

Silence descended once again. It was uncomfortable, suffocating.

"I'm sorry I wasn't here before yesterday, Cade," she told him softly; afraid that was the reason he was angry with her. He had been unable to get hold of her. She and several of her friends were at Greg's that night, studying for a test. She hadn't learned of Grandpa Joe's death until the next morning.

"There was nothing you could have done." He shook his head.

"I could have been here for you." She laid her hand on his arm. "I would have been."

He looked down at her hand lying on his muscular arm as though surprised she had touched him.

"The will was read the night before you returned home," Cade informed her suddenly. "I'm sorry, but Joe never got around to changing it—"

"I never expected him to leave me anything." Marly moved her hand back at his cold tone. "He hadn't liked me from day one. So it doesn't matter."

It merely reaffirmed what she knew. Grandpa Joe had truly hated her. Hated her so much, that he was determined that nothing he had would go to the little waif he had taken in. Sometimes, she wondered why he had done so at all.

"It wasn't dislike," Cade began.

"No, it was hatred," Marly rebutted. "And there's no sense in us arguing over it now that he's gone. I didn't want anything he had. I want nothing you have. That's why I'm going to college, to learn how to provide for myself."

Cade sighed.

"You'll always be taken care of Marly, I've ensured that," he told her softly. "You won't have to struggle."

"Then you can unensure it," she told him calmly. "Because I don't want it, Cade."

Greg was practically gaping at them now, drawing Cade's fierce look once again. He dropped his gaze, but his brown eyes were still rounded with surprise.

"I could have sent the limo," Cade muttered, and she knew he was talking about her decision to bring Greg. Marly frowned at his rude behavior. She had never known Cade to act so surly, so hard to get along with.

"So you could have. But I didn't want to be alone Cade, and no one was offering to come after me."

That had hurt her. Marie, their former housekeeper, and now sometimes cook, had been the one who had informed her of Grandpa Joe's death, Cade had been unable to even place the second call, or leave a message in her apartment. She knew he would have been busy. But she also knew he would have been considerate enough to do it for Sam and Brock.

"If you had asked, one of us would have," he told her quietly, glancing at her in surprise.

"Had I been offered, I may have taken you up on it," she snapped back. "But I wasn't, and I didn't want to ride alone. Greg kindly offered to come with me."

Marly smiled sweetly at Greg in thankfulness. She watched in amazement as his chest seemed to puff out two extra inches. What the hell was up with this? Evidently, Cade saw it too, if his look of disgust was anything to go by. Sam barely contained his mirth as she glanced at him, frowning. Brock, as always, was quiet, but when his glance met hers, Marly saw the edge of amusement in it.

Marly shook her head at them all. The moon phases must be really out of whack today, she thought. Every man she had met with seemed to act like they had rocks for brains. It was disconcerting to say the least.

* * * * *

Cade didn't know why he was so furious with Marly. It wasn't her fault that the old man had a nasty, perverted mind, or that he was a depraved monster. That he had seen emotions and needs in Cade that couldn't, shouldn't be there. It wasn't her fault that her legs were gorgeous, and any man with eyes in his head would be more than impressed. It wasn't her fault he could barely control his own body's response to her, or the swift hardening of flesh between his thighs every time he saw her.

She had been raised as his niece. She was growing up whether he wanted to admit to it or not. She had likely already had sex, most girls her age had. Cade wanted to clench his fists at that thought, and barely restrained the need. She may even be having sex with the little punk sitting across from him.

Cade stared at the boy, not caring as that narrow face paled and the hazel eyes widened behind the lenses of the glasses. Greg swallowed tight and hard, giving Cade a measure of satisfaction.

"Please, Cade—" Marly's voice wrapped around his fury, pleading, desperate.

Biting back an oath, Cade stared resolutely into the tinted glass that separated the driver from the family. He was in a lousy mood and he knew it. He wasn't fit company for man or horse, and he should have driven himself to the cemetery alone. But Marly was riding with the family, and he was damned if he hadn't missed her this past year and a half since she started college.

She only came home infrequently, despite the short distance to Dallas. Christmas, Easter and birthdays. Three weeks total if you added it, and he hated it. The house was so still, so silent without her laughter, or her girlish tantrums. No more Marly sneaking into his study at night when nightmares plagued her to sleep on the couch while he worked. He wondered who soothed the nightmares now. His gaze sliced to the James boy, but his head was lowered as he stared in fascination at a loose thread on his jacket. The little jerk.

Cade hadn't expected her to arrive with a friend. And he sure as hell hadn't expected a male friend, considering how wary she was of men. She always had been, since her stepfather, and her Grandpa Joe.

Cade's teeth gritted with renewed fury. She carried a scar on her leg from the first and only whipping she had ever received in his house. A whipping Joe had administered that first month Marly had lived with them. Cade would never forget his horror that day when Marie had run screaming to the barn that Mister Joe was whipping Miss Marly. Oh God, Mr. Cade, she had screamed, he's gonna kill her.

Cade had rushed to the house, horrified to see his father beating the tiny girl with a leather strap. Joe had been enraged, furious, demented with anger. Cade had nearly killed him that day.

He had whipped her when he overheard her telling Marie that some little boy at school had attempted to kiss her. An innocent kiss on the cheek by a child with a crush on her, and Marly had paid in a way that left her unable to attend school for two weeks, until the deep bruises and lacerations on her legs and buttocks healed.

"Cade?" Her worried voice interrupted his thoughts, her soft hand on his arm made his skin heat. "Are you okay?"

He covered her hand slowly as his head turned and he gazed into the deep pools of those mysterious blue eyes. She drew him in, her innocence and lack of guile soothing the raging beast in his soul. How in the name of God would he survive when she left again?

"I'm fine, honey," he sighed, his hand covering hers, holding it close to him when she would have moved it. "Just thoughtful. I'm sorry I've been such a grouch."

Her head went to his shoulder, strands of riotous curls falling over his chest where they had escaped from her braid. He laid his cheek against her silken hair and breathed her scent in deeply.

"It's okay, Cade. I understand." It wasn't a little girl's voice anymore. A child years younger than her actual age as she had been when she came to them.

The voice was sweet and lyrical. A woman's voice, and he knew from watching that damned James boy what it did to the male race to hear the sexy sound.

"I've missed you, Munchkin." He sighed against her hair, feeling a sense of warmth replacing the cold knot of fury that had filled him.

"I've missed you too, Cade." There was a note of regret in her voice. A sigh of wanting that he didn't want to delve into too closely.

Stretching his arm behind her, he pulled her close to his chest as the limo moved towards the ranch. The cemetery Joe had wanted to be laid in was hours from the ranch, and completely disconnected from it. Joe had no friends; no family laid to rest in that hallowed ground. He had wanted nothing to do with the ranch at his death, having hated it so much during his life.

Marly's hand was laid at his chest now, just below her head. Trusting, warm, she lay against him, a fragile weight as cherished to him as any could be. He couldn't imagine never having her in his life, not needing to hold her, to be assured she was okay. She was still tiny, barely five four to his six four. She was slender and light, with a thick mass of black curls that flowed past her shoulder blades and very nearly to her hips. She didn't cut it because he loved it so much. She had sworn over the years that if it weren't for Cade, she would have shaved her head bald.

And he did love her hair. When she was little, Cade had brushed and braided it every day until she was sixteen and started getting fussier with her it. Even then, though, there were times she would ask him to brush her hair. Many times when she sought him out in his study deep in the night, she would carry the silver brush he had bought her. She would lay it on the table beside the couch, and he would come to her and brush her hair until she could sleep.

And on that couch, she would sleep until he went to bed. Then he would carry her to her own room, tuck her into the lacy canopied bed and kiss her cheek before going to his own room. The last time he had done so had been the night before she left for college. The nightmares had been bad that week.

"I want to stay home a while," she whispered now against his chest. "Spring break starts tomorrow, and I thought I'd just stay on until school starts back."

She had been spending the breaks studying, pushing herself through summer and holidays in her studies.

"Stay home with us then, honey," he answered her, ignoring Sam and Brock as they watched them quizzically. "You can let your friend take your truck back, and I'll drive you back to school when you need to return."

"No, Greg needs a break too." She yawned as his arms tightened against her. "We're both gonna stay. Do you care?"

Cade moved his gaze slowly to the suddenly nervous Greg James.

"Th—th—that's okay, Marly," Greg stammered. "Really. Fine. I can go back."

"Absolutely not." Marly shook her head against Cade's chest. "I remember how excited you were about spending the week here. We'll stay and just laze around and enjoy ourselves. Besides, you know you don't want to return to your sister's house."

Cade read a thread of anger in Marly's comment. The boy just shrugged and looked at Cade beseechingly. Dammit, did all kids have that look in their eye, that plea for understanding when faced with Marly's resolve?

"You're welcome to stay, Greg." Cade wasn't about to incite Marly and cause her to move from his hold.

It had been too long since she had let him hold her. He didn't want the boy there. Didn't want to know if his sweet, innocent Marly was sleeping with such an incompetent youth, but he would allow the visit to keep his tenuous hold on her now.

"Thank you." There was a vein of regret, of deeply laced loneliness in the boy's voice.

Dammit, Cade thought, another kid was the last thing he needed right now. Marly made him crazy enough. She didn't need help. He didn't need someone else helping her to push him over the edge. She was doing just fine all on her own.

Chapter Three

ജ

Dawn was barely streaking across the horizon the next morning when Marly ventured from her room and headed for the kitchen. Cade would most likely be up and gone already, but she knew he always made a fresh pot of coffee before leaving the house for Sam and Brock. It was a cup of the strong, heady brew she was after.

Still dressed in the big shirt and thick heavy socks she had stolen from Cade the day before, she padded drowsily into the room. The socks dwarfed her small feet, but kept them warm and snug. The shirt fell almost to her knees, the soft tan cotton covering her well, and making her feel closer to Cade somehow. She rarely slept in anything other than his shirts.

"I was wondering what happened to that shirt. Did you know it was one of my favorites, Marly?" Cade's amused voice had her stopping short, her gaze going to the corner of the room where Cade sat at the round kitchen table.

He was hunched over a steaming cup of coffee, the crumbs of his breakfast in a plate before him as he watched her. His eyes were light, amused; his lips tilted in a sort of half smile that made her heart beat hard and fast.

"Figured you would have already been out working." She hunched her shoulders beneath the cotton, hoping he would forget about the shirt.

"I got a late start." His gray eyes were dark as they went slowly over her body. "My socks too huh? How many pairs did you steal this time?" The edge of exasperation in his voice was softened with affection. It was routine, a game. She stole his shirts and socks and he pretended to care how many she made away with.

"Just one." She shrugged. "It's not like you'll miss them." Marly hid her smile as she turned her back on him, her senses tempted by the smell of hot, steaming coffee. Her body tempted by the sight of the sexy, drowsy man.

He was silent as she poured a mug of coffee, then took a sip of the hot liquid. Her eyes closed as the caffeine hit her tongue, anticipating the rush it would bring her later.

"You should still be in bed," he told her softly as she stood at the counter, her hands wrapped around her cup.

"I usually get up early," she told him sleepily, smothering her yawn. "I didn't sleep well last night."

She fought the blush she could feel just under her skin. She hadn't slept because each time she closed her eyes visions of Cade and his arousing mouth danced before her eyes. His lips were full, with a rough, hard edge. His gray eyes were always direct, the thick, black lashes framing them giving him a carnal, sexy appearance.

"Yeah, I was restless too." He lowered his head, sipping at his coffee.

She had heard him in his room. She had watched the door, praying he would come to her. Marly took in a deep, hard breath. He looked sexy and dangerous, if a bit on the drowsy side. She wished the sleepiness had been caused from something other than pacing the floors all night.

"Missing Grandpa Joe?" She took her coffee to the table, sitting down in the chair beside him as she watched him.

Cade grunted. "Hardly. That old bastard held on a lot longer than he should have."

Marly winced. She hadn't particularly liked Joe herself, but she hadn't known Cade was so bitter towards him as well. The ring of hatred in his voice was bitter, consuming.

"He wasn't a happy man." She hunched her shoulders, trying to find a way to comfort him.

Cade's expression shuttered, but Marly glimpsed an edge of pain and fury in his eyes in that last second that made her breath stutter in her throat. How had she not known, in all these years, the anger he felt toward Joe?

"Don't make excuses for him. He was a bastard and we all knew it. But he was my Father, I had to put up with him." In Cade's voice was years of regret and hopelessness. And pain.

Cade shouldn't hurt like that. Alone, the emotion carefully hidden beneath the surface, like a dark, angry beast roaring in pain, with no one to hear. That thought had tears pricking at her eyes, at her heart. He had always taken away the pain in her life. She wanted to remove his as well.

Marly looked up at him, seeing a vein of sadness running through his eyes. A sadness he could no longer hide. She moved from her chair before she thought of it, and before Cade could stop her, was cuddling into his lap.

She felt him accept her with a surprised start, his arms going around her, clenching around her as he pulled her close. He buried his face in her hair, rubbing his cheek over the top of her head slowly. Her arms were wrapped around his neck, her head on his shoulder, and Marly wanted to cry because it felt so warm, so good to be in his arms.

"I've missed you, Cade," she whispered softly, her lips touching the underside of his jaw. "I've missed you so much."

She felt his hands clench on her. One at her waist, the other at her thigh. The heat of them was like an erotic brand on her skin.

"I've missed you too, baby," he said, his voice rough. "More than you know."

The material of the shirt had ridden up her thighs, leaving an indecent amount of skin bare. His hand rested there, just below the hemline of the shirt, his thumb rubbing over her skin softly. It was like fire against her flesh, the heat of the caress driving her crazy.

"You're going to have to stop stealing my shirts, Marly," his voice was husky, amused as his fingers rubbed the cotton at her waist. "This was one of my favorites."

She fought to control her breathing, the blood thundering through her veins.

"Maybe I'll let you borrow it sometime." She smiled against his chest, tortured by the feel of his big hard body against her, and loving it.

She felt his smile against the top of her head and bent her head back to look up at him. God, he was so handsome, so dark and rough it made her heart beat out of control. His eyes met hers, the color darkening and swirling in a way that made her mouth dry, her knees to weaken.

"You're so pretty." His hand lifted from her thigh, those long fingers cupping her cheek as they caressed her skin.

Marly swallowed tightly, then licked her lips nervously as her body weakened against him. He watched her in a way he never had before, his gaze fierce, searing into her very soul as he stared at her. Tenderness reflected in his eyes, but she could also see the hot core of desire. It had to be need. Desire.

"Cade—" She couldn't bear the need, the longing. She was dying to feel his lips against hers.

His lashes lowered, his gaze centering on her lips. Tension, thick and hot swirled around them, drawing her in, leaving her nearly gasping in his arms. He would have kissed her. She knew he would have. But at that moment Brock and Sam grumbled into the kitchen.

"Dammit, too early for this shit." Sam made a beeline for the coffee maker, as Brock bumped along to the stove where Cade had left a plate of bacon and biscuits. Neither man appeared awake, or aware. Though they were dressed and trying to fake it at least.

She sighed, her gaze dropping from the still, dark intensity of Cade's as she glanced over at the brothers.

"Hey Cade. Marly." Sam nearly fell into his chair, his bleary eyes barely registering life as he glanced at them.

Marly felt Cade sigh roughly. Then he was patting her thigh before his hands grasped her waist to help her from his lap.

"Get it together, you two," he growled as he came to his feet and finished his coffee with a grimace. "I'll be in the barn waiting on you."

Without another word he moved away from the table and left the kitchen.

"Dammit, we have a chauffer driven limousine, more money than any of us can spend, and he still works us like ranch hands." Sam shook his head, showing his feelings of injustice over that fact. "No cook, and we do our own laundry. That man was a born slave driver."

Marly smiled, shaking her head at his morose look.

"Cheer up, Sam. At least he doesn't make you clean the stalls anymore," she told him as she rose to her feet as well. "See you guys later, I'm going to try for a few more hours of sleep."

Not that she thought she would get it. Her body still tingled, heat and longing zipping harshly through her veins. But she needed to get away from Sam and Brock. She needed to think about what she had seen in Cade's eyes, the swirls of emotions, the darkening of desire. It had to be desire.

Cade leaned wearily against the side of an empty stall seconds after entering the barn. A deep, weary sigh exhaled from his chest, and his eyes closed in misery. His body pulsed, hard and tormenting, his flesh throbbing for ease. Son of a bitch, he thought, another second with her in his arms and he would have done the unthinkable, the unconscionable. His hand flexed at his side, the feel of her smooth thigh imprinted there forever. Her skin had been warm, supple, textured like the softest silk.

He leaned his head against the wall, shaking it in resignation. There was no denying it any longer. He lusted after Marly, and he had for years, just as Joe had accused him. The dreams were bad enough. The stolen moment in her bedroom last night, criminal. But this, this was more than he could bear. Only a few minutes with her in his arms and he had been ready to throw her across the breakfast table and have her, rather than the cooling bacon and biscuits waiting on the stove.

He dragged his hat from his head, thrusting his fingers through his hair in growing frustration. He couldn't take her. He knew that. The things he wanted to do to Marly would terrify her. Hell, they terrified him.

He wasn't an easy man. His sexuality was hard driven, and sometimes rougher than even he liked. He was intensely dominant, in all ways, especially sexually. He never hurt his partners, but he knew the acts he wanted to perform with Marly would leave her shaking in fear. The ways he wanted her would shock her. And she had done the one thing guaranteed to destroy his will. She had waxed the flesh between her thighs. She tempted him with fresh, damp silk and the sweet heat of her body.

It was smooth and silky, coated with the desire growing from whatever dream tempted her. Who was her dream lover? His teeth clenched in jealousy. Who was the man who had left her slick and hot, her inner body preparing for her penetration?

Fury was like a bitter acid eating at his stomach now. His erection was like a snarling beast beneath his jeans, demanding release, demanding Marly. Not just any woman, Marly. Sweet and hot, her innocent eyes dark and adoring as she gazed up at him. He wanted them dark and needy, her moist lips opened for his, or wrapped around his hard flesh.

He wanted to hear her cries, echoing around him as he pushed into her, thrusting into the hot little portal that haunted his dreams. He wanted to fuck her until she screamed, begging for more. He wanted what he knew he couldn't have from her. His sexual demands would terrify her, and he knew it. He wanted to scream with the loss of his own decency, taken from him, stripped from his soul long before she had come to his home.

A groan was wrenched from his chest at the thought of taking her. Perspiration dotted his brow, and his erection was a torturous demon pulsing between his thighs.

"I need to get laid," he muttered, knowing he wouldn't, knowing there would be no true satisfaction in another woman's body.

"Cade, you in here?" Brock called out as he entered the barn.

Shaking his head, Cade forced the need back, praying the hardness between his thighs would lessen, at least enough to finish his work for the morning.

"Back here." Cade picked up his saddle from the bench at the back of the stall and headed back into the main part of the barn. "Get saddled. Fences need repaired."

He ignored Brock's grimace.

"Fences," his brother muttered. "Hell, I was hoping for an easy day."

So was he, Cade thought, but it didn't look like one was forthcoming. He wanted to get finished before lunch. He had to be finished, because he didn't know if he could wait until evening to see Marly again.

"You finally decide to open the back pasture?" Brock surprised him with his question as they saddled the horses.

"Not yet." Cade patted his horse fondly after tightening the cinch. "Why?"

"Curious. Thought I saw someone up on the rise this morning. Must have been one of the hands wandering around." Brock shrugged. "I was hoping to get some of the mommas out there before they calve."

"That's my intention." Cade nodded. "I haven't sent any of the boys out yet, but they have just been checking it early. Did you see who it was?"

"Naw just saw the horse." Brock led his horse into the ranch yard, glancing back at Cade as they left the barn. "I'll find out who it was later. Make certain they checked that old den that wolf was using last winter. I don't want to lose any more calves to that wily ole bitch."

Cade nodded, glancing up at the small hill that rose behind the ranch house. With its slope, it covered the better part of the back pasture, and on the far side, wolves were prone to use the natural cavern there for a den. They tried to keep it cleared of the animals, yet they always managed to find a way in.

"Let me know what they find." Cade nodded, then turned his horse and set it into a quick canter along the fence line. Several miles away the barbed wire and wood fence was wearing.

Cade enjoyed keeping the white painted planked fence in place near to the ranch house. Marly had loved it when she was just a child, proclaiming that it made it look more like a home. That made it worth all the aggravation in the world.

Thinking of Marly again only made his dick throb. He shook his head, trying to push the sight of her in her bed, out of his mind. The feel of her, slick and hot, the taste of her sweet and tangy. He gritted his teeth. Dammit, it was going to be a long day.

Chapter Four

∽

It was good to be home. Marly stood at her bedroom balcony, overlooking the swimming pool and the flower gardens out back and inhaled the sweet scents of spring. The soft peace of the late afternoon shimmered around her, easing the restless yearning in her body only slightly.

Below, the heated pool shimmered with a glimmer of mist from the rising warmth, and the flower gardens were showing bursts of green. The renewal of the Earth. She loved spring. The days were cool, the nights crisp and clear, and all around, it seemed the air pulsed with energy.

She could hear the muted sounds of the ranch yard out front. The cowboys working out at the barn to the side of the house, the call of the horses in the pasture. The sounds that had comforted her in the years since her mother had left her with Grandpa Joe and Cade. She hadn't seen her mother since. Not a phone call, a card or a letter. There were Christmas presents under the tree each year from her, but Marly suspected that was Cade's doing. He had always done everything he could to ease the pain of that desertion.

She loved him. Marly closed her eyes on the bittersweet thought. From the first day she had seen him, his eyes swirling with emotions, his harsh face softening at the sight of her filthy appearance, she had loved him. At first, it had been the simple, sweet love of a child who knew that if there was one person on Earth who would protect her, it was Cade.

But somewhere, the feeling had changed. Over the years, it had deepened, grown, and no matter the arguments against it, she loved him. She wanted him. It wasn't even the desire she had as a teenager, filled with visions of kisses and warm touches. It was a need that throbbed in her, filled her, made the nights she spent beneath his roof intolerable.

He slept in the room adjoining hers. He always had, in case she had nightmares. Sometimes, she could hear him moving around in his room, late at night, restless. She would listen, and imagine him coming to her, sliding into the bed beside her, his hard body moving against her, over her. But he never did. He never seemed to see her as anything more than the little child he had raised.

She was abnormal, Marly thought. She was as sick as Grandpa Joe had always accused her of being. A woman marked with the sins of her mother, and forced to suffer the same unnatural needs. Marly had always wondered at those unnatural needs; until she realized what she felt for Cade wasn't what she was supposed to feel. She wasn't supposed to ache, to dream of him touching her, moving over her, inside her. She wasn't supposed to hurt for him until the hurt was like a physical pain, driving her mad with its intensity.

She shook her head, feeling the heavy weight of the braid at her back. Cade loved her hair. He always did. And once, just once she had glimpsed something deep and dark in his eyes as he brushed it late one night. As his hands ran through the unruly mass, slowly, caressingly, she had glanced back at him, and she knew she had seen desire. She could have been certain. Then it was gone, and he hadn't touched her the same since.

"Marly?" Greg's voice called through the door as he knocked tentatively. "Are you dressed?"

Marly smiled fondly at his hesitant voice.

"Come on in Greg, I'm naked as hell and ready." She laughed as she reentered her room, calling out her standby answer, knowing his face would flush and his expression would be strictly disapproving.

The door slammed into the far wall, causing her to cry out in shocked surprise. Greg was there, pale and shaking in the grip of a madman. Cade's eyes were so dark they were nearly black, a flush rising along the upper edge of his cheeks, his face tight with fury.

"Cade?" Surprise flowed through her.

"Ready are you?" He growled, his voice low and vibrating with his anger.

Fury seemed to pulse in his body, vibrating along his muscles as he stared at her with stormy eyes.

"Yeah, you better believe it." She blinked at him in surprise, only barely managing to keep her composure. "Could you let Greg's neck go, Cade? The closest chiropractor is a quack, and I think you're hurting him."

Cade's hand gripped the back of the boy's neck, his hands were almost white with the strength of it, and Greg didn't seem to be breathing very well. Cade looked down at the boy, then released him with a growl of disgust. Greg nearly crumpled to the floor.

"Greg, are you okay?" Ignoring Cade's fury she rushed to her friend, her arm wrapping around his waist as she led him into her bedroom and sat him on her lacy bed. "Did he hurt you? I'm sure he didn't mean to."

Marly cast Cade a furious look. Neanderthal. What the hell was wrong with him? He was staring at her as though he were possessed, fury tightening his body, his eyes narrowed on her, glittering with an emotion that sent her body trembling.

"The boy is fine, for now." Cade fumed audibly.

She had never seen such an expression of demented anger on his face. He was like a stranger. His dark face set in savage lines, his dark brows lowered over darkening eyes.

"You've lost your mind, Cade." She bit out. "What would cause you to act that way? Don't you think I'm old enough to have sex yet?"

She wasn't expecting his reaction. He flinched as though a whip had been laid to his bare back, his face paling beneath his tan.

"God. No. No. We don't have sex." Greg was frantic as he shook his head, looking at Cade beseechingly. "This woman is possessed, Mr. August. On my parents' graves I swear I've never touched her. Never."

Marly's eyes narrowed on the fear in Greg's expression.

"Oh Greg, he's not really going to hurt you." She rolled her eyes at his terror.

Cade wasn't going to really hurt him. He should realize that. If Cade wanted him hurt, he would have been lying on the floor broken and bleeding already.

"Marly, shut up. He already has." Greg pleaded hoarsely. "Please tell him we don't have sex, Marly."

She had never heard him use the 'S' word as he called it, so easily. He usually stammered over it for an hour before getting it out. Her eyes narrowed on Greg, then turned to Cade. He was breathing harshly, his fists clenched as he watched her with a dark, violent look.

"I was only joking about being naked and ready, as you can tell." She held her arms out to indicate her jeans, and long sleeved sweater. As she did so, Cade's eyes went to the strip of bare belly that the raised sweater was showing. Uh oh. The gold ring in her belly button was clearly visible, as was the slender gold chain that wound around her waist and clasped into the ring.

Cade frowned darkly, his fists clenching and unclenching as though he was going to do physical damage. Rather than scaring her, the look excited her.

"Downstairs." His voice was harsh and grating, his gaze locked on the small ring and its connecting chain. "Downstairs, now."

He turned on his heel and stalked from the room as Marly watched him with a frown.

"God Marly, what kind of game are you playing?" Greg was rubbing the back of his neck as he groaned out the question pleadingly. "I'm going back to my sister's. At least there it's just words. That man is gonna kill me."

"Cade won't kill you," she murmured, still staring at the door. "Do you think he acted interested, Greg?"

"Interested?" Greg's voice was incredulous. "Marly, you can't be serious?"

Marly ignored the rough disbelief in Greg's voice as she still watched the empty doorway.

"Hmmm, just curious," she said thoughtfully. "I better go down and see what his problem is. I'll meet you outside in a little while. Maybe we can go swimming."

Since there was no longer any need to try to hide the belly ring, she could enjoy the pool. Marly licked her lips nervously as she left the bedroom. Cade had nearly flipped when he saw the ring. It had been there in the flush on his cheeks, the disbelief in his eyes. She liked it, though it had hurt like hell getting it. She especially liked the thin gold chain that went around her body and connected to the ring. It made her feel sexy, even if no one else ever glimpsed it. Until Cade.

He was waiting on her in the study, where she had known he would be. She closed the door softly behind her, watching him as she neared his desk. He was standing at the sliding doors, staring out at the pool. The liquor on his desk was opened, and he was holding an empty glass in his hand.

"Don't you think you're overreacting just a little bit, Cade?" Her voice was soft, questioning. "It was just a joke. Greg is easy to tease —"

"So you tease him?" Cade turned to her slowly. "How far do you go to tease him, Marly?"

Marly blinked. He was really furious. She felt a small flare of unease, but mixed with it was an excitement she couldn't define. It made her knees weak, made the muscles of her stomach clench in anticipation. She could feel the tender portal between her thighs heating, readying itself.

She shrugged uneasily. "I'm not mean to him Cade. And I don't tease him badly. You know I wouldn't do that."

"Do I?" He refilled his glass. "You've changed Marly, while at school. How much have you changed?"

Marly licked her lips, trying to ignore the flare of hurt feelings his tone and his look caused within her.

"I'm not a child anymore, Cade," she whispered. " I don't do anything that would embarrass the family, but I'm not a kid."

Marly had always been very conscious of the family's good name. She had always fought to make certain she brought no shame to it. To Cade. She didn't want him to be ashamed of her, yet he was acting as though he was.

Cade didn't answer her. He threw back the liquor as though it were water, causing her to swallow tightly. She had never seen Cade so upset.

"Are you having sex with that incompetent little prick?" he finally asked her harshly, refusing to look at her.

Marly swallowed tightly, suddenly nervous in Cade's presence. She had never seen him like this, enraged in this way. His emotions seemed to pulse just under the surface, ready to erupt.

"I haven't had sex with anyone, Cade. And Greg is a nice guy. He's very lonely, and he's my friend." Marly heard the tremble in her voice and hated being so weak in front of him.

The pupils of his eyes dilated at her announcement. A hard breath racked his chest and his hands clenched.

His gaze speared into hers. "Never?" He asked her harshly.

"Never, Cade." She shook her head.

"Are you going to have sex with him?" He turned away from her as though he couldn't bear to look at her.

Marly felt tears well in her eyes. He was so handsome. His jeans rode low on his hips, belted with wide leather, and emphasizing his hard stomach and broad shoulders. His legs were long and muscular, and he had a smooth, rolling walk that made her crazy. She needed him, wanted him, but he still saw her as a little girl.

"I'm a woman," she whispered again, ignoring his flinch. "I don't know how to answer your question. If I fall in love with him, yes I will. Do I love him now? No, I don't, except as a very dear friend."

Cade sighed deeply, running his hands through his hair as he turned to her. The look on his face was agonized.

"Marly, don't cry," he groaned, and only then did she realize the tears were running down her face.

She was dying. Marly knew she was. She wanted him so desperately she couldn't stand the ache. She wanted him to touch her, hold her. How much longer did she have to wait? She had waited a lifetime already.

"I'm sorry," she whispered as she wiped at her cheeks, shaking her head. "Maybe I should go back to school. I don't cause any trouble there."

She had been causing trouble at home since she had started dating. As though Cade expected any minute to walk into his home and encounter an orgy.

"God no. Baby, I've missed you so much." He pulled her into his arms, and the pain of needing him was like a physical blow to her stomach.

Her arms wrapped around his waist, her hands holding tight to his back. He was so warm and hard. So male she wanted to scream out her need for him. His scent, a combination of spice and pure male heat wrapped around her, infusing her. She felt her breasts swell beneath the lace cups of her bra, her nipples hardening. She held onto him tighter, knowing how desperately she had missed his rare hugs in the past two years, the feel of his hands stroking over her head.

"The belly ring was a surprise," he whispered at her ear, his lips barely caressing the lobe, making it nearly impossible to suppress her shiver. "And that chain is decadent, Marly."

Cade's voice was husky and deep. It pierced her stomach, and beyond, making the ache all the more sweeter. His hands caressed her back slowly, his fingers running over the thin gold at her waistline. His hands were hot, setting fires along her body wherever he touched her. She needed. God help her, how much longer could she live with this aching need?

* * * * *

Marly was soft and warm in his arms, her hands clenched at his back, her breathing rough as he tried to calm her. Slowly, he stroked her back with one hand, then both. His palms smoothed easily over the soft material of her sweater. He could feel the chain at her waist, and the sight of it flashed before his eyes. The glitter of gold against pale skin, the waist of her jeans riding low, the little gold ring drawing his gaze as surely as a bolt of lightning would have.

Cade had become so enraged, so furious that she would have bared her stomach for a stranger, endured having such a sensitive area pierced, that he had barely been able to contain the violence already flowing through his system.

Her soft, husky voice inviting that little turd of a boy into her room, where she was naked and ready, had already brought red to the forefront of his vision. He had wanted to kill that boy. Slowly, surely. And Marly's confusion, the hot flare of excitement in her eyes as she saw him, had been nearly more than he could bear. Why had she been looking for a fight with him? And there was no doubt she had been. Her eyes had glittered with her own battle-ready senses as she stood up to him, where she never had before. She was pushing him, and he didn't think he could take the pressure.

His own needs, fury and fears would destroy him. Cade admitted that silently as he enjoyed the feel of her smooth flesh as her sweater rose a scant inch over her waist. He was drowning in the scent of her, wild and sweet. His blood was still coursing through his veins, and he wanted nothing more than to pull her tighter into his arms. He had missed her. He had missed her too damned much.

He missed holding her, watching her laughter and feeling the warmth it brought to him. He hadn't known how much she filled him until she had gone away. How much her presence alone soothed the ragged, wounded edges of his soul.

His fingers played with the chain that ran around her back, strumming against her skin, feeling soft satin flesh beneath the thin, cool band of gold. Warm satin, so damned soft his fingers relished the touch of it. Over and over again, he stroked it, until his hands were running beneath the sweater by a hands width as he soothed her. Her breath was still hitching, her breathing harsh. He hadn't meant to upset her so deeply. He had gone crazy. Driven past any limit he could handle at the thought of her naked, inviting, smiling up at him as he moved over her. Wedging between her thighs. Her hips arching to him. Her voice a husky murmur as she pleaded —

Marly moved against him, and Cade felt the erection growing stiffly behind the fly of his jeans. She moved against him slowly, feeling the hard length pressing into her soft belly. Cade knew she felt it when he heard the low, needy whimper that came from her throat.

"No, Marly," his protesting whisper was a breath of sound as he felt her lips at his chest, her hot little tongue stroking his skin. "Son of a bitch..." His head fell back as his hands pulled her closer, his knees bending as he lifted her nearer, driving the cloth-covered erection against the vee of her thighs helplessly.

He couldn't believe she was doing this. That she was reacting this way, reaching for him, needing him. He couldn't let her. His control was already shaky at best, and he had to protect her. He had to protect himself from the hatred she would surely feel for him later. But right now, he had to fight for breath. Her lips were warm, her little tongue moist and hot against his skin.

Cade gritted his teeth, fighting the compulsion to take over. To pull her against his body tight and hard, and show her what she was asking for. His cock was pulsing, so tight and hot beneath his jeans he was in agony. The need coursed and rose inside him, drawing his body so taut he felt as though he would shatter at any moment.

Marly rubbed against him, a little sigh of desire, of want whispering over his skin as he gripped her hips, pulled her closer and bent to press his erection between her thighs.

"Cade." Her hoarse, lust-filled cry made his brain explode with the furious need to fuck. To slam his cock inside her, to feel the ripple of soft wet velvet encasing, gripping him.

"Is this what you want, damn you?" he growled down at her fiercely, watching her eyes glaze with shock as he rocked against her. "Is this what you want Marly, because I swear to God, I'm within an inch of driving it into you."

He was angry. Angrier than he had ever been. She was teasing him, tempting him, pushing him past reason. Or was she? Lust, hot and carnal clouded his brain as he watched her nipples peak beneath her sweater. He pulled her against him harshly once again, grinding his flesh into her as her eyes closed on a ragged whimper. Need or fear?

Shock, hot and remorseful seared his very soul. His hands dropped from her and he turned away quickly, going instantly for the bottle of liquor at his desk. His hands shook as he poured the drink, his chest heaved. He felt like screaming in frustration.

"Cade?" He closed his eyes as her voice speared through his body.

Hot, husky, needing. God, he was so far over the edge that he was lending to her his own unnatural desires. He had raised her for God's sake; he had no business acting this way.

He had no business stealing her innocence and drawing her into his nightmares.

"I'm sorry I—" Cade lowered his head, watching desperately as the liquid filled the glass. "I promise, I'll not jump so quickly to conclusions from now on. You're right, you're a woman..." he couldn't go on.

He downed the whisky, welcoming the burning that tore into his gut and almost replaced the other heat searing him from the inside out.

"So I can sleep with whoever I want?" Cade knew he was imagining the bitterness in her voice. A bitterness seeping into his soul.

"I can't stop you." He shook his head, taking another drink desperately, praying to God that something, anything would wipe the sight of her welcoming some bastard to her bed, out of his head.

"What if I want you, Cade?" Her whispered question seared his skin.

His hand shook. Cade had to take precious moments to control the instinctive reaction in his body to her soft question.

"No, Marly." He shook his head tightly. "You don't want me. Not really. You just think you do."

There was silence behind him now. Tension flowed around him, choking him, making his stomach rebel at the amount of liquor he was consuming. Surely to God he would drink enough soon to drown this awful ache.

He needed a woman, Cade told himself desperately. That's all it is. A woman. He wondered how long it had been since he had taken one to his bed? Years, he knew. He couldn't remember the last time he had tested the wet heat of a woman's desire. He had been busy; he excused the lack of desire in the past years. The ranch, Joe's illness. There were a million details to go over every day and he just hadn't had time. And once again, in his mind's eye he saw Marly, inviting, open. But it wasn't the pale little puke of a boy upstairs moving between those slender thighs that he saw. It was him, covering, moving over her—God help him, it was time to get laid before he did something stupid.

"I have work to do, Marly." His voice was harsher than he meant it to be as he sat down at his desk and began riffling through the drawers for his address book.

Surely it hadn't been so long that he couldn't find a willing woman.

"Sure, Cade." There was no mistaking the anger in her tone now. "I wanted to go swimming anyway. Sorry I put you out."

"Marly." He stopped her before she could turn away.

Turning slowly, breathing harshly, he fought to explain.

"I didn't mean—" he didn't know what the hell to say. "I've been without a woman—" he shook his head. Dammit.

"You're just horny and I was just here. Right?" She nearly snarled the answer for him. "I'm the same as your niece, and please don't read any more into it than that." Her voice was mocking and cold. "Save it, Cade. Because it's not something I want to hear.

She turned and stalked from the room as he finally raised his gaze. Good thing she didn't want to hear it, he thought morosely, because it sure as hell wasn't what he wanted to say. As she stalked from the room, he had a perfect view of her round buttocks and lithe, jean-clad legs as she left the room. He closed his eyes tightly, fighting for control, fighting to halt the visions rolling through his head. If he didn't do something soon, the steel hard erection in his jeans would take control for him.

His father's accusations haunted him now. The old bastard had known how much Cade wanted her, had seen it when no one else had. Seen it, and tormented him with it.

Cade felt bitter fury churn in his stomach. God, he couldn't be as demented, as depraved as that old bastard. He wouldn't allow it. The past had almost destroyed him once before, he wouldn't let it finish the job now.

Chapter Five

ဆ

Marly laid a hand to her trembling stomach, the imprint of Cade's arousal still burning her flesh. And he had been aroused; there had been no mistaking it. She felt alternately giddy and furious that he had pushed her away at the exact moment she felt it. As though it were dirty, she thought with a frown, her fingers running lightly over the flesh of her stomach. She trembled, remembering his fingers on her back, his calloused flesh running warmly over her skin. His fingers playing with the chain as though he couldn't help himself. She shivered again.

It was the first time he had touched her in any way other than a child. The first time his own breathing had been harsh, his heart thudding roughly beneath her cheek. She had wanted so desperately to turn her face up to him, to tempt him to lower his head, to touch his lips to hers, but she knew he wouldn't, and she hadn't wanted it to end. It had ended much too quickly the way it was.

"Hey Marly, are you okay?" Greg knocked at her door again, his voice softly questioning.

Walking over to the door, Marly pulled it open. Looking past Greg she checked the hallway quickly, then stood back for him to enter.

"Get in here." She gripped his arm and pulled him into the room.

Greg's eyes widened in surprise as he moved past her.

"Are you okay?" His gaze went over her face quizzically, as though he expected bruises.

Marly rolled her eyes as she closed her door quickly.

"I'm fine. Cade has never laid a hand on me and he never would." Well, at least not to hurt her, she thought with a shiver.

"Then what's up?" Greg shook his head as he sat down in the large chair by her bed. "He was really pissed, Marly. You shouldn't play with him like that."

Greg's earnest face matched his warning tone. Marly breathed out roughly.

"I can handle, Cade." She shook her head, almost laughing at herself. Yeah. Right. She could sure handle him. She had him right where she wanted him and she ran.

"I'm glad one of us can." Greg rubbed the back of his neck with a grimace. "I'm still thinking I should go home."

"No. You can't leave." Marly spoke before stemming the desperation that bled into her tone.

Greg glanced up at her, his eyes narrowed speculatively on her face.

"What are you up to, Marly?" He asked her slowly, his gaze suspicious.

"I'm not up to anything." But something had been up on Cade. Marly knew she was going to burn herself alive just thinking about it.

"You're not convincing me," Greg sighed roughly. "Marly, you aren't going to try to use me to make Cade jealous, are you?"

Marly blinked at him. She hadn't thought about that.

"Uh oh, your mind's working." Greg shook his head, fear shadowing his eyes. "Stop Marly, you know how that always scares me."

"Wimp." She crossed her arms over her chest. "And besides, you have no idea what I'm thinking."

Greg grunted. "I'm not stupid Marly, I saw the look on your face after Cade nearly killed me. You enjoyed that too much, if you ask me."

"He was interested." Satisfaction seeped through her, shivering over her skin.

"I know he was, Greg."

Greg blinked at her in amazement. "You wanted him to be interested?" he asked her as though she had lost her mind. "You've lost your mind Marly."

"You just don't know Cade yet. You'll love him once you get to know him." She waved her hand dismissively at his comment. "But now I have to figure out how to make him realize he's interested."

Greg shook his head as though he feared he was imagining this conversation.

"Trust me, Marly, he would know if he were," he assured her a bit mockingly as he watched her.

Marly frowned.

"Maybe not," she mused with a grimace. "He still sees me as a baby. The little girl he raised."

This was the part that Marly couldn't figure out how to get past. Cade insisted on treating her like she was still twelve years old. There had to be a way to make him realize she wanted to be treated like a woman, not a child.

"Marly, what if he doesn't want that with you?" Greg asked her gently. "Men react sometimes, even when it's not the woman they really want. What if that's all there was to it?"

Marly looked at him, her stomach protesting the idea with a wave of pain. She had waited too long, that couldn't be it. Cade would want her, the same way she wanted him. If he didn't, she didn't know if she could survive the pain.

"He will," she told him quietly. "He has to, Greg."

Greg sighed roughly. He watched her with his quiet eyes, his face somber as she tried to convince him how much this meant to her.

"Honestly, Marly, I don't know how he could resist you." He stood to his feet, and walked to her, hugging her gently, briefly. "Now, what about that swim you promised me. I even brought shorts. But don't you dare tell anyone I wore them. All right?"

He smiled down at her, and Marly glimpsed the sadness in his eyes.

"You're next Greg," she told him softly. "You watch. We're gonna find you a wonderful girl to love you."

He laughed as he moved back from her.

"Find someone who doesn't mind a string bean then." His smile was more a grimace as he shook his head. "My dad was built just like me, only older. He cried over it all the time before he died."

"Well, I think you're wonderful," she assured him brightly, and she knew he was. He was the best friend she had ever had. "Now, go get those shorts on and I'll meet you in the pool."

And hopefully, Marly thought, Cade was still in the study, and he would get the full effect of her new thong bikini if he still happened to be watching. She breathed out roughly. Seducing him wasn't going to be as easy as she had hoped it would be.

* * * * *

That wasn't a bathing suit; it was a walking excuse for sex. Cade watched Marly dip her foot into the heated pool, then glance back at the kid following her to say something. She wore a dark blue bikini, with thong bottoms. He closed his eyes tightly, praying he wasn't really seeing her bare ass cheeks with that slender piece of material running between them. But there they were when he opened his eyes again. The pale, perfect globes of flesh glistened in the weak afternoon sun and sent his body to throbbing heatedly.

He wanted her. His erection throbbed, hot and hard, making him crazy with need. He knew if he didn't have a woman soon, then he wouldn't be able to keep himself from taking Marly.

"Damn if she ain't getting prettier every day," Brock remarked softly as he moved behind him to look into the pool area. "I bet she has that boy so damned hot he's ready to explode."

"Not if he knows what's good for him," Cade growled, fighting his anger.

Damn, this wasn't going to work.

"She's a grown woman, Cade. You can't keep her a baby all her life," Brock told him quietly. "And the way she looks, if that boy ain't having sex with her now, he will be soon."

"How can you talk about her like that?" Cade turned on his brother wrathfully.

"We raised her, Brock."

Brock was silent for long moments, then Cade heard the deep breath he drew into his lungs.

"Yeah, we raised her, but she's no blood of ours, Cade. If I didn't know how hard you got every time you looked at her, then I'd have already tried to get her into my bed."

Cade turned on him slowly, anger eating him alive.

"Are you fucking crazy?" Cade asked him hoarsely. "She's our niece—"

"No niece of mine." Brock glanced down, and Cade knew there was no hiding the raging hard-on that ridged his jeans. "And not yours either by the looks of it."

"The way she's dressed, a saint would get a hard-on," Cade bit out, gritting his teeth as she faced the French doors. Her breasts were practically spilling out of that damned bikini top.

Full and firm, the cold hardening her nipples until they poked against the cloth in a way that had Cade's mouth watering. He could almost feel them in his hands, in his mouth. He fought the desire, knowing it was useless.

"I need to get laid," he sighed harshly, moving away from the doors. "It's been too long since I've been with a woman."

"Bout a year or so." Brock nodded.

"How the hell do you know?" Cade bit out. "And when did you start keeping tabs?"

"The night you rushed Marge Cline outta the house after Marly ran from your study crying after catching you two on the couch. The next day, you burned the couch and bought a new one. You haven't had a woman since."

He was right. Cade cursed silently, remembering that night. He had just fucked Marge into a screaming climax when Marly walked into the room, her hairbrush in her hand, tears tracking her cheeks from another nightmare. She had walked into a living one.

Cade remembered the look on her face, the way her eyes had settled on his erection when he jumped to his feet, the fury that stole across her face.

"How could you?" She had thrown her hairbrush at him, aiming at his jutting arousal, and barely missing. *"How could you do that with her? Don't you know she tells everyone?"* And she had run from the room, her sobs echoing through the house.

Marge had been amused by the display, quietly informing him, as she dressed, of her sister's claim that Marly believed herself in love with Cade. Cade had denied it, forcefully.

But he had seen the look in Marly's eyes. He had seen her pain, and her possessive fury. He had seen the want in her gaze as her eyes widened at the sight of his steel hard flesh.

"She was shocked—"

"Shit. She was jealous as hell." Brock laughed in genuine, affectionate amusement. "Come on, Cade. The girl's been trying to get your attention for four years now. Why not just give into it?"

"What are you, her pimp?" Cade snarled. "Since when were you so eager to get her fucked?"

"Since you turned into a snarling bear every time she's around," he grunted. "Dammit, a person can't get along with you anymore, Cade. If Marly's around, it's even worse. And she's no better. She eats you with her eyes every time you turn your head, and you do the same to her. Fuck her already, and get over it."

The whisky glass Cade held shattered against the wall as the last syllable left Brock's mouth. Cade turned on his brother, seeing red as anger, white hot and barely controlled, surged through his body.

"Shut up," he snarled, realizing it as the rumble of words left his mouth. "Shut the hell up, Brock. And if I catch you touching her, I'll kill you."

Brock's lips kicked up in a grin, small though it was, the amused look had Cade forcefully restraining himself from kicking his brother's ass.

"Well, I see you're going to be just as easy to get along with as you always are when she's home," Brock sighed with exaggerated tolerance. "And damned stingy for a change, too. You're getting greedy in your old age, Cade."

Cade wanted to growl. He contented himself with pouring another shot of whisky and downing it quickly. He wasn't getting as greedy as Brock thought he was. That was the problem. God help him, and Marly, if he didn't get a handle on this.

"Well, I'm outta here. I have a hottie waitin' in town. After watching Marly's little show out there for you, I'm primed and ready for her." Brock chuckled at his own humor as he sauntered out of the room. "Have a nice evening bro. I'll catch you tomorrow."

Cade turned back to the French doors, his eyes narrowing as Marly stepped up to the diving board. As her lithe body poised to begin her jump, her gaze met his in the glass. He watched her cheeks flush, her nipples harden. His gaze went back to her face, and her pink little tongue ran over her pouty lower lip slowly. Then she jumped. Her body cleaved smoothly through the water, and Cade felt his stomach drop. He was a goner.

He lowered his head, somber, saddened. His past was ugly, the results of it even darker. He was an animal, a craven bastard that would shred her innocence, and her purity with the demands he would make on her. Brock knew, as did Sam, and he knew they were eagerly waiting the day Cade would give into his own dark desires. He loved her, he always had. But he also knew there was no way Marly would see his love as the tender, gentle emotion she needed. She would come to see it for what it was. A ravenous, decadent emotion that would feed from her desires, increase them, darken them. He was damned to hell, Cade knew, for what he would eventually do to the love she offered him.

Chapter Six

ळ

Torn, restless and discouraged, Marly went to bed early that night. Cade was indulgent, treating her gently, seemingly amused by her attempts to be close to him. He had foiled her at every turn, making her feel like an obtuse teenager rather than a beautiful woman.

She finally had enough, retired to her room and showered, then crawled into bed. Sleep wasn't long in coming, but if she had known the nightmare would hit her that night, she would have stayed up longer.

It washed over her, the leering gaze of her stepfather, the demonic look in his eye as he jerked her over his lap. Her buttocks were bare, and he enjoyed spanking her as he described in graphic detail what he would do to her when she was older. She screamed, fighting him, knowing he was drunk, praying she could get away from him.

"You're mine, Marly." His evil whisper didn't sound drunk. Intent, cruel, but not drunk. "I'll have you girl. I'll have you soon."

She fought to get away from him. She kicked out, her foot connecting with flesh. She scratched at hard arms, fought to scream. She wanted to beg, plead, but knew it wouldn't help.

"Cade!" she screamed out in desperation, her throat finally unlocking as she felt hard fingers pushing at the tender lips between her thighs.

Marly awoke when she fell from the bed, scratching and clawing as she fought for balance to reach Cade's room. The bedroom was cold, or she was. So cold, she shivered and cried, nearly paralyzed from the instant chill that hit her body.

"Son of a bitch. Marly." Cade was there. His big warm body was suddenly close to her, jerking her into his arms, holding her against his bare chest as she cried out his name, trying to convince herself that the demon was gone, and the nightmare was over.

"What the hell have you done to yourself?" He wrapped her with a blanket, leaving her for a moment on the floor as something slammed. "Dammit, you went to sleep with the balcony doors open, Marly."

She had? She looked around wildly as he picked her up in his arms, carrying her quickly to his warmer, safer room. But she hadn't had the doors open.

"You're soaking wet." His voice was gentle, soothing as he sat her on his bed. "Sit here, baby. Let me get a towel."

He moved away from her, and Marly knew he was watching her closely. She was shaking. Shaking so hard her teeth chattered. Her body hurt, and the echo of remembered pain could be felt on her bottom. She tried to clench her teeth closed as Cade knelt in front of her, wiping her face with the towel, then her hair.

"What have you done to yourself, Marly?" He sounded agonized, and his expression in the harsh light of the room was worried, inexpressibly concerned.

She could only shake her head. Trying to speak only caused her teeth to chatter harder.

"You're still freezing." He moved up beside her, wrapping her in his arms, pulling her close to him.

The warmth of his big body seeped through the blankets and into her skin.

"Jesus, Marly, that was a bad one." His fingers were moving through her hair, combing through the tangled curls as he tried to calm her.

Terror still strummed through her body, making her blood rush and her body shake. She couldn't seem to get totally warm, no matter how hard she tried. She kept shaking, shivering harshly.

"I'm scared," she finally whispered tearfully, shaking in his arms. "Oh God, Cade. It's like he was right there this time. Like I couldn't escape." Tears ran from her eyes as his arms tightened around her.

"It's okay, Marly." He rocked her gently, like he used to when she was young and screaming, unable to separate reality from nightmare. "Look what you're doing to yourself, baby. You have to stop this."

"I didn't do this," she cried out, trying to burrow closer to him, to steal as much of his warmth as she could.

"Didn't you, Marly?" he asked her gently, tipping her head back as he looked down at her. "Think about it, baby. You're pushing yourself into believing you want me, but you don't. Are you scared I'm going to throw you out if you don't sleep with me? What's gotten into your head?"

Shock of another kind held her immobile now. She shook her head slowly, her body now shuddering with misery. He thought she was having nightmares because she wanted him? It made no sense. Why would he use this against her?

"How can you use that?" she whispered painfully, a harsh sob tearing from her chest. "Are you so desperate to deny what you want yourself, that you would use my nightmares against me, Cade? That wasn't about you."

"But it was the worse. You're shaking like a leaf, and damned near froze to death. You aren't thinking straight," he accused her harshly, though his grip was still gentle.

"Evidently I'm not thinking at all." Dammit, why couldn't she stop crying? "I'm throwing myself at a man who doesn't even want me. I think its time to find someone who does. Would that suit you better, Cade? Would you feel better if another man were in my bed?"

"I'd kill him." The words sounded torn from his chest.

"Listen to you," she accused him harshly. "You don't want to touch me, but no one else can either. Dammit it, Cade, I'm twenty years old and I've never had sex. Not even oral sex. I can't save myself for you forever."

He was suddenly breathing harshly. His hands were on her arms, his fingers firm on her flesh.

"Never?" he growled, as though it seemed inconceivable to him. "Nothing?"

"Nothing," she bit out, more angry than frightened now. "And I'm sick as hell of waking up to nothing but empty dreams. I won't be a nun for you, so you can hide from this."

"I'm not hiding from it." He shook his head harshly. "Dammit, Marly. I'm not one of your teenaged boys. The things I want to do would send you into hysterics. The things I want you to do would destroy you and any love you have for me."

He didn't want that. He couldn't have that. He needed Marly. Needed her love and her laughter more than she would ever know.

"Try me," she challenged him harshly. "Don't keep turning me away Cade. I need you. Please, I need you."

His lips swallowed the last of her words as they covered hers. Swift and sure, making no concessions for innocence or nightmare as he jerked her to him, one hand holding her head securely, the other thrusting the comforter away harshly as his arm went around her waist.

He kissed her like a man possessed. His lips eating at her, his tongue staking his claim on the moist interior of her mouth. She moaned against the invasion, allowing her tongue to tangle with his, her hands to clutch desperately at his shoulders.

"You'll kill me," he whispered as he tore his mouth away, his lips running over her neck.

"Touch me," she panted, shuddering as his teeth nipped at the skin of her neck. "Cade. Please, please touch me."

He drew back only enough to gaze down into her face.

"Have you ever come for a man?" He growled. "Tell me now if you have, Marly. I need to know how to make it easy for you. Don't lie to me, not about this." Savage and intense his eyes snared hers.

She shook her head harshly, her arousal sweeping over her mindlessly.

"Never," she gasped. "Never, Cade. No other man has touched me. Please make me come. Please."

He clenched his teeth, his breath rumbling from his chest as he fought himself. Then he was pushing her down on the bed, coming over her as his lips clamped on the tip of her breast, his tongue curling around her nipple, rasping the ultra sensitive nerves with a stroke of fire.

"You want to come for me, baby?" He parted her thighs, moving over her as his lips moved to her stomach, his tongue painting her skin with need as his lips sent her body trembling with passion.

"Yes," she gasped, her fingers in his hair now, her head twisting on the bed as he moved swiftly down her body. "Only you, Cade. I only want to come for you."

He paused the moment his lips were poised over the vee of her thighs. Marly opened her eyes, watching as he gazed down at her.

"Oral sex," he groaned. "This isn't oral sex, Marly, it's a feast for kings, and I'm about to devour it."

His head lowered, then his tongue touched her. Marly cried out, arching to the soft stroke of his tongue as it circled her clit. His hands pushed her thighs further apart, his lips settling on her, suckling her in time to the slow flicks of his tongue.

Marly panted for air. Her heart was ready to burst out of her chest her excitement soared so high. She was no longer cold, no longer frightened. She was so hot she felt on fire. Cade's tongue was an instrument of pleasure so intense it bordered on pain. Sweeping through the velvet folds of skin, licking sensually at her clit, then suckling it firmly. She was bucking against his mouth, hanging on an edge that was both terrifying and exhilarating as she fought the mindless sensations ripping through her body.

Cade didn't protest her heaving body. He merely gripped her thighs in his hands, held her hips steady and proceeded to torture her in a way that left her breathless, pleading. Then that devilish tongue moved lower. It dipped into the soft recess of her body, thrusting inside her, making her cry out harshly.

She was disoriented, shaking in need as he growled, rose from the delicate feast he was making of her, and turned her quickly to her stomach.

"Cade?" She felt his hand smooth over the soft rise of her buttocks.

"Shhh. Baby, what did you do to this pretty little rear?" He groaned. "It's so damned red I'd swear someone smacked it."

Marly flinched. She had been whipped in her dream. She would have questioned him, but suddenly she felt his lips on the tender flesh. She groaned, shuddering as his palms smoothed over her, pulling the rounded cheeks apart tenderly.

"Scared yet, Marly?" he asked her roughly, his fingers holding her apart, his breath hot and moist at the tender bud she knew he sought.

"No," she cried out harshly.

Her head tossed as his lowered. His tongue swiped over the area quickly. From the clenching, drenched vaginal opening to the tight little hole of her anus. His tongue licked her over and over again, dipping into each entrance with slick deliberation as his hands spread her thighs further apart, smoothing over her skin, making her tense, groan, and push against his mouth for more.

Then he turned her to her back again, raising her thigh, his tongue penetrating her with a smooth, deep thrust that had her bucking against his mouth.

"Scared?" he groaned, his head raising, his voice dark, harsh.

Scared? Terrified he would stop.

"More," she begged. "More, Cade."

His fingers joined his mouth, moving the drenching lubrication of her body to her anus. His finger dipped in with each pass, pressing against her, easing his way into her body. Marly was on fire. She panted, fighting to relax, to further invite the invasion of his finger into her body. When it came, she nearly screamed from the bite of bliss that seared her.

His finger was inside her now, stretching her, moving smoothly as he tongued her cunt to delirium, spreading the silky liquid back, keeping the entrance hot and easy to access as he drove her higher, always higher.

She was falling. Dying. The harsh ring of the phone on the table beside Cade's bed was barely noticeable until he reared up with a virulent curse.

"No," she gasped, clutching at him, her body slammed suddenly back to earth, the edge of oblivion shattered.

Growling, cursing, he jerked the phone from the bedside table.

"What?" His voice was so harsh, so graveled that even Marly flinched.

"Then get the fuckers back in the damned pasture." He raked his fingers through his hair, his chest heaving. "Shit. Shit. I'll be right there."

Cade slammed the phone down, then turned and looked down at Marly. She looked drunk, high and dazed.

"Cattle are filling the yard. They got out of the pasture." He raked his fingers through his hair again. "I have to go, Marly."

She was fighting for breath, her fists clenched beside her, her eyes large, dark and pleading. She had been so close. So fucking close, but not close enough to throw her over before that damned phone would have disturbed her.

"Cattle?" she gasped, closing her eyes.

Her body was tight, once again damp with sweat and trembling. Trembling in need. It was a shimmer through her body that echoed in his. A need to release. He couldn't leave her this way. He dropped to the bed again, his mouth going to the saturated flesh between her thighs and began to feast on the creamy nectar.

With his thumb on her sensitive clit, rasping it with gentle strokes, he moved his head lower, then plunged his tongue swiftly inside her melting vagina. One thrust and she heaved. On the second she tightened, arching high and hard. The third had her screaming, convulsing mindlessly as the sweet essence of her release began to fill his mouth and his own hollow ejaculation spilled to the sheets.

She collapsed to the bed long moments later, boneless and spent, her hands falling from his shoulders. Cade rose painfully from her body, and shook his head in disbelief. She was asleep. Damn it all to hell, but she was asleep. He flipped the blanket over her body, and went quickly to the bathroom to clean up. Ten minutes later he was dressed and running down the stairs to meet Sam and Brock at the front door.

"What the hell happened?" Sam mumbled sleepily.

"Cattle's loose in the yards. Bret says it looks like the whole herd is busy munching the lawn grass," Cade bit out furiously, not even certain why he was so pissed. Cattle got loose all the time. "Get out there and get them herded back, then we'll find the break in the fence."

"Damn, thought we had cowboys hired," Sam sighed.

"We do, and they need help, so get your ass out there." He pushed Sam none too gently out the door, then stared in amazement at the sea of bovine guests. "Dammit to hell." His curse rang through the yard with his disgust. "Get these damned animals back the hell where they belong."

There were days, or nights in this case, Cade thought, that he wondered if Sam was right all along. Surely to hell he could pay someone to put up with this shit.

* * * * *

They dragged into the house long after dawn, dusty and tired, with nerves fraying at the ends. Entering the kitchen, he found Marly and Greg seated at the kitchen table, laughing at some joke as they finished breakfast. Eggs, ham, biscuits. He was starved.

"Well, at least the two of you are comfortable," he snapped, eying them suspiciously.

Once again, Marly was dressed in only one of his shirts and a pair of his socks. Her legs were crossed, in the boy's line of vision and it infuriated him. Especially considering the fact that it was all the James boy could do to keep his eyes off them.

Marly blinked in surprise.

"Um, I need to shower, Marly." Greg jumped to his feet, uneasy in Cade's presence anyway, the sight of his anger was enough to leave him scurrying.

"What's your problem?" She frowned as she rose to her feet.

"What could be my problem?" he growled, stomping to the coffee pot. "You leave your balcony door open all night then awaken me screaming like a banshee. Some moron let the cattle out, and I walk in here to find you two cozying over breakfast. At least be good enough to do it in private."

He watched the surprised hurt that crossed her face.

"I don't have time to baby-sit you today either," he bit out. "I have work to do."

"I didn't ask you to." Her lips trembled, but she held her tears carefully in check. That made him even angrier. Damn her. He'd had her screaming out into the night with her orgasm, and here she was the next morning acting as though it had never happened.

"Make sure you don't," he growled.

"Damn, Cade, go get laid or something. You're an asshole," Sam bit out. "Leave Marly alone."

Marly paled, blinking in shock as her gaze flew back to Cade.

"Maybe that's just what I need," he said furiously. "A woman for a change."

He didn't wait to see the tears building in her eyes fall to her cheeks. He turned and stomped from the kitchen, disgusted with himself, furious at Marly, and unable to make sense of any of it. He knew if he didn't get away from her, before he took her, then it would kill him later to see the fear in her eyes.

He stalked through the house, his body trembling with lust, fatigue and fury. She was too young, too innocent and the wrong damned woman. Dammit, when was he going to convince himself of that?

"Ahh hell, Marly, he didn't mean that." Sam grabbed her as she made to run out of the kitchen in tears, pushing her head against his chest as he rubbed her back soothingly. "You know what an ass he can be when he's stressed."

Marly's breath hitched as she fought the tears. She knew why Cade was attacking her; she just didn't know it would hurt so badly. She held onto Sam, feeling his hands at her back, petting her through the silk of Cade's shirt. He was warm, comforting. She liked the way he soothed her, holding her. She blinked, sighed. She was so hot for Cade that even

Sam's touch was turning sexual. His big hands roamed her back, pressing her against him.

She moved away nervously. Rumors, sexual and otherwise reared their ugly heads, but didn't terrify her as they should have.

"I'm okay." She rubbed her arms quickly, fighting back the ache between her thighs.

She had been waiting on Cade, hoping to tempt him, to experience the breathtaking heights of pleasure he had taken her to once again. Instead, she was allowing Sam, her beloved friend and confidant, to only stoke the embers higher.

"Sure you are, honey." He hugged her close, his arm wrapped around her waist, his fingers lying below her unbound breasts. "And you will stay just fine. Just you wait. Cade will get over his little mad spell and everything will be fine."

Had his fingers accidentally raked over her nipple as he moved away, or had it been deliberate? Suspicion raised its ugly head even as she beat it back ruthlessly. Cruel rumors, that was all they were. Wasn't that what Cade had assured her years ago when she questioned him about it?

"I need to go." She shook her head; fighting the insanity Cade was filling her with. "I'll see you guys later."

She rushed from the kitchen, her head down, her body rioting. Maybe she was the one that needed to get laid, and quickly, before she did something stupid.

Chapter Seven

෨

"Did I ask you to think, Devon?" Cade's voice echoed through the house on a note of rising anger.

Marly stopped just inside the hallway as she exited the staircase, watching as Cade pulled the door open for the furious cowboy.

"All I asked you to do was to get the new foals in. I didn't ask you to think, and I sure as hell didn't ask you to contradict my orders. Do you think you could manage that much?"

"I sure as hell can, boss." Devon shoved the hat back on his head as he stalked to the door. "And I sure as hell can leave as soon as I do. I didn't sign on for this shit."

The cowboy stomped from the house, and Marly flinched as the door slammed harshly behind him.

"Another one get fed up with your temper?" She leaned against the wall, crossing her legs slowly as he turned to her.

His eyes were narrowed, heavy lidded and brooding as he watched her.

It had been almost two days since he had nearly taken her in the bedroom. Two long, torturous days where his temper raged alternately cold and silent, or hot and loud. Even Greg avoided him, staying at the stables with Sam or Brock when he wasn't studying, but rarely venturing anywhere near Cade. Marly was the only one brave enough. It made her feel guilty for pressuring him to stay. She had honestly thought he would enjoy the visit.

"Why aren't you dressed?" he growled, his gaze darkening as it went over her body.

Marly glanced down at the short bronze dress and matching high heels. Silk thigh-highs completed the outfit. She knew she looked good. Knew the dress would make him notice her.

"I am dressed, Cade." She smiled up at him, slowly, daring him to notice her. "Why aren't you in a better mood? You keep stomping around like a mean old bull and I'm going to go back to school where it's peaceful."

"You hate school," he growled. "I don't even know why you enrolled. You could have taken classes here. At home."

He neared her slowly, his jeans riding low on his hips, and from the brief glance, with a steadily growing bulge beneath the cloth. Marly's knees weakened. The white cotton button down shirt he wore and the wide leather belt that encased his hips emphasized his hard stomach.

Marly felt her mouth go dry, then moist. She wanted to taste his skin. Badly.

"Still playing games?" he growled, as he stepped closer to her.

Marly raised her gaze, arching a brow in way she knew would only infuriate him. "Still horny? What, your little black book missing?"

His lips tightened. He stared down at her, the gray of his eyes darkening, the color swirling like thunderclouds ready to burst.

"It's a fine line you're treading, Marly," he whispered, staring down at her, his expression dark and dangerous. "If anyone in this world knows me, it's you, and you know you aren't ready for what I'd dish out to you."

Heat slammed into her stomach, making her knees weak.

"I've dreamed about you dishing it up, Cade," she whispered, touching his chest with the flat of her hand, feeling his heart thunder in his chest, much as hers was. "I've waited for it for two long years."

She watched his jaw clench.

"You don't know, Marly," he growled. "You can't know."

"I know how hard you like it," her voice was husky, smoky and raw with desire. "Rough and hard, your women on their knees, submitting to you. I know you like things most women would run screaming from. I don't run easily, Cade. You know that."

His hand covered hers, his fingers pressing them against the shirt, to feel the heat of her flesh sinking into his skin.

"Then you know I don't do little girls." Ragged and tense, his voice belied the anger he tried to project.

She laughed richly, then shrugged. "I'm still a virgin, but not stupid. I know you want me, Cade."

His eyes narrowed, his lips thinning ominously.

"It would terrify you."

"It might at first," she admitted. "But just think, you could teach it all to me. How you like it, where you like it, when you like it. I haven't had any other lovers, Cade. No one else has taught me how to do that."

"What have they taught you?" His voice was low, curling through her like a flame.

She licked her lips. She was treading on dangerous ground, and she knew it. Cade was like a volcano, ready to erupt. When he did, she knew he would burn her alive with his touch. But she didn't want his anger. She wanted him to need her, to accept that need. She didn't want him angry over it.

"You'll just have to find out I guess," she told him, smiling secretively. "Experiment, so to speak, and see if you can find out what's been taught to me, and what hasn't."

It was a challenge. She knew what a challenge did to him. He may not take her up on it now, but he would. She knew he would.

He was breathing harshly. It turned her on to watch him struggle for breath, to know she was doing to him the same things he did to her.

"If you know so damned much, then you know I like my women submissive," he growled. "I don't like to be challenged, not in sex or in life. Jump when I command, fuck when I want."

"I never said I would be just like them." She moved against him, her body brushing his, feeling the heat coming off of it. "I said I know what you like. And most of it, I can accept. But I won't be a submissive, Cade."

"You come to my bed and I'll enslave you," he swore darkly. "Is that how you want it Marly? A sexual slave, begging for me, and learning to love the degradation I inflict on you? Is that how you really want it?"

He grabbed her roughly, pushing her into his study, then against the wall behind the door. He held her there, her stomach and breasts pressed into the wall, his hips pinning her tightly. The dress was jerked to her hips, his hand clamping on the bare cheek of her rear as he groaned harshly at her ear.

Then he smacked her. Marly cried out, bucking as the stinging flare of heat seared her butt.

"Spread your legs." He didn't give her time to comply; he simply jerked her legs apart, then smacked the other cheek lightly, yet hard enough she knew to redden the flesh.

"Take your panties off." He smacked her again, making her jerk, making her body hum with an arousal she hadn't expected.

Dear God. This wasn't what she had expected. Thrown into arousal so hot and intense she was ready to come now. His hands, hard but not hurting, held her still. His breathing, harsh against her neck, had her trembling in painful awareness of his strength.

Moving awkwardly, she slid her hands in the waistband of the thongs and pushed them over her hips and thighs. She stepped out of them slowly when they pooled at her feet.

His hand smoothed over her rear, hard and warm, his fingers running slowly down the crack, pausing at the tight pucker lower, then dipping quickly into the heated, slick crease of her female channel. Marly cried out, her head falling back on his chest as his finger pushed forward slowly. He gathered the slick essence, massaging it from her crease back to her tight little rear then back again. She was so wet, so slick and hot he had her lubricated quickly.

"You don't know me, Marly," he growled at her ear. "Not like this. Not sexually. No matter what you've heard, no matter what you think, you don't know."

His finger rasped over the pucker again, slick and hot as he drew the moisture from her cunt.

"I'm hard and thick, baby, and all I want in this world right now is to hear you scream in pleasure as I slide my cock up your tight little ass. I'll take you there. Do you know that? Are you ready for it?"

She flattened her hands against the wall; her back arching as his fingertip slid in then retreated.

"I want you. However you want me, Cade. Wherever you want me." Her head tossed. She knew he would want this. Knew it was a favorite sexual practice of his.

Marly's heart was thundering in her chest, her breathing ragged, almost a cry as he kept moving, lubricating both areas slowly.

"Take a deep breath," he commanded harshly. "Now."

She breathed in deep. She knew how to do this, made certain her body would be ready for it when he wanted it. But still, her eyes flew open, her mouth opening on a gasp, then a cry as his finger slid deeply into her anus. She heard him moan harshly behind her as her muscles eased around him, accepting him, then gripping tight.

It was so good. She couldn't stop the need to push back against him, or the strangled cry as the fingers of his other hand moved to her clit. She was on fire. So hot, so ready for him, she didn't know if she could survive it.

"Who's fucked your ass, Marly?" There was fury ringing in his voice now. "That little prick upstairs?"

She shook her head, unable to speak as she felt him pull back, then add another digit.

"Who?" He growled.

She shook her head again, gasping as he pushed deep now.

"Tight. So damned tight." His voice was tortured, ringing with lust now.

He thrust inside her again, causing her to cry out at the pleasure, to buck in his arms and to need.

Cade stilled behind her. His fingers were lodged deep, then sliding smoothly away from her, leaving her aching, almost begging for more. She cried out in protest, on the edge of oblivion and gasping to fly into it. And he was denying her. Again, he was denying her.

"I don't like this game you're playing with me," he accused her roughly, his mouth at her ear, low and furious. "Stop it Marly. Stop it now, before I do something else we'll both end up regretting."

He jerked her dress down, and she felt him turning away from her. She stayed where she was, hiding her disappointment and her tears.

"I have work to do." He turned to his heel heading for the door. "Change your clothes dammit. You're making my cowboys crazy. I'll end up having to kill one of them."

Chapter Eight

ဆ

It must be the night for nightmares. Cade heard Brock's strangled scream. Seconds later the other man's bedroom door slammed and he stalked down the hall. Dressed, heading for the night. They all headed for the night after the nightmares. The darkness, the shadows, hiding from the demons that stalked them continually.

He breathed deeply, tired. He stared at the ceiling, feeling the familiar weight of grief and guilt that tore through his belly every time the twins suffered from the dreams. He didn't know how to ease the pain. Didn't know how to ease the grief. He carried his own, and only found oblivion in sex. In the hard driving edge of lust, sweat and ragged cries. There was no solace to be found in the night. The wide-open spaces did nothing to ease the confinement of a locked cage, the helplessness of being totally at another person's mercy.

He rose from the bed and dressed, knowing he would never sleep until he made certain Brock still held to his sanity. It was a fine line, holding onto something they had lost for precious months, long ago.

The night was dark, moonless. Cade stepped onto the porch, smelling the acrid bite of tobacco from the shadows to his right. The demon glow of a lit cigarette flared in the darkness, a sharp exhale, a strangled gasp as a man fought for control.

"You okay?" Cade leaned against the porch post, still several feet from the shadow-darkened form.

"Fine." Brock's voice was hard, tight.

"It's over Brock." Cade didn't know how to reassure him. How to make it better. "We have to get past it."

There was a broken growl of cynical laughter. Like an animal, a dying creature fighting to accept. Cade clenched his teeth against the fury that sound brought.

"Get past it huh?" The cigarette tip flared again. "So tell me brother, are you past it yet?"

Cade tucked his hands into the pockets of his jeans. The sky was as black as he sometimes thought his soul was, but he still looked for the light. The tiny pinpricks of brilliance that proved there was at least the hope that life existed.

"We have to keep trying." It was all he had to hold onto. That someday, the bloody memories would ease, and give him peace.

"He knew, Cade." Brock's voice was hoarse with his knowledge, with unshed tears. "He knew what that bastard was going to do to us. I don't care what he said. He knew."

Their father. Joe August. Yeah, Cade always suspected the same thing, despite Joe's pleading vows that he hadn't known. Despite the lengths he had gone to cover the blood Cade had shed, he knew. There was no way either Joe, or their mother, couldn't have known what was happening to them.

"I know, Brock." Cade hunched his shoulders, frowning into the night.

"I wanted to kill him." Brock's voice shook. There were no tears. There hadn't been since those weeks after the nightmare had first begun. Brock hadn't cried since.

"I couldn't have hid it." If he could have, Cade knew he would have killed Joe as well if it had been possible. That need had lived in him for years, like a monster, fanged and enraged, ready to escape.

"I need her Cade." The loneliness in Brock's voice was searing. "God. Damn it to hell and back, Cade. I need her."

Cade flinched.

"We can't do it to her, Brock. Not to either of them. Not to Marly or Sarah. You know that."

"Then someone else," Brock growled, furious. "I hate this Cade. I hate this fucking feeling more than anything in the world. Goddammit, it's killing us all."

"Would anyone else ease it, Brock?" Cade heard the mockery in his tone, but did nothing to filter it. "We tried that, more than once. It didn't help."

This was their life. Fury ate at Cade, just as he knew it ate at Brock. They were alone. So isolated within themselves and the black secret they carried, that there was no ease, no comfort, with the exception of one thing. Marly. Marly, or the woman whose name Brock refused to mention. One denied him, and therefore better left forgotten.

Cade lowered his head, hearing a lighter strike, smelling a new cigarette filtering through the air. Brock rarely smoked, but when he did, it would take him hours to stop lighting.

"Have you fucked her yet?" Cade heard the longing in Brock's voice.

Cade closed his eyes, fighting it. Fighting it but needing it just as much as his damned brothers did. They were monsters, all of them, though Cade never accused them so harshly. It was his fault. His guilt that he had been able to find no other outlet for them.

"No."

"You have to, Cade. Soon."

"She'll leave us, Brock. Is that what we really want?"

"She'll leave you anyway," Brock predicted. "She's a woman, I told you that. She wants you, and whether you accept it or not, she'll accept me and Sam. I've seen it. I know she will. Especially if you explain."

"No," Cade denied the idea outright. He wouldn't tell her, and he would kill whoever did. He couldn't bear the guilt, but even more the shame. He couldn't bear to see the knowledge in Marly's eyes that he was less than invincible.

Screams echoed through the night, but they weren't the screams of reality. They were the distant thunder of the past, washing over him. The helplessness, the agonizing pain, both physical and mental. The unwashed smell of sweat, blood, fear and semen drifted on the air.

"Was it our faults?" Brock and Sam had both asked that question. The same tone of voice, the same remembered rage.

"You know it wasn't, Brock," Cade reminded him. "We did nothing to cause it. You know that."

A sigh, softer, no longer strangled as smoke drifted through the night.

"You won't be able to stop this," Brock told him as he took a deep breath. "Just like Sam and I can't stop wanting her. It's going to happen."

If he took Marly. If he fucked her, and made her his woman in any way, then Cade knew it would as well. For the first time since he had found a way to save them from the brutality of the past, he hated it. Not because it meant sharing the woman he loved with the brothers he no longer knew how to love, but because he wanted it so fucking bad. Wanted it, even though he was terrified it would destroy Marly. Destroy her, and any love she would still hold in her heart for him.

"If I lose her, it will kill me," Cade told him, shaking his head. "Do you know that Brock? It will be the one thing I won't be able to survive."

"Then we're all doomed, Cade," Brock told him, his voice bitter, lost. "Just as we were from the beginning. Fucking doomed."

Chapter Nine

Marly watched from the corral the next morning as Greg and Sam worked inside with one of the horses. Greg's smile was so big it nearly covered his face as Sam taught him how to ride Beanie, their gentlest mare. For the city boy with no riding experience, she knew this was a dream come true for Greg. And though she could tell he was excited, he was strangely serious about it as well.

"You wanna ride out with us, little sister?" Sam neared her on the large buckskin he rode. "You could saddle one of the horses up right fast."

"Not today. You and Greg go on." She waved him away, smiling as Greg shifted in the saddle, frowning down at the horse with a look of concentration. "I'll go next time maybe."

"Okay." Sam nodded, glancing behind her. "We'll be back in a bit then."

He turned his horse, cantering back to Greg as Marly felt Cade move up behind her.

She stiffened, feeling the heat of his body as he braced his arms on each side of her.

"Those skimpy dresses are going to drive my cowboys over the edge, Marly." His breath feathered the loose hairs along the side of her braid.

"The cowboys are gone for the day. Remember?" She said huskily, remembering his same charge the day before.

"That dress shows more of your ass than the one you wore yesterday." He leaned close, his breath warm at her neck.

Marly took a deep, harsh breath. Then it stalled in her chest as one hand dropped to her waist. She closed her eyes, feeling the tension in his body, a strange intent emanating from him.

"Still haven't got off yet, Cade?" Her voice was strained. "Man, must be tough finding an available woman at your age. All of them married now or what?"

His hand clenched at her waist, then his teeth scraped her neck. Marly whimpered as her knees nearly buckled. A breathy sound between a moan and a cry was torn from her as his teeth clenched about her skin, his tongue stroking over the flesh he held captive.

"Cade?" One strong arm wrapped around her waist, pulling her against him as she cried out. Another pushed passed the hem of her dress, zeroing on the smooth bare cheeks of her bottom.

"Damn thongs. They need to be outlawed." His fingers pushed past the fragile elastic, until two were pushing into the tight, soaking depths of her vagina.

Marly came. She couldn't believe it. Right there, no sooner than she felt the pinch of his entrance, those two large fingers pushing into her, she climaxed with a sharp cry. She felt the slick release of moisture that she knew must be coating his fingers, dampening the bare flesh of her quivering cunt.

The arm wrapped around her waist moved, his hand cupping her breast, pinching the nipple of one between his thumb and finger. His fingers moved inside her again, slow and easy, pulling back, then thrusting into the hot depths until they met the barrier of her virginity. Over and over again. Long, smooth sliding motions that had her trembling, gasping for breath.

"I want you on your knees, with my cock in your mouth," he whispered seductively at her ear, his teeth nibbling the skin there. "I'm hard Marly, and hurting, and you know it. Stop pushing me or you'll get something you're sure as hell not prepared for."

His fingers moved from the soaked depths of her pussy, back to the tight little bud of her rear and back again. Marly trembled. Shaking. Weak and on fire. She knew what was coming, and she craved it. Each time his fingers passed the little bud, pushing her moisture into it, deeper with each pass, she pushed against it, needing it inside her, needing to give him anything, everything he wanted from her.

"I could tear that piece of cloth from your body now, and fuck you until you're screaming," he panted, pressing his erection into the smooth, bared crevice of her rear, the jeans material scraping her soft skin.

His fingers dipped into her wet channel, then moved back again. And again, until the tight little entrance was giving easily to the fingertip pressing smoothly against it. Marly cried out, fighting to stand upright as his finger tormented then retreated, then two fingers pressing inside her vagina again, only to repeat the maneuver over and over again.

"I could push you to your knees, and fuck your hot little mouth, or bend you over and take you from behind. I can do it, girl. Stop flashing your ass at me. Stop showing me those pretty hard nipples, or I'll do just that." His finger sank into her nether hole deeply, eliciting a sharp, shattered cry from her as her muscles clenched around him.

Marly was dazed. Shocked by his actions. He bent her over his arm, thrusting his finger into her again, and again, ignoring the arching of her back, the tight grip of her body as he taunted her. Then he was turning her in his arms, his arm curved around her, his finger refusing to release her from the shocking impalement.

He lifted her against him as he leaned against the barn, holding her steady as he lifted her nearly off her feet, his thick finger sinking deeper, making her gasp as her damp need began to soak the jean-covered thigh he pushed between hers.

One hand tore at the bodice of her dress, jerking aside the fragile cups until her breasts were bare. Marly screamed out as his head lowered, his teeth nipping at her nipple, then his mouth covering it, sucking it, laving it with his tongue.

His finger pulled back, then thrust inside her again. Marly arched, pushing her breast deeper into his mouth as the little pain the thrust caused made her ride his thigh harder.

"You want it bad, don't you baby?" He growled against her breast, holding her steady as he moved into the barn.

The finger he had shoved up her ass pulled free as he entered the dark confines of the nearest free stall. Then he was fighting with the buttons of his jeans, freeing them with quick, jerky motions.

"Cade?" Her voice trembled as his cock sprang free. It was long and thick, and angry looking as her eyes widened at the sight.

"No." He closed his eyes, tormented. "Don't Marly. Don't get scared on me. I just want you to suck it baby. Please...I just want to feel your hot little mouth around it."

He pushed her gently to her knees, leaning weakly against the wall of the stall as he watched her with a savage, hard expression.

"I swear to God I won't hurt you, but I can't take anymore, Marly. Suck it now, baby. Suck me until I come in your mouth."

Fear, excitement, hot pulsing lust mixed and merged inside Marly as the thick erection was pushed against her lips. Cade was moaning, his gray eyes nearly black now as he watched her mouth open for him.

"Yes. Yes," he hissed. "Open your mouth, Marly."

The head of his cock slid slowly in. One large hand wrapped around the base of it, and the other half sank deep into her mouth, nearly touching her tonsils as she fought to take him.

"Suck it," he ordered her harshly, pulling back, only to slide past her lips once again. "Now Marly."

Her lips tightened on him, one hand moving to cover the base of his cock with her own hands, gripping him tightly as her mouth covered the remaining flesh begging for attention. It stretched her lips, made them feel bruised as he thrust against her, but the feel of him in her mouth, his deep groans echoing in the barn spurred her on.

Hollowing her cheeks, slurping on his flesh, her lips caressing, her tongue stroking him, she began a rapid bob of her head. His free hand clenched in her hair, making her move her head faster as his hips fucked his flesh in and out of her mouth, over and over again.

Marly loved the feel of his flesh, so hard and hot, filling her mouth, stretching her lips. She stared into his face, watching the flush that mounted his cheeks, the way his eyes darkened, filled with lust.

"Suck it hard," he bit out fiercely. "Suck it hard, Marly. I'm going to come, baby."

Two hard thrusts later she felt the thick jets of his semen pulse into her mouth, sliding down her throat as he buried his cock deep. His body jerked in time to the hot pulse of his release, his gasps harsh and agonizing as she kept sucking, drawing every drop of his release from his tight, hot sac.

Suddenly, just as quickly as he had thrust his cock in her mouth, he jerked it free. He stared down at her, his eyes dark, almost frightening, his flesh still hard as he breathed roughly.

"Is this what you want, Marly?" He groaned as though in pain. "Is this really what you want? Because I swear to God, I don't know if I can handle it."

He stuffed his still hard cock back into his pants, buttoning them swiftly as she stared up at him. She ran her tongue over her lips, tasting the salty residue of his orgasm there. Cade stilled at the movement.

"Your lips are stained with my come," his voice was tormented. "You look like a whore, Marly. My whore."

He turned his back on her, stalking from the barn as Marly felt her face pale. She lowered her head, fighting the tears that began to fall from her eyes, the sense of shame that filled her body. Slowly, she pulled herself up from the hay-scattered floor, fixing her dress, her panties, and walked painfully back to the house.

Cade stood in the doorway of his study as she walked in, a bottle of liquor in his hand as he watched her. She met his gaze, though it took every measure of strength she could pull into her to do it.

"I'll leave tonight," she whispered, then moved past him.

Before she could stop him, he had jerked her against him, staring down at her in fury.

"No you won't," he bit out. "You promised me the full Spring Vacation Marly. Two whole fucking weeks, and I'll be damned if you'll cheat me out of them."

Her eyes widened as he jerked her into the study, slamming the door behind them.

"No!" Marly jerked away from him, fury filling her at the treatment he had given her. She faced him, fury surging through her, drying the tears threatening to fall from her eyes.

"Come here, Marly." She could see the intent in his eyes, the bulge beneath his jeans.

"So I can whore for you again?" She nearly strangled on the words. "You bastard. You're too cowardly to admit you want me as much as I want you, instead, you want to hurt me with it. Teach me a lesson."

He ran his fingers through his hair in a gesture of intense frustration as he grimaced heavily.

"Marly, please. I'm not trying to hurt you," he whispered, shaking his head. "You're killing me, and you refuse to see it. For God's sake, please stop. Before I hurt both of us."

"I can't be a child again," she screamed out at him, the tears finally falling. "That's what you want, Cade. Admit it."

"Hell yes. God. Damn, yes it is." The bottle went flying, crashing into the wall, the heavy scent of liquor washing through the room. "I fucking raised you Marly. I didn't raise you to fuck you."

Marly shook her head, sobs shaking her body now.

"I won't." Her fists clenched as she stared into his tormented features. "I won't Cade. I love you too much. I need you too much to ever play a role for you so you can hide the fact that you need me too."

"No." He grimaced at the accusation.

"No?" She questioned him with an amazed laugh. "So whose hard-on did I have shoved down my throat? Whose finger was pushed up my ass, Cade? I could have sworn it was yours. And I could have sworn it was me getting it. Are you fooling yourself into thinking it's someone else?"

Her voice rose with her anger as she faced him, ignoring the storm brewing in his eyes, the fury gathering in his expression.

"Stop," he bit out. "Just stop this, Marly."

"What about me, Cade?" She stepped close to him now, her body vibrating with the injustice of what he had done to her. "You left me kneeling in the dirt, the taste of your climax still in my mouth, needing you. I needed you too. Where was my orgasm, you son of a bitch?"

"Horny, Marly?" He threw her own, earlier words back at her.

Marly drew herself up stiffly, ignoring the tears and the pain.

"Hell yes, and I'm woman enough to admit to it," she said slowly. "And you know what, Cade? I'm woman enough to do something about it."

She shoved past him roughly, heading for the door. She turned the knob, ready to throw it open when his voice stopped her.

"What the hell does that mean?" There was danger in every syllable.

She turned back to him, her smile mocking and bitter.

"Simple, Cade. If you can't put out the fire you started, then fuck you. I'll find someone who will."

She jerked the door open as she spoke, turned and ran headlong into Sam's chest.

She raised her eyes, seeing the quiet anger in his face, the sympathy in his eyes. He had heard it all. She shook her head, her face flaming in shame.

"Hey, Munchkin." He lifted her face up, his thumb touching the corner of her lips briefly, then staring down at the creamy residue he had wiped from it. Marly felt sick, overwhelmed with humiliation and fury.

Sam raised his gaze, looking over her shoulder as his expression hardened.

"Sam," Cade's voice was warning him not to interfere.

"Come on, Marly." Sam drew her outside the room, his arm wrapping around her shoulders in a gesture of brotherly concern. "Greg and I decided on pizza tonight. You can go with us to get it."

"Sam." Cade's voice was harder now as he started towards them.

"Stop." Sam pulled Marly out of harm's way, pushing her towards a silent, grim-faced Greg. "Leave her the hell alone, Cade. I think enough is enough. Go wallow in your liquor, if there's any left from your temper. I'm getting Marly out of here for the night."

"Marly, don't leave." Cade stared at her darkly. "We aren't finished."

"Yeah, we are." She shook her head, moving for the door. "At least, for tonight we are."

Chapter Ten

🍧

The night was dark. Even though Marly had left the curtains open to her balcony, the cloud-filled sky filtered the glow of the moon. The nightlight was on, though. It cast a soft light over her bed, over her pale naked body as she slept restlessly. Cade entered the room, pacing silently to the chair at the side of the bed and eased himself into it with slow, weary motions.

Sam had kept her out late. Cade knew his younger brother was furious with him, so angry he refused to speak to him. Cade hated it, but for the life of him, he could think of no way to fix it. His conscience and his lusts were tearing him apart to the point that here he was; sitting silently in her room, staring at her, because he couldn't have her any other way.

Her slender body was stretched out on the mattress, one arm bent over her stomach, the other laying at her side. Her thighs were parted, her bare mound glistening. Damn, did she stay wet? His body throbbed at the thought.

He stifled his groan, rubbing his hands over his face, denying the need to shed his soft sweat pants and crawl into the bed with her. His cock demanded it, his head refused, and his heart was torn. How do you fuck the woman you spent eight years protecting and raising? What kind of pervert did that make him? He leaned back in the chair, watching her painfully.

He used to do this when she was a child. Knowing when the nightmares would come and wanting to be there for her if they did. He'd had none of these thoughts then. No lust for her. She had curled innocently in her bed, sleeping while he tried to protect her. She had been so damned tiny as a child.

Still was. With those big blue eyes and all that hair. He had loved her the minute Annie had brought her to the door that day. When had it changed?

He couldn't pinpoint the day he had started lusting after. He knew it hadn't begun before her eighteenth birthday, but he knew when it started it had been hard and quick. He remembered the day he realized it. Right after her graduation, at the pool with her friend Lexia. He had looked at her, a brief glance out the doors of his study, and lust had consumed him. It had been all he could do to keep from stalking out to her, picking her up and thrusting into her then and there. And it had gotten worse since then.

"Cade?" Her sleepy voice was questioning as his gaze met her heavy lidded expression.

She didn't jump to cover herself, didn't seem to care that she was naked and he was hard, hurting with his need. Her blue eyes were dark, her lips full and sensual.

Her nipples hardened as his gaze centered on them, puckering for him, the sweet mounds of her breasts hardening. His mouth went dry.

"Did you get off?" He growled, unable to get away from the anger of her earlier words to him.

"Not unless you count masturbation." Her voice was amused, but soft and sweet with drowsiness. "Does that count, Cade?"

He swallowed tightly. Then his breath left his throat as her fingers, slender and graceful caressed the flesh between her thighs.

"That counts," he growled, moving quickly to forestall her movements.

Her hand lay under his, the humid heat of her body like a brand to his fingers.

"Want to help me?" Her voice was thicker, smoky and hauntingly sexy.

His index finger lay impossibly close to her clit. He swore he could feel the little knot of nerves throbbing. He was nearly laying beside her now, staring down at her, helplessly caught in the glittering sensuality she exuded.

"I want to eat you up." He heard the catch in her breath; saw the sharp rise of her breasts as excitement flared inside her. "But I can't."

Why? Why? The question tore through his brain, his body. His lust demanding a reason.

"You fucked my mouth until you came. You owe me." Her hips rose against his hand, causing his finger to glance her clit. He felt it swell, harden.

His erection throbbed at the reminder of her hot mouth. Tight and suckling him like she loved it. He wanted to close his eyes, remembering the hot pulse of his release, but he couldn't look away from her. She licked her lips slowly.

"You think you have me, don't you, Marly?" His hand cupped her, pushing her hand back, covering the entire area of her silken, soaked cunt. "You think you can dominate me, make me heel."

"No, Cade," she protested on a breathless cry as he tightened his grip on her, enough to make her clench with pleasure. "That's not what I want."

He thrust his middle finger into her vagina, his palm rubbing her clit as she jerked and moaned roughly.

"What do you want then?" He thrust his finger inside her again, then allowed another to join it.

He watched the heat mount her cheeks, her eyes grow darker as her firm breast moved against his chest with her body's demand for increased oxygen. Her thighs splayed apart, her hips rose and fell against his hand as her hand clenched at his wrist as though trying to hold him there.

"I just want you," she cried out.

"Then tell me the truth, Marly," he whispered. "How did you learn to take my fingers so easily up your tight little butt. A virgin would have run away screaming."

"No," she cried out, painfully. "It's not like that."

He could see a flare of shame in her eyes.

"Then what was it like?" He rubbed her clit harder, bringing her close, never letting her go over. "Tell me, Marly. What was it like?"

"I knew you liked it," she gasped as he licked her nipple, his eyes never leaving hers. "I had to learn how to do it, so you wouldn't refuse me."

Jealousy boiled inside him.

"Who showed you, Marly?" His eased his caress against her clit, knowing she was desperate to come.

"Don't stop." Desperation flared in her expression. "Please. Please, Cade. Don't stop."

"Tell me what I want to know, Marly." His touch was lighter, but he didn't leave her. "Who taught you? Who took you there?"

"I did," she cried out miserably.

Shock held him rigid.

"What do you mean, you did?" He asked her slowly.

"I watch movies, and read books. I bought stuff—" She tried to turn her head, but he refused to allow her.

"Dildos?" he asked softly, his body hardening impossibly.

"Yes," she answered miserably.

He went hot all over.

"Plugs?" His voice was soft.

She bit her lip, her face reddening further.

"Yes."

Cade closed his eyes.

"You're still using them?" He asked her harshly.

"Yes." He could barely hear her, all he knew was that Marly, his sweet innocent Marly was, at any given time, walking around with a device inside her body intended to prepare her for him. He shuddered, his finger moving from her vagina down.

Disappointment speared his gut as he realized she wasn't using it now.

"Where is it?" He could barely speak. He was so hard he was hurting. So tortured he could barely stand it.

Shock flared in her eyes, panic rolling over her expression.

"Cade?" There was an edge of fear in her voice. Damn her, it was the wrong damned time to get scared.

"Where? I won't ask you again, Marly." He demanded harshly.

She flinched, but he could read the arousal in her eyes at the demanding tone of his body. Damn her, she wanted him like this, and he couldn't seem to fight it. She was driving him crazy with it.

"The side table. Under the books." She glanced at the table beside her bed.

Cade rose up. He jerked the drawer out, throwing the books to the floor until he found what he was looking for. His stomach muscles clenched as he found the tube of lubricant and the thick plug used to stretch and widen the anal muscles. Beside it lay a rubber dildo, nearly as thick as his cock, yet not as long.

"Son of a bitch." He lifted the plug and the lubricant from the drawer slowly then turned to her.

She was watching him anxiously, her eyes wide now, flickering to the articles then back to Cade's face.

"Turn over," he ordered her roughly. "I want to see you take it."

He was dying. Cade knew he would never survive the night.

"Cade." She trembled against him. "I'm sorry. Please don't be mad at me."

Mad. He was furious. So agonizingly furious he could barely stand it. At both of them. Her for wanting it, and him for wanting to give it to her so damned bad.

"Roll over, Marly. Now."

He watched her shiver as she rolled over, presenting the pretty curves of her backside.

"On your knees." He moved behind her, watching as she moved shakily, pushing her hips into the air.

He couldn't resist. He lowered his head, spreading the cheeks of her ass apart as he stared at the small pink hole a second before spearing his tongue into it. She cried out harshly, her hips jerking in response to the heat of his mouth, the thrust inside her. Then he went lower until he could repeat the movement into the soaking depths of her vagina.

She overflowed. Her sweet juice filled his mouth, making him drunk on her. He moved back, taking the plug and lubricant from the bed.

"How long since you used it?" He didn't want to hurt her, but he had to see her take it. He had to see her filled with it.

"Yesterday," she cried out as he began smearing the thick lubricant over the little hole, then placed the nozzle at her opening and squeezed.

She shivered and shook. She cried out as perspiration covered her skin. Then he carefully lubed the thick device, applied the head to her small opening. He pulled the cheeks of her ass carefully apart, watching with narrow-eyed wonder as she groaned in arousal, spreading to accept it, crying out in pleasure as the thick base lodged completely inside her.

"Marly." His hands caressed the pale globes as he stared at the flared knob that kept it from entering her further. "Marly baby. You're killing me."

He turned her over on her back, staring in awe at the dazed pleasure on her face, the long, hard nipples flushed and needy. He raised himself over her, his lips covering one of those hard tips as her hands clasped his head and she cried out in pleasure.

His hand moved to her cunt, so wet and hot, massaging her clit as she thrust herself against him, nearly screaming as lust consumed her. Within seconds her body was shaking with her climax, surprisingly triggering his own as his erection rubbed against her thigh. The quick ejaculation surprised him, terrified him. He had never come so fast, so hot without the grip of a tight, female body.

He jerked away from her. He stared down at her spread thighs, the end of the plug clearly visible, her lips flowered open, her slit wet and slick. His pants were stained with his release, his hands shaking with need.

"Damn. Damn you." He felt like a monster. He was a monster. This was Marly. His Marly. And he was taking her like the common whores he had used over the years.

His hands went through his hair in frustrated agony as she whispered his name. She still wanted. She still needed. Just as he did. It was killing him, this need.

"You've turned me into a monster, Marly," he whispered, tortured. "Look at me, shaking to take you there, to take you anywhere. I raised you. Like my own, Marly. I raised you. This is wrong. It's just wrong."

He turned, stalking from her room, ignoring her cry of pain. He couldn't stand it. He had to think, to figure out what he was doing, and how to stop it. If he could stop it. He had a terrible feeling it had just passed any limit where it could ever be halted.

Chapter Eleven

ဢ

The next afternoon was just as unsettling as the previous one had been. With Cade stalking the house and ranch yards, his dark eyes watching Marly every chance he got. He was like an animal, ready to snap. He refused to smile at her; to even talk to her. He looked at her as though he didn't even know her. It was enough to make her want to pack up and go back to school, but Sam was certain it meant she was making headway. He just had no idea of the previous night, and she couldn't tell him. And Cade refused to hear her when she mentioned returning. But watching Sam now, Marly was certain her idea was the best course of action. He was going to get her killed.

Sam, Greg and her were going to end up stripped bare of flesh when Cade got finished with the tongue lashing he would surely inflict on them, Marly thought as she sat silently through lunch. Sam was his usual, 'tactless' self, acting on impulse and stirring waters better left alone. Marly had never imagined he would go so far. Especially not after yesterday's debacle.

"Come on, Marly, surely you have a few boyfriends in college. You don't spend all your time studying?" Sam pushed her; his eyes alight with mischief and a hidden message to lie if she had to. She knew that look. Sam was more than pissed with Cade. He was out for revenge.

Marly fought her grin, ignoring Cade's brooding looks from the head of the table. She aimed him a look from beneath her lashes. Sam had spent hours teaching her how to do that in the mirror that morning. They had both decided to fight Cade's fire with more of their own.

At first, Marly had been hesitant. Cade was enraged already, stomping around the house like a mad man. But upon reflection, and Sam's insights into the stupidity of a male mind, she had reluctantly agreed to go along with him.

She shrugged slowly, shaking her head. There really weren't any boyfriends.

Cade gave Greg an evil glare when she didn't answer. Marly almost laughed out loud as Greg paled. He was terrified of Cade. They would all be lucky if he didn't give the game up out of fear.

"You remember that one little creep you were so hot for a few years back?" Sam asked her with a frown.

Marly's eyes widened as she almost choked on her food. There wasn't anyone she was hot for. What was Sam doing now? She shook her head desperately to convince him to stop now.

"Yeah you do." He leaned forward intently, frowning at her action. "What was his name? Let me think—" He narrowed his eyes intently. "Dillon wasn't it? Dillon Carlyle? I thought it was him when I was talking to him yesterday."

Oh Lord, no! Not Dillon. He was Madison County's most revered playboy, even to this day. Marly didn't choke on her food this time, but Cade seemed to wheeze as he gave her a furious glare.

"Damn good thing she didn't tell me about it," his voice was low and angry, his eyes hard as he glanced at her.

Sam seemed surprised.

"Damn, Cade. I told him he could come over tonight. He mentioned wanting to see her in town yesterday, so I told him to come on around." Sam was frowning, distressed. Who knew he and Dillon were such pals? "Besides, I think Marly needs a break from you. See what it's like to be treated right by someone who knows what a woman is."

Cade laid his fork carefully on his plate as his gaze rose to meet Sam's. The need for violence pulsed in the air around him. Thankfully, he chose to ignore the last remark.

"Are you crazy?" he asked him carefully. "Dillon is not fit company for Marly."

"Dillon's damned near as rich as you." Sam began to tick off the man's qualities on the fingers of one hand.

"Not even close," Cade bit out.

"He's looking for a wife, and he would make a good husband." Point two.

"He's a hound dog that wouldn't know fidelity if it bit his ass," Cade snarled.

"He's well respected —"

"By the women he beds, or his business partners. No one else." Cade was growing coldly furious.

"Who else would matter?" Sam chuckled, his male wit out of control. "Oh come one, Cade. He just wants to see her. Marly's a big girl now. A woman. Let her decide."

Marly watched as Cade paled when Sam said those words.

"He's too old for her," he sneered. "He's older than I am."

"Just by two years." Sam lifted his shoulders in unconcern. "He's mature. She doesn't want a kid, Cade." His eyes sliced to Greg. "No offense intended, kid."

Greg choked on laughter or anger, Marly wasn't certain.

"None taken," he assured Sam tightly. Maybe it was anger, Marly thought.

"Marly?" She jumped as Cade's voice boomed through the room. "Tell Sam to cancel it. I won't have you going out with that pervert. It's hard telling what diseases he's packing with him."

Marly opened her eyes wide; affecting what she hoped was pure amazement.

"You won't have me?" She asked him carefully. If he would have her, they wouldn't be having this problem. "Cade, you're forgetting, I decide who I go out with and who I don't. And since you obviously want to treat me like a child, I think it would be nice to be treated as a woman instead."

Silence, complete and overwhelming rippled through the room. Sam watched Cade carefully, while Cade glared at Marly. Greg was nervous, his Adam's apple bobbing frantically. Marly appeared calm, but her stomach was in violent protest. Brock was sitting back in his chair watching it all as though it were some strange movie he had to figure out the plot to.

"Dillon Carlyle's out of your league, Marly," he bit out.

"Out of my league?" she asked him curiously. "I was unaware I was in one, or that you would know what it was if I were."

Ouch. Cade's brows drew together sharply, the muscle in his jaw flexing in fury as he watched her.

"So, it's okay if he shows up?" Sam asked Marly as though Cade weren't even there. "He seemed really interested in seeing you."

"I think it would be fun." She smiled merrily though she could still feel Cade watching her, a thick cloud of fury hovering over her. "When's he supposed to be here?"

"Tonight." Sam leaned back in his chair with a grin. "Better wear jeans though, I think he's bringing that new Harley he bought. He's a grinning fool over that machine."

Cade rose suddenly from the table and stalked from the room. Sam smiled in contentment as he heard the door to Cade's study slam shut with a vicious sound.

"Act one completed," he breathed in satisfaction. "If I were you, I'd stalk right in there and ask him what the hell his problem is."

Marly widened her eyes in complete amazement.

"Are you crazy, Sam? He's completely furious. You know what he would do," she told him as adrenaline surged through her at the thought.

"Aw, he won't hurt you, Marly." Sam shook his head. "He's not pissed enough to yell at you yet. He's mad at me. He thinks you're an innocent bystander." Sam laughed at this. "Man. He has no clue."

"Dangerous game the two of you are playing," Brock suddenly spoke up quietly, reflectively. "I wouldn't push Cade so far so fast if I were you. Especially after yesterday. Whether you two are aware of it or not, Cade's staked his claim on her. He won't let another man have her, and anyone else is only going to get hurt."

Marly, Sam and Greg glanced at him in surprise.

"Only a blind man wouldn't see what you're up to, Marly. All of you." He shook his head at them. "Fortunately for you, Cade is real damned blind right now. Push him too far, and when he opens his eyes, it might be more than you can handle."

"What would you suggest?" Sam frowned angrily. "He treated her like shit, Brock."

"Hitting him back is only going to make things worse." Brock rose to his feet, moving carefully from the table. "Our Marly's a beauty, and the feeling's already there Sam. Let it come to him naturally, or someone's going to get hurt." Brock moved away from the table, his stride casual and easy.

"How often is he right?" Greg asked them curiously.

Sam frowned. "I don't know. He's never done anything like that before."

Brock had always left Sam and Marly to their pranks, standing back, watching with a tolerant expression when they messed up.

"Do you think he's right?" Marly asked worriedly. "Cade was furious, Sam. Maybe someone less dangerous than Dillon would have been a good idea."

Dillon was nearly as tall as the August boys, with dark brown hair and vivid green eyes. He was lean and muscular, and the worst flirt Marly had ever met.

"Dillon's a pussycat." Sam laughed. "The rumors are false for the most part. I know. Those orgies in the mountains he's accused of have actually been fishing trips with me and the boys. I can't tell you the times we've laughed over that boy and his growing reputation, and the fact he hardly does a thing to deserve it."

Marly looked at him in surprise. "Does Cade know that?"

"Hell no. He'd ruin it all, Marly. Dillon loves his reputation. Let the boy enjoy it while he can." Sam was utterly complacent in his part in it all. "You just get dressed up real pretty for that ride he's gonna take you on. I promise, he won't try anything. He knows I would kill him."

The utter confidence in his tone was a good indication that Sam had laid out a heavy threat to the other man. Marly just wondered how he had convinced Dillon to join the game.

"So all that talk about me being able to handle him was just talk." She grinned at his deception.

"You couldn't handle a kitten in a wet paper bag," he grinned. "And none of us would trust another man not to hurt you, except one of us. So it's a damned good thing you chose Cade to go after."

"I'd like to point out that Cade may not agree with you," Greg said softly in concern. "What if Marly gets hurt in all this, Sam?"

Sam frowned. "No way in hell. We can't stand to see her cry, least of all Cade. He'll take care of her, boy. Just you wait and see. Trust me." They all winced.

* * * * *

He was going to end up killing Dillon Carlyle. Cade flung himself into his desk chair and stared across the room in growing fury. But first, he was going to kill Sam. What had possessed his normally protective brother to allow Marly within ten miles of the depraved creature Dillon was? Not that the guy didn't have his good points, but Cade knew he would commit murder if he dared to touch Marly. His control wouldn't be able to handle it. And damn her, she better be wearing more clothes when Dillon showed up than she was wearing now. That short dress, despite the long sleeves, was a killer. The stretchy silk clung to every curve of her body like a second skin. And her damned nipples were hard again. Didn't she wear a bra?

He groaned, closing his eyes. He wouldn't think about it. He wouldn't. But he couldn't forget either. The sight of her kneeling at his feet, his flesh hard and thick sinking into her mouth as she watched him with dazed desire. The sounds of her suckling, her moans of need as he spurted harshly inside her. The memory of the night before seared in his brain. Bent over before him, her lovely rear bare and vulnerable to him, that fucking plug stretching her, driving him crazy. He groaned, his head pressing into the back of the chair as his fingers gripped it tightly. God, he wanted her. Wanted her so desperately he was in danger of hurting her if he managed to get his hands on her again.

Next time, he swore. Next time he had her soft and hot, he was going to fuck the living hell out of her before he ever let her away from him. No. He shook his head roughly. Dammit. He couldn't take her like that. Not like he had the women before her. His sexuality was like a beast when set loose. Marly deserved gentle, sweet loving, not the dominating sexuality he couldn't rein in when it was given a chance to free itself. And there would be no controlling it. There was never a way to control it, especially when the need was riding him this hard.

Yet, he couldn't force himself to call any of the available women he knew. The thought of it was instantly reprehensible. A betrayal. He shook his head. That wasn't true, this attraction to Marly was the betrayal, and he was going to have to remember that.

But he couldn't convince his body, or his unruly brain. He closed his eyes, and instantly he saw her, naked and willing, soft and inviting. He would move over her, parting her thighs, lowering his head. His tongue would touch and taste, his fingers would explore and invade. He remembered the feel of her tight little rear clenched around his finger and wondered—no. He opened his eyes, breathing harshly, fighting to contain the lust.

As he sat and brooded over his present predicament, a firm knock at the door interrupted his dark musings.

"What?" he barked, unconcerned that his temper showed in his voice.

The door opened, and one of the ranch hands, Bret, stepped hesitantly inside the study.

"Boss, we just found one of the mares injured. You want to come out and look at her?"

Cade rose quickly to his feet. "Which one?"

"Storm's Promise. She came in from pasture a little bit ago and she's hurt." The cowboy scratched his jaw in confusion. "She was fine yesterday."

Storm's Promise was Marly's horse. Grabbing his hat from the corner of the desk, Cade shoved it on his head. He only hoped no one had told Marly about the horse. The old mare was too fragile to ride anymore, but Cade knew she was attached to it.

"What's wrong with her?" He kept his voice low as they left the house and rushed toward the barn.

"She's been shot, appears to me like." Bret shook his head. "I put a call in to the vet, he should be here any time now. He was just out at Carlyle's ranch and fixin' to leave anyway. Strange thing is, Cade, none of us heard any shots, and that mare wasn't far enough away that we wouldn't have heard it."

Damn Carlyle, now he was using Cade's vet too. The man was fixing to get hurt.

When Cade stepped up to Storm's stall, he bent slowly, inspecting the long gash along the horse's flank. It was raw and bloody, and deeper than he would have expected. The wound wasn't very old, only hours at the most, Cade thought.

"Wasn't she in the home pasture?" he asked softly, referring to the grazing land around the house.

"Was last night." Bret Wayne leaned against the stall door, watching Cade as he examined the wound. "And like I said, there ain't been no shots put off today, period. We would have heard them."

"The wound isn't very old." Cade touched the fresh blood on the horse's side. "A few hours at the most."

"Yep. She was limping heavy when she came to the barn, sweaty and breathing hard. Looks like she had run as far as she could after she was hit."

The pastureland around the house extended for miles all around the ranch yard. But the retort of a gunshot wouldn't have been missed, even at that distance. Cade straightened up, frowning down at the mare as she shifted painfully, her head tossing as her hoofs stamped against the hay-strewn floor.

"Vet's on his way, then?" Cade frowned at the wound.

"Should be here within the next little bit, he said." Bret nodded his shaggy, dark blond head. "I told him we needed him extra quick, so he shouldn't be long."

"Get a couple of the boys together, have them begin inspecting the pasture, make sure none of the other horses or cattle have been hit," Cade ordered him as he moved back to the stall door. "Could have been rustlers looking to wound her enough to catch her. Have them check for any breaks in the fence or anything unusual."

As he moved through the stable, Cade stopped, checking the other horses carefully. Most were in for treatment for minor problems. Sprained foreleg, vaccinations. They had several dozen horses on the ranch, and at any time the stalls could be filled with animals. But this was the first time one had wandered in from a gunshot wound. Coyote or wolf attack, even bear, but never wounds like this.

"You wanna see the doc when he gets done?" Bret followed along behind him.

"Not unless there's something I need to know," Cade told him quietly. "Have him clean and dress it. I'll call him tomorrow for details."

"Sure thing, boss." Bret nodded as Cade walked through the ranch yard, heading back to the house.

His frowned, thinking about the wound, the lack of sound that indicated trouble. There was no doubt about it, a gun shot would have echoed for miles, and had one been heard the cowboys working the pasture would have headed out to inspect it.

The only way that wound could have been made was with a rifle, silencer attached. Rustlers didn't usually possess such expensive weapons, nor did they bother with old horses. The young, well-trained ones were what they sought. It bothered him that it had been Marly's horse that was hit, as well. Cade wasn't a big believer in coincidence. Considering the circumstances behind Marly's childhood, he was even more uneasy.

His gut was roiling with warning, but he hadn't heard from Annie, and she would have called if Jack had found her. Unless she had been unable to call.

Cursing softly, he strode quickly into the house, and called Sam and Brock into the study. He didn't know if it was warranted, but he would warn the boys; make sure an extra eye was kept on Marly. Because God above knew, he didn't know if he could handle it if anything happened to her.

Chapter Twelve

ജ

Dillon Carlyle was as handsome as he ever was. His thick brown hair was longish, with just enough curl to make it wavy and his dark green eyes were still filled with laughter. Marly had never had a crush on the handsome rancher, though, even during her younger, more impressionable years. She remembered the aloof figure from gossip and brief glimpses in the small town of Glaston, but his image had never really impressed her.

He was standing in the entryway talking to Sam and keeping a careful eye on Cade's glowering expression, when Marly descended the stairs. Dressed in jeans, a thick sweater and a leather jacket, she knew she looked more than ready for a ride on his new Harley. Not that she was looking forward to it, but anything to further the cause.

"Great, you're ready." Relief was thick in Dillon's voice as he shifted beneath Cade's regard once again. "It's not too cool this evening, so you shouldn't get cold."

Marly smiled sweetly at him, glancing at Cade beneath her lashes. He was watching her silently, broodingly, as Sam fought to keep from smiling. Darkly handsome, his gray eyes probing and intense, he was the epitome of the strong, dangerous male. Damn, she wished he were easier to seduce.

"I shouldn't be late, Cade." She walked over to him, standing on her tiptoes to plant a slow, brief kiss on his jaw. He was warm and hard, and mad as hell. "But don't wait up on me just in case."

She turned just in time to see Sam wince.

"If you'd like to stay out a little later, I know a wonderful place over by the county line that looks out over the bluffs,"

Dillon offered quietly as they headed for the door. "You won't see a prettier skyline there."

"It sounds wonderful—" Marly began.

"Dillon." Cade's voice stopped them at the entrance.

Marly took a deep breath as she and Dillon both turned back to face Cade.

"Yeah, Cade?" he asked warily.

Cade's gaze flickered to Marly, hot and furious.

"Marly better come home in the same shape she's left in. You understand me?" There was a deadly, hard edge to Cade's voice.

Marly watched tensely as Dillon's eyes narrowed, his expression becoming blank as he watched Cade.

"She'll return in whatever shape she wants to Cade," he finally said softly. "She's a woman, not a child for you to watch over."

"Dillon—"

"Cade, don't you dare start this 'he-man' stuff." Marly narrowed her eyes on him warningly. "I won't tolerate it. At least try to be nice."

"Oh, I am being nice, honey." He smiled, all teeth. It was a frightening sight. "And I will be waiting up for you, Marly."

"Damn, he acts more like your lover than your uncle." Dillon chuckled, taking his life in his own hands. "Come on, Marly, before he sprouts horns and starts breathing fire."

Dillon placed his hand in the small of Marly's back and escorted her from the house. Marly could feel Cade's gaze on her back, burning past Dillon's hand into the flesh below. Singeing her flesh, making her skin itch. She was starting to wonder at the wisdom of pushing him like this. Maybe Brock had been right.

"Damn," he muttered as the door closed behind him. "I'll have to talk to Sam about combat pay."

Marly muffled her laughter as he laid his hand at her back once again and led her to the huge motorcycle.

"How did he talk you into this anyway?" she asked him softly as he helped her onto the back of the machine.

"Don't ask." Dillon laughed, shaking his head. "It's too strange, and it would likely get us both killed. Now stay still while I do this right. Sam was pretty specific about what to do before leaving."

Marly smiled up at him, sitting still as he lifted the helmet and fitted it over her head, then adjusted and buckled the strap slowly. His fingers trailed over her cheek in a parody of affection. It was all Marly could do to keep from checking to see if Cade was watching from the front room window. Then Dillon was pulling his own helmet on and straddling the beast beneath them.

The motor revved, hummed, vibrating between Marly's thighs as he lifted the kick stand and headed down the ranch road.

"Hang onto me." His voice came through the small speakers at her ears.

Leaning forward, Marly wrapped her arms around his waist, the added height at the back of the seat allowing her to prop her chin on his shoulder.

"Do you do this often?" She asked with a smile, glad that the small mic at her mouth made speaking possible.

"What? Take out the nieces of my friends to piss their adoptive uncle off?" He laughed, glancing back at her. "Naw, I gotta admit, this is a first for me. But the least of the sins added to my name."

Marly laughed at this. She was well aware of the list of sins added to his name.

"So, wanna tell me the game, Marly-love?" he asked her with a thick thread of amusement. "I can be a hell of a team player if the rules are right."

* * * * *

Cade paced the floor. He growled when he spoke to anyone and drank too much liquor for his state of mind. He had drunk more whisky in the past few days than he had drank in the past few years. Marly was driving him crazy.

How could she leave the house with that orgy-loving pervert? How could she even consider being with another man? Because he told her he couldn't take her. Because his guilt was so deep that he refused her. If he didn't have the guts to take what he wanted, then another man would do it for him. He growled harshly as he stood in the front door, his body tense, tight. Fury, complete and overwhelming surged through his body. She was his, and when she returned, he would show her she was his.

He closed his eyes, imagining how tight her body would grip him, how hot and sweet she would be as the velvet walls of her vagina clenched and soaked him with her release. She would scream when he took her anally, beg for more, cry out with the pleasure of it. He fisted his hands, fighting the need to go after her now. He was going to make her pay for tonight. When he took her, she would scream in need, the sound echoing around the house until everyone around it knew who possessed her. He'd make her beg for release. He would show her who had the upper hand, and who would submit.

He walked out on the porch, his whisky glass in hand, and sat down on the porch steps. Night was crowding in, and she had been gone for several hours with the debauched playboy of Madison County. The self-proclaimed heartbreaker was late bringing her home too. They were most likely parked along the bluffs, Marly's hair blowing in the wind as she sat on the back of that damned Harley, Dillon turning to her —

Cade took a deep, fortifying breath as he plowed the fingers of one hand through his hair. Then he sipped at the whisky and wanted to hit something. Someone. Preferably that darkly handsome bastard out with his Marly.

He closed his eyes. She was making him crazy. He knew he was in trouble when he started drinking again. At this rate, he would get drunk before midnight. Hell, no he wouldn't. If Marly wasn't home in the next hour then he would collect his rifle and go hunting for her. And he would take Sam, just to show him how he dealt with the bastards who wanted to hurt Marly. Touch her. Take her.

Cade groaned. He had lost his mind.

"Hey, Cade." Sam stepped out on the porch, watching him questioningly. "What are you doing out here?"

He looked up at his younger brother; the affable expression on Sam's face was enough to make him want to wipe it away with his fist.

"Waiting on Marly," Cade snapped. "Since you threw her to the wolves I thought at least one of us should be concerned."

Sam sat down on the step beside him, leaning back on the porch, his elbows braced on the floor.

"Aw hell, Cade, Dillon will take care of her. He's a good guy," Sam protested.

Cade knew better. He didn't know who Sam thought he was fooling, but it wasn't Cade. He had been to enough of Dillon's parties himself; he knew just how perverted the man could get.

"He's a pervert, and a lying tomcat that doesn't care anything about a woman after he gets his rocks off," Cade bit out. "Where are your brains, Sam?"

Sam was silent for long moments, and Cade could feel his brother's gaze centered on him intently.

"And you're any better?" Sam grunted, his anger thickening once again. "How stupid do you think I am Cade? I know what happened yesterday. I know what you did to her. Which would have been fine if you'd been smart enough to at least accept it for what it was."

"This is none of your business, Sam," he growled warningly.

"Wrong. When you fucked her mouth and left her crying, you made it my business, bro." Sam turned on him furiously. "She's not just yours, she belongs to us all. And I know that's what scares the hell out of you. It does me too. But Marly's not stupid; she's heard the rumors by now. She knows what's coming."

"We protected her," he bit out.

"And we can't protect her forever," Sam told him harshly. "Dammit Cade, she's so horny she's dying for it, and if you don't give it to her soon, she'll turn to me or Brock. Do you really want one of us to be the one to take her virginity, to claim her first?"

They would eventually claim her, though. Cade knew it, and his body hardened further at the thought of it. Marly, stretched out, screaming in pleasure while the men who loved her most took her in every way a man could take a woman.

"She'll leave. She'll run." He shook his head. "That's what I don't want, Sam."

"I don't think she will," Sam disagreed quietly. "Not if you handle it right, Cade. Not if you ease her into it. I know. I've watched her. She gets horny for all of us to some degree."

Cade rubbed his face furiously. Dammit it, he wanted to go back and kill the monster who did this to them all over again. Then he wanted to kill his parents himself for turning them over to the bastard. Then he wanted to kill his father himself for turning them over to the bastard. He couldn't cry for them, he had lost that ability years ago. He couldn't do anything but try to protect them, and show them in the only way he knew how, just how much they meant to him. By sharing Marly. And it was what he wanted, what he needed. An extension of his love for her, and his love for his brothers.

"Son of a bitch, I ought to just kill us all and get it the hell over with." He rose to his feet then, stomping furiously into the house.

Sam hid his grin, whistled a soundless tune and leaned back against the porch as he waited on Marly as well. As he relaxed, watching the road that led into the ranch yard, he heard the distant sound of Cade's phone ringing.

Chapter Thirteen

ॐ

Marly stared in dazed fascination at the swirling stars in the sky. They moved haphazardly, streaking and impacting, bursting in a kaleidoscope of color and pain. She was lying on her back. Why was she lying on her back? She could hear the motorcycle throbbing in the distance, whining, a drone that grated on her nerves and made her stomach roll with fear. There was something wrong with that sound. Something she should know, should understand.

She tried to shake her head, but it felt as though a cement block was wrapped around it, choking her. Damn, Cade was gonna be mad. Real mad this time. At least in the other accidents she had the full body of a car around her. She had never felt as though every bone in her body had been whacked out of place.

"Cade?" She called out his name in fear as she blinked dazedly, fighting to understand the pain radiating through her, to make sense of the disorientation that whirled in her head. Where was Cade? He was always there when she hurt. She knew she was hurt. Knew she had somehow wrecked again. That was what always happened when she was hurt.

"Marly." Grating, evil, the voice whispered at her side.

A hand touched her breast above her jacket, making her recoil in terror. God, why couldn't she see?

"Marly, you're mine." The voice again, cutting through the pain in her head, making her mad with fear.

That wasn't Cade. Marly trembled, shaking as the voice echoed in her head again. Then she screamed out in terror and pain as harsh hands gripped her arms, pulling her, dragging at her body. Someone was trying to take her away. Cade couldn't find her if someone took her away. She couldn't let them take her.

Marly curled her fingers into claws, raking bare skin, fighting to get free of whatever bound her head, her body. She screamed out into the night, trying to ram her head into the person dragging her across the ground, and though she felt the impacting agony in her head, there was a curious sense of something wrapped about her head. Smothering her. Cutting her off from the world.

Then suddenly she was released. She was thrown to the ground, her breathing harsh as she heard another male yell out, a scuffle, the sound of tires squealing in protest as a vehicle accelerated away.

"Cade." She tried to crawl. To pull herself to her hands and knees, but the weight on her head was dragging her down, hurting her.

"Marly." She didn't recognize this voice either, but it was frightened, concerned. "God, Marly, Cade's gonna kill me."

Gentle hands lowered her to the ground, a husky, worried voice sounding above her. Marly fought to see the man touching her, trying to gentle her. Her eyes were opened wide, yet all she could see was a dark gray world of shifting shapes.

"I can't see," she screamed, trying to claw at her face, but something kept her hands blocked, kept her from reaching her eyes. Dark and unyielding as she fought to tear it from her head.

"Easy, Marly. For God's sake, let me get it off you." A body straddled hers as hands, firm and resolute worked beneath her chin. Then the hard covering was jerked from her head and she was watching Dillon's face swim above her.

"It's okay," he soothed her as his expression remained strained with worry. "Are you okay, Marly? Is anything broken?"

Broken? She hurt all over. How the hell was she supposed to know if anything was broken?

"Son of a bitch just ran us off the road." He dug his cell phone from his jacket pocket, his fingers keying in numbers with shaky speed. "I think he was trying to help you till he saw me, then he just lit off. Crazy bastard."

Marly couldn't make sense of what he was saying. No, something evil had touched her, dragging her to the pits of hell. She blinked, fighting to clear her memory, to make sense of the pain and the swirling lights.

"Hurt...no bones broken...get here." She heard his voice from a distance.

"Cade," she whispered his name again. Why hadn't he come yet? Where was he?

"He's coming, Marly," Dillon swore, tearing his jacket from his body and laying it over her. "It's gonna be okay, honey. Just relax."

His hands began running over her limbs, testing, questioning her. No, it didn't hurt in any one particular place. Yes, she could feel her arms, her legs. "Where is Cade?"

"Cade's coming, honey," Dillon promised her again.

Slowly, the fuzziness receded and Marly moved sluggishly, rolling to her side, then pulling herself to her knees.

"Marly, lay back down until the paramedics get here," Dillon urged her harshly. "You could be hurt."

His hands touched her arms. She shrugged him away with a cry. Where was Cade? She had to get to Cade.

"Let me go." She jerked away from him, nearly falling flat on her face as she tore from his arms. "I want to go home."

She had to get to Cade. Dammit, he should have been here by now. Where the hell was he? She was hurt and scared, and so cold she couldn't stop shivering.

"Dammit, Marly, stay still." He gripped her arms again, pulling her to the ground with him, wrapping her in his arms, holding her still.

She fought him. Bucking against him, crying out against the restraint, her hair whipping around her, blinding her, her body screaming in pain. Or was that her screaming? Growling. Rage echoing through the night, and suddenly she was free.

"You bastard!" She heard his voice, rough and furious, like a demon gone mad.

"Cade." She fought the cascade of hair raining over her face, nearly falling to her knees before hands caught her, pulled her close.

She fought to get free, screaming his name, terrified that suddenly her vision was once again darkened. The waves of hair wouldn't move, wouldn't be pushed aside. She pulled at the mass desperately, scared that she couldn't remember what had happened, where she was. Why wouldn't Cade help her?

"Marly." It was Cade, his voice agonized, tormented. He pulled her into the warmth of his chest, his hands shaking, trembling as he gently pushed the hair back from her face, his expression streaked with tears, with rage when she blinked up at him.

"It hurts," she whispered, her head falling to his chest, the fight going out of her, knowing Cade would keep her safe. "It hurts, Cade."

An animalistic growl sounded beneath her ear as he swung her up in his arms. Lights were swirling again, yellow and white and blue, making her head splinter with pain. Marly buried her head against Cade's chest, fighting the nausea welling inside her, and the fear that throbbed in her chest.

"It's okay, baby. The ambulance is here. Everything's okay. I promise." His voice was husky and deep, ridden with pain.

"No ambulance." She jerked in his arms. "No hospital, Cade. Promise me."

Her hands dug into his shoulder and back, holding on as tightly as she could, terrified he would let go of her.

"Baby, they need to check you out," he told her fiercely against her hair. "You could be hurt Marly. You have to go to the hospital."

"Stay with me." She held on tighter, scared. If he took her to the hospital he would have to leave. She would be alone. Defenseless. The monster was still out there. "Don't leave me, Cade."

"I won't leave you, baby." He lowered her onto a stretcher, staring down at her with such a worried expression that she felt fear tear through her again.

"Swear, Cade." She gripped his hand hard. "Swear you won't leave me."

"I swear, Marly." He leaned close, his mouth brushing her trembling lips for the barest second. "I swear, if you'll just calm down, I won't leave you."

"Not ever? Promise me." She felt sick. Her head was whirling again, and Cade's face looked so fuzzy.

"Not ever, Marly." His voice was distant, dark, as was his face. Then the darkness washed over her, her eyes closing as the pain rolled in like a dark, suffocating wave.

* * * * *

Cade was in a violent frame of mind. Dillon was being treated for minor injuries, the least of which was the broken nose Cade had bestowed on him. Marly was asleep, pale but unhurt in the hospital bed, under close observation for the concussion she had sustained the night before. She had some bruising along her back, her left leg, but nothing serious. The full helmet Dillon used had protected her head from the impact with the road. Without it, she would have been dead. It didn't change the fact that there wouldn't have been an accident if she had been home where she belonged.

There wouldn't have been an accident if he had gone with his gut instinct and forbidden her to get on that damned motorcycle. He knew letting her leave that house was a bad idea.

But since when had he ever denied Marly anything? He grimaced at the thought. It terrified him, this all-consuming need he had to make certain she had anything, everything she wanted. But she never asked for anything. A new outfit, maybe. That damned Jeep she had wrecked last year. But at least it had been a relatively inexpensive used Jeep. They had learned over the years to never buy Marly a new vehicle. It never failed that she ended up wrecking the damned thing, new or used. At least no one else had ever been involved in her accidents. At least, no one outside the vehicle she was in.

Cade shook his head. For eight years, every year, one way or another she ended up in the damned hospital. The first year, it had been double pneumonia. Every year after that it had been a concussion. A fall from a horse. A fall from the roof, and only God knew what she had been doing up there. The manner of the accidents were never the same, the outcome usually was. Her head. Damned good thing it was a hard one.

"Cade." Dr. Barnett entered the room, his portly body moving with surprising grace, his homely face creased in a smile, his gray hair standing on end.

He had been Marly's doctor since her first visit to him; just days after her mother left her on the ranch. Cade still refused to allow anyone else to treat her.

"Hey, Doc." Cade wiped his hands over his gritty face. His jaw was bristled with a day's worth of beard, and he hadn't had a shower yet.

"You look tired, Cade. You should have gotten a room at the motel last night at least." Dr. Barnett frowned at him in disapproval. "I'll have you in here next, at this rate."

Cade grimaced. He had promised Marly he wouldn't leave her, no matter what. She had awakened a few times through the night, scared, calling out for him. He had been there, moving close to her side, leaning close to her so she would know she wasn't alone.

"I'll be fine." He shook his head wearily. "When can Marly go home?"

"Soon as she wakes up this morning. They just wanted to keep her for observation. The concussion was pretty bad. You know the routine, though. Keep an eye on her; wake her up once every so often after she goes to sleep for another forty-eight hours. Plenty of fluids and rest."

It wasn't Marly's first concussion. It wasn't even the second. Cade doubted seriously it would be her last.

"I can wake her up then?" He just wanted to get her the hell out of there and get her home.

"Go ahead and wake her up." Dr. Bennett nodded. "I'll have a prescription brought to you and the sign out papers by the time she's dressed. Take her home and let her rest, it's the best thing for her."

Dr. Bennett made several notes on the board he carried, then nodded a farewell to Cade as he left the room. As he left, Sam and Brock walked in carefully. Cade glanced at Sam's bruised face. He almost regretted hitting his brother the night before, but not enough to apologize. It was his fault she was on that damned motorcycle to begin with. He should thank his lucky stars his nose wasn't broken too.

"Did you bring her clothes?" he snapped out. Marly's clothes had been trashed the night before, even her beloved leather jacket. They had been nearly ripped from her body, bloody and streaked with dirt and grime.

"Here." Brock handed him the bag. "We bought her a new jacket, too. The bomber kind she keeps hinting at for Christmas."

Cade took the bag, peeking in. There was a loose cotton dress, white canvas sneakers, and her jacket. Her usual garb for leaving the hospital. This habit of hers was going to have to stop. Her head was only going to take so much abuse.

"Get out of here then, I'll get her up and dressed. Did you bring the limo?" He snapped out the question.

"Outside waiting." Sam nodded cautiously. Cade bet that black eye hurt. Served him right.

"Anyone find out who hit them?" The question of the day.

All Dillon could remember was the black four by four pickup and some guy trying to help Marly into it. He had dropped her and went running when Dillon had picked himself up from the dirt in the field they had run into and went running towards them. It was too dark for a description, and he hadn't recognized the truck. After the accident with the horse, Cade wasn't in a coincidence frame of mind.

"Nothing yet, Cade." Sam glanced at Brock who shook his head as well. "There was no one else on the road that night that the police have been able to find out."

Cade laid Marly's clothes out carefully, frowning over the information he had received. He didn't like the feel of this at all.

"Where's the James boy?" He asked them.

"He's waiting outside. He's pretty scared of you after that episode at the wreck. We just can't convince him that you always hit someone whenever Marly gets hurt." Sam shook his head as though it made perfect sense to him.

"Especially the one responsible." Cade grunted. "Get the hell out of here while I wake her up. Make sure the limo is running and warm, and I want it right outside the front door when we bring her down. You understand me?"

"Sure Cade." They should know the drill well by now, Cade thought.

"Go on then. I'll wake her."

The two other men filed out of the room, glancing back at Cade with a frown. Cade shook his head; he had tired of trying to figure out the twins a long time ago. Their brains just worked differently than anyone else's. Except Marly. He sighed wearily. These yearly accidents were going to have to stop. If this one had been an accident.

Chapter Fourteen

∞

"Man, Marly your life is just too exciting here." Greg shook his head as he packed his bags, his voice carrying a rich vein of bemusement. "Honest. I don't understand it. You never had problems at school."

Marly contained her laughter, her head still hurt too badly to be laughing out loud. But she smiled, lying comfortably on Greg's bed where Cade had carried her after she had awoke that evening and been informed that Greg was returning to Dallas.

"You aren't able to study are you, Greg?" she asked him with a smile.

Greg paused, shaking his head wryly. Marly knew Greg was determined to hurry and get through college as quickly as possible. Anyone who knew him knew this. He was desperate to find a way to support himself, and to begin paying off the student loans he was accumulating.

"I'll miss you," Marly sighed. "You fit in well here."

And he did. When Cade wasn't brooding over the younger man's presence, Greg lightened up and actually had fun watching how the ranch was run. He had even learned how to ride a horse.

"It's a great place, Marly." He shook his head as he zipped his suitcase. "I don't know how you bear to leave it for even a day."

She heard the thread of longing in his voice, his need for a home, a place that welcomed him. Marly knew that since the death of his parents years ago, Greg hadn't had that sense of 'home'.

"I wouldn't if I didn't have to." Marly yawned, shifting on the bed as she closed her eyes. Her head was pounding. "This is home, Greg."

And it was. She missed the house, and the family terribly while she was away. She knew, though, that the day would come that she may not have a choice but to leave. If she couldn't get Cade to see sense, make him see that he loved her as more than a niece, then it would no longer be her home. He would marry eventually, moving another woman in, and there would be no way she could live here then.

"Mr. August is having one of the ranch hands drive me in, so you'll still have your truck when you want to come home," he told her as he sat down on the edge of the bed. "Do you know when you'll be back?

"Hm, next Monday," she answered him drowsily. "Gotta test."

A test she needed to be studying for and wasn't. She had a few days, though, she assured herself. Besides, this damned medicine Cade kept poking down her throat left her too dazed to try to study. Not that he would let her anyway. He was like a mother hen trying to anticipate her needs since bringing her home that morning.

"Is she asleep?" Marly heard Cade's voice as he entered the bedroom.

"Not really, mostly just drifting." She heard Greg's worried answer.

"Bret's ready to take you back whenever you want to leave," Cade told him softly as he looked down at Marly. "You don't have to leave, Greg. She'll settle down now with that concussion. For a few days at least."

"I swear, I've never seen her like this," Greg said with a shake of his head. "She's always so quiet and contained at school. She never gets into trouble. Gets strange ideas sometimes, but no real trouble."

Marly heard Cade grunt and imagined the look of disbelief on his face. She was always getting into trouble here at the ranch.

"She's never quiet and contained, and she stays in trouble somewhere, somehow," Cade told Greg with patient tolerance. "But we love her, so we deal with it."

He sounded like an uncle again, she thought in disgust. She hated it when he did that.

"Well, I guess I'm ready to leave then," Greg sighed. "I've had fun Mr. August, thank you for allowing me to accompany Marly."

"Thank Marly," Cade's voice was amused. "It's her home too, Greg, and she brings who she wishes. Thankfully, she has good taste in friends."

Marly wondered why Cade had glowered at Greg ever since they arrived if that was the way he felt? The man was such a contradiction she wanted to smack him.

"Thank you. She's a good woman, Mr. August. A good friend." Greg's voice retreated from the room.

"Yes she is, Greg. You take care, and we'll see you again sometime." Marly would have peeked to see the expression on Cade's face, but her eyelids were just too heavy.

She knew Greg had left, though. His steps were muffled as he went down the hallway, and soon she heard the front door close as he left the house. She hoped he would be okay. Their housemates were away for vacation as well until Sunday, and Greg would be all alone at the house. He forgot to eat sometimes when he started studying.

"Come on Sleeping Beauty." Cade lifted her into his arms gently. "You can sleep downstairs where I can keep an eye on you."

On the couch, where she had spent most of the nights during her childhood, curled up, waiting on Cade to finish his bookkeeping before going to bed. He had always had to carry her to bed. Tucking her in tenderly, kissing her forehead, sometimes sitting by her bed for long minutes as she drifted off to sleep once again.

"Are you my Prince?" She asked him softly as he carried her down the hall.

She felt his heart race at her question. Oh yeah, she thought, he wasn't totally unaffected.

"Is that what you want, Marly, a Prince?" He asked her as they went down the stairs.

"No," she sighed. "I just want you, Cade. All of you."

"And what would you do once you got me, Marly-love?" There was an edge of sadness in his voice. "You're too young to want someone as hardened as I am."

Her hand curled into the edge of his shirt, the heat of his skin burning her fingers. It was a strange sensation, caught somewhere between waking and dreams, her body cradled against his as he carried her to his study.

"You could show me what to do," she suggested, a smile curving her lips at the thought of that.

Marly felt his body jerk as though a shock of electricity had shot through him. His breath caught, just as hers did, at the thought of that.

"You're dangerous." He lowered her, her body sinking into the plush contours of the blanket-covered couch, her head lying gently on a soft pillow.

"I can get worse." A smile curved her lips.

Her favorite fantasy. She would sneak into his bedroom while he slept, naked and warm. She would slip silently under the blankets, her body pressing against his heatedly. He would turn to her. Kiss her. Touch her. She wanted to moan at the need such an image generated in her body.

"I have no doubt you could," Cade growled.

Suddenly, she felt his lips at the corner of her mouth in a brief kiss. No, not brief. She hurt, she needed more. Her head turned slowly, her lips seeking his hesitantly. Cade stilled, though he didn't pull away. Marly's eyes opened, her gaze meeting his as she fought to keep them open. He was staring down at her, the color swirling in his eyes as her lips trembled beneath his.

Then she did something she had always longed to do. As long as she could remember she had wanted to taste him. Her tongue slid between his lips, touching his as she watched the pupils flare in his eyes. His lips opened, his tongue meeting hers as his head slanted, his lips covering hers experimentally.

Marly didn't close her eyes, she couldn't. Her gaze was snared by his, held in a trance-like fascination as he caressed her lips softly.

"Is that what you want, Marly?" He raised his head enough to whisper against the rounded curves.

Marly was breathing harshly, fighting to draw air into her lungs, to convince herself this was real and not another erotic dream come to taunt her.

"More," she whispered against his lips, the headache nearly forgotten as his tongue slid slowly over her lips.

Marly cried out. She shook with need.

"We have to think about this, Marly," he whispered as she felt his hand at her waist, the other braced by her head. "We have to talk about it. I don't want you to get hurt."

He spoke against the lobe of her ear, then his lips slid slowly down her neck. Marly groaned with the sensations of it. Hot, like fire racing across her skin, making her crazier for him than she already had been.

"Shh," the sound whispered over her skin. "I want you to rest, Marly. To get better, so we can talk about this."

His teeth sank gently into the skin bared by the fallen sleeve of her blouse. Lightning raced from her shoulder to her thighs, making her arch her hips.

"Cade." Her hands rose to his shoulders, then his head, her fingers spearing into his hair. "Kiss me right. Please, Cade."

"Shush, Marly," he whispered, licking the small bite sensually. "A little bit at a time, slow and easy, until we find out where we're going. Okay?" He rubbed his cheek against her upper arm, and Marly wanted to scream out in frustration.

"Just once," she pleaded desperately. "Please, Cade. Just once."

Cade cursed harshly, then his lips were covering hers, his tongue driving deep and hard, the kiss so carnal it made her blood pressure skyrocket. Her hands tightened in his hair as his lips slanted over hers. Her body arched against him, her inner flesh melting in a heated plea. And his hands weren't still. His fingers caressed her waist for just a moment, then cupped the firm weight of one thrusting breast.

"Son of a bitch." His curse rang through the room as he pulled back quickly.

"No," she moaned as he pushed back from her, taking his heat and passion, leaving her bereft.

"Easy, baby," he groaned roughly, holding her hands as she reached for him. "You're in no shape for kisses, let alone what I could do to that hot little body of yours."

She watched him drowsily, seeing the flush that mounted his cheekbones, the swollen fullness of his lips. She wanted those lips against hers again, tasting her, taking her.

"Cade—" Love welled inside her, nearly bursting her heart with hope.

"No, Marly." He laid his fingers against her lips, halting the outpouring of devotion. "Don't say it, don't say anything. We have to talk first."

Marly stared up at him, breathing raggedly, seeing the flare of desire in his eyes, in the way he watched her heatedly.

"Rest for now," he told her gently, moving away from her as he pulled the light blanket from the back of the couch and laid it over her. "Rest. We'll talk when you're better."

Chapter Fifteen

ഇ

Cade watched her sleep. He wasn't getting any work done, the accounts lay forgotten before him on the desk, but he was content to watch Marly. Watch her and ache and worry. And try to find a way out of the damned mess he found himself in.

The touch and taste of her was intoxicating. He should have never kissed her, should have never touched her in the shape she was in. But he had seen her need in her eyes, felt it in her body. The drugs took away her inhibitions and she watched him like she craved the touch, the taste of him.

He leaned back in his seat, his eyes never straying from her pale face, her relaxed body. She had kicked the blanket off her, leaving her clad in the long shirt she had stolen from him at least a year ago. Damn girl wouldn't sleep in the hundreds of gowns he bought her over the years. She stole his t-shirts, his flannel shirts, and even the damned silk dress shirt to sleep in.

Charcoal gray silk now covered her body, and should have gone to her knees. The shirt could have wrapped around her three times at least it was so big on her, but as she lay there, the silk conformed to ripe breasts, her flat stomach, and rode along her silken thighs. He had covered her twice already, trying to hide the sight of her. He wasn't getting within touching distance of her again.

He blamed himself for that accident. She was going out with Dillon to get to him, she had admitted that while delirious with concussion. To make him jealous. To make him want her as desperately as she wanted him.

Cade wanted her. His body was so hard and hot for her; he could barely stand the constriction of his jeans. But did he love her the way she needed him to love her? Or had he just gone so long without a woman that he was going crazy for the only one that seemed readily available? Was it love, or lust?

He sighed wearily, dragging his hands through his hair in a gesture of desperation. He couldn't take her until he knew. Not until he could make sense of the sensations and needs storming his body. She would be going back to school soon. He would have three months to weather the storm inside his body, to figure out what he felt himself, to be certain she knew what she wanted. Three months was a damned long time, but the rest of their lives was even longer. If he took her, he would have to marry her. He had to be certain of her because Cade knew he couldn't bear the thought of losing her.

Marly shifted in her sleep, a low moan coming from her lips as her body protested the movement. One arm curled gracefully above her head, emphasizing the full breast thrusting against the material of the silk. Her long, silken curls fell from her head to the floor. Her head was too tender to braid the mass, and it flowed around her, making her appear wanton, inviting. As though she needed the hair to contribute to the overall picture. He was going crazy as it was.

Letting her go was going to be next to impossible. Somehow, someway he was going to have to stay away from her until Sunday. Until she left for school again. If he took her, he would never be able to let her go, and he knew it. And the thought of it terrified him.

She whispered his name in her sleep. Cade swallowed hard as her nipples hardened beneath the silk, a fine sheen of perspiration suddenly coating his skin. Things had changed too damned fast, and he wasn't comfortable with it. He had hid from his desire for her for two long, lonely years. Pushing it back where he didn't have to examine it, didn't have to see it for what it was. The dark, pulsating monster of need that made his flesh harden and ache, made his soul weary and tired.

For years he had feared she would fall in love with one of the pimply-faced little brats she dated. Young men too filled with themselves to care about her, to know how to touch her and to please her. And he knew now that was why he hated every young man that fought to secure a date with her. Hated them. Glowering at them and doing everything he could to frighten them away. Even the ranch hands knew better than to approach Marly. Several had found themselves without a job after trying. He didn't tolerate it. He wouldn't tolerate it.

Cade was possessive and brooding, and had fought to assure himself for years that it was because she was so special. He had raised her. Fought battles for her. Tended to her illnesses and her scraped knees, and once even played Santa Claus for her. Just to see her eyes light up, to see the joy that crossed her face. And God, he would die right now to see her expression lost in passion, the awe and wonderment when he brought her to climax. He wanted that so much he could barely stand the need.

He had given her all her firsts in her life since she was twelve. Her first bicycle, her first car, her first prom dress, her first prom. She had been without a date, and he had been unable to stand her tears. She swore she was the envy of every girl there when he danced that first dance with her. He had been as uncomfortable as hell. But he couldn't stand to see her cry. Now he wanted to be her first. Her first lover, her only lover.She was watching him. Her eyes slumberous, dark and inviting. She hadn't changed position; she hadn't moved a muscle as his gaze roved slowly over her body.

"We're in trouble, Marly." He was breathing roughly, on the verge of doing something he knew he would regret.

Her breasts were rising quicker, her breathing accelerating. He could see the excitement in her eyes, in the flush staining her cheeks.

"Am I dreaming?" Her voice was husky, calling him to her in a way he could barely resist.

"Yes," he groaned. "Your worst nightmare. Go back to sleep so you can wake up and make everything normal again."

"Come kiss me again so I know it's not a dream." She smiled at him, slow and soft, dreamy with her emerging sensuality.

Marly knew now the power she held over him. He clenched his fists as he fought her request.

"Go back to sleep." He tried to smile back at her. "Maybe I'll kiss you goodnight when you go to bed."

"I'm ready to go to bed, then," she whispered with innocent seduction. "Tuck me in, Cade."

The flesh between his thighs hardened, nearly bursting from his jeans as her husky voice tore through his body.

"Marly," his voice was soft, the protest lacking strength.

"You could just let me sleep with you and keep me warm. You know how cold I get at night." Her legs shifted, the shirt riding marginally higher from the movement.

He had slept with her one night, right before she went off to college. That night was seared into his brain, as was his father's words when he found Cade there the next morning. It had been innocent. She had been depressed over leaving home, crying. He had only tried to comfort her. But the hand wrapped around her breast, beneath the material of yet another of his shirts hadn't been. Neither had the hard-on beneath his sweat pants been in any way innocent. That event had begun his downfall, and Marly wasn't even aware of it. That he knew.

Cade breathed out roughly. He wouldn't survive a night with her in his arms now. He knew it, and it terrified him. He watched as her hand pressed against her stomach, and he wondered if the ache in his gut was echoed in hers.

"Sweet Jesus," he moaned, closing his eyes and shaking his head at the suddenly erotic pictures flashing through his mind. He would burn in hell for this. Surely as anything, he would.

The knock at the study door had him jumping with a guilty start. His gaze flashed to her as she hastily jerked the blanket over her body, her face flushing in embarrassment. Shaking his head he watched as the door inched opened, wondering if her thoughts had somehow mirrored his. Praying not, because if she actually did it, he knew his heart would explode.

"Cade. Got a minute?" Sam was standing in the doorway, his bruised face unusually serious.

Hell, he was going to have to stand up.

"Yeah, a few." He stood, thankful that he had pulled the tails of his shirt from the waistband of his pants earlier. There would have been no way to hide his arousal if he hadn't.

Marly swallowed tightly as Cade left the room, closing the door behind him. Her body was pulsing beneath the blanket, shivering with the look in Cade's eyes. She had never seen anything so hot, so achingly possessive and wanting as that look. As he watched her fingers move lightly over the silk of her stomach, she had seen his needs, his desires. She closed her eyes. She knew what he wanted. She knew he would have never been able to resist her if she had.

Regret filled her as her fingers stilled on her stomach, the blanket lying at her hips. She had been tempted, but terrified. She cursed her own immaturity and lack of experience. Other women would know how to entice him, how to give him what he wanted without being hesitant or frightened.

Cade was a very sexual man. She had heard that when she was as young as fourteen. He had been a young man, but even then, careful to keep his women away from Marly. But that hadn't kept her from hearing the rumors. It hadn't stopped the women he bedded from whispering the tales they heard. How he could go all night. His touch slow and sure, his kisses hot and wild, his hands bold and his desires as carnal as original sin. She had hated the rumors, jealousy eating her up inside, but she had listened. She had listened and fought to understand what they meant. She had known, even then, that she loved Cade and that one day she would have to know the needs of the man, as well as the friend.

Could she do it, she wondered? Could she tease and tempt him as those other women had done? Did the older Cade still enjoy the sights and sounds that the younger Cade had, from his women?

"That look on your face is killing me." His voice was raw and husky, and when she opened her eyes, his gaze was a liquid flame centered on her hand and the fingers still rubbing over the silk softly.

He was standing beside the couch, his dark face flushed, his eyes glittering and centered longingly on that hand.

"What look?" Marly couldn't breathe. She felt too warm, too excited. She needed his touch too damned much to wait any longer.

"Marly," he whispered warningly. "You don't know what you're doing."

Marly licked her lips.

"When I was sixteen, Kari Black told me about that little fling you had with her sister," she said softly.

Cade's eyes widened in shock.

"Sisters talk. I was so mad at you, Cade. Remember? I wouldn't speak to you until you quit seeing her."

"I remember." His tone was guttural.

"Her sister told her all kinds of things Cade, and I listened. I hated it, but I listened, because I wanted to know how to please you. How to make you need me so badly you couldn't resist me."

"No," he whispered weakly, his eyes greedy, transfixed as her fingers went to the buttons of her silk shirt.

Marly was breathing roughly. All shame, all sense of decency deserting her as Cade's gaze became riveted by her slow movements, his hands mirroring hers as he began to unbutton the shirt he was wearing.

One by one the buttons were undone, until the edges lay neatly down the center of her body.

"Marly," he said thickly, roughly as she moved her hand, her fingers trailing in the slowest caress from the cleavage of her heaving breasts down.

His shirt was shrugged from his powerful shoulders as he watched her, his face flushing with desire, with helpless fascination as her fingers met her stomach. He fought himself, fought his need for her. Then her fingers reached the line at her hips, touching the waistband of the lacy thong panties.

"God, Marly." His fists clenched as her fingers played with the waistband deliberately. "Do it, or stop. Your choice, but decide now."

Her fingers disappeared beneath the waistband, but she knew it didn't halt the knowledge, the clear sight of where they touched. Then they pulled back, running over her flesh above the silk of the panties, leaving a damp crease down the center of the triangle of fabric.

Cade licked his lips, watching her, mesmerized as he went to his knees beside her.

"Do it right," he whispered, his fingers hooking in the waistband of her panties and pulling them quickly down her legs.

Marly cried out weakly, her thighs falling apart at his urging, feeling the brand of his gaze centered at her most vulnerable point.

"No," he growled. "Let me see you, Marly. Let me see you."

She touched herself, crying out as his hands touched her thighs, his long fingers moving closer.

"Tell me what you want, Marly," he growled as her fingers ran slowly over the humid curves of her own desire-slick flesh. "Tell me, Marly."

Tell him? God, she couldn't breathe, let alone speak.

"Now." His voice roughened as one fingertip touched the dew of her need. "Tell me what you want now."

"Kiss me," she panted harshly, wishing he would do anything. Something. She was dying.

He looked up at her, his eyes nearly black now as a finger slid smoothly past the folds of skin, lodging at the entrance of her body.

"Where?"

Marly whimpered as her thighs trembled, her inner muscles clenching in agonized need.

"Cade," she cried out weakly.

"Did Tara tell you about that Marly?" He asked her softly, his lips going to her thigh. "Did she tell you how I would kiss you? Taste you?"

He was teasing her, tormenting her. His tongue touched the satin flesh his lips caressed, drawing higher by only slow degrees.

"You didn't kiss her there." Marly shook her head, nearly crying in pain at the thought. "No. You didn't."

"No, I didn't," he agreed. "But by God, I'm going to kiss you there."

Before she could cry out he was between her thighs, his lips covering her, his tongue spearing into her. Marly lost her breath. Stars exploded all around her as he held her hips steady, thrusting into her repeatedly, driving his tongue deep and hard into the very center of her body as she exploded into so many fragments she thought she was dying.

When she opened her eyes again, Cade was kneeling before her, his gaze hot, his hands working frantically at the button fly of his jeans. Then he was spreading the edges apart, pushing the material over his hips as the thick length of his erection sprang free.

"God. Damn, Cade." Sam's shocked voice was like a bucket of ice as Cade leaned forward.

Chapter Sixteen

ॐ

"Why didn't you just lock the fucking door?" Sam's hushed voice was filled with understandable shock, an hour later.

"Shut up, Sam." Cade shifted in the saddle, staring into the inky blackness of night as they moved through the pasture. This was not the ride he had been expecting.

"Damn." Sam was still shaking his head. "I just didn't expect that."

It wasn't the first time Sam had made that comment in the last hour.

"Shut up, Sam," Cade growled warningly.

Cade could still smell the sweet scent of her, the heat and desire, hear her cry of release as it rained over his tongue. He was dying. His erection was like a steel hard spike an hour later. He hurt until he could barely stand to sit in the saddle. If it didn't go away soon, he'd be walking the damned horse.

"I just didn't expect it," Sam said again. "Not yet."

"If you don't shut up, I'm going to kick you out of that damned saddle," Cade gritted out between clenched teeth.

"Yeah, like you could do that with that hard-on killing you," Sam snickered in amusement. "I say I'm safe for several hours yet."

Asshole, Cade thought. He didn't have a brother with a lick of sense; he had one that was a moron who just didn't know any better.

"I didn't glimpse any protection there either, bro," Sam whispered just loud enough for him to hear. "You know the dangers, right?"

Shit. Cade closed his eyes, remembering the fiery heat of her dew slick flesh against him as he positioned himself to enter her. Hell no, there hadn't been any protection. He shifted uncomfortably, the thought of that worrying him as nothing else could have. He had never forgot to use protection in all of his adult life.

"Cade, you're gonna be careful next time, right?" Sam asked him somberly. "I mean, you're not going to take a chance, are you?"

Cade was silent. The thought of Marly, pregnant with his child, was heating through his body. Her soft belly rounded with life, her face glowing with it. He didn't think it was possible, but his body only hardened more.

"Don't worry, Sam. I'll take care of Marly. Now do you want to tell me one more time why we're out here on these damned horses?"

An hour later, they drew abreast of the two cowboys waiting on them. The ride had been a slow one due to the darkness of the night and the need to protect the horses' legs from hidden holes or unknown rocks. Behind them rode half a dozen other cowboys, their horses snorting quietly in the still air of the late night.

"Bret." Cade dismounted, drawing abreast of the two riders waiting on them. "What's up?"

"Sorry to drag you out here like this boss, but I was afraid the 'copter would give us away, and the trucks too. I think you need to see this and I don't know if you want to let anyone know we've found it."

One of the old, unused line cabins was tucked into the shelter of the hill rising in front of them. The door was opened, and only a faint light showed as the door cracked open and the men walked in.

"Didn't want to wait till morning. It's also why I told Sam to make sure one of you stayed with Miss Marly."

They walked into the cabin, a building that should have been forgotten, unused by man or beast in the years since Cade had bought the helicopter. But here was proof that someone had used it. It, and many other areas of the ranch. But what struck terror into Cade's soul was the pictures scattered out over the table.

Marly. Every picture there was, was of Marly. And all of them were taken in just the past two years. Some were taken while she was at school, at home. There were pictures of her riding her horse, driving her truck, laughing up at Cade, lying out beneath the steam of the pool, Greg at her side, the bare cheeks of her rear glowing in the glossy paper.

There were pictures of her in his arms outside the barn. That first touch, the power and passion of it appearing crude and somehow vulgar when viewed through the lenses of the camera. She was perched on his thigh, his hand tucked between the cheeks of her rear, the position of his finger clearly visible, buried deep inside the tight little hole.

Cade felt something freeze in his soul. It wasn't the only picture of him and Marly either. There were dozens displayed out on the table. Cade raised his gaze, staring at Sam as his blood beat sluggishly through his body.

"Call Brock, make certain Marly's okay. Tell him to lock her in a room and stay with her."

"Already took care of that." Sam nodded but pulled the cell phone from the holder at his hip anyway. Quickly, he keyed in the numbers. "I told him before we left. Before I knew what Bret found."

Cade listened silently as Sam spoke to his brother. Sam's voice stayed steady and calm, indicating there were no problems at the house. As he continued the phone call, Cade walked around the cabin, the beam of the flashlight picking out more signs of habitation. The boxes of ammunition, several of which were halfway empty. Gun oil and cleaning squares, saturated with the efforts of cleaning and maintaining more than one weapon.

The bed in the back was neatly made. On it laid another picture. One of Marly staring into the direction of the camera from her balcony, her expression dreamy, her blue eyes shadowed with emotion as she braided her hair. The picture must have been taken the summer before, because she was barefoot, propped against the railing and enjoying the morning.

He walked back to the table slowly, staring down at the pictures once again, a wave of fury washing over him. The bastard was watching her, violating her. The son of a bitch was obsessed by her.

"Is this the way you found them?" Cade waved his hand over the table and the pictures it contained.

"We ain't touched anything, boss," Bret assured him. "We found this right after dark, checked the area over and then called Sam. I figured it was your call what we did."

Cade breathed deeply, fought to do so steadily. His heart was beating out of control, fear snaking like an evil wind down his spine.

"Looks like whoever it was, was here not too long ago." The other cowboy, Jake, moved to the side of the room, along the wood stove. "These ashes ain't old, the stove barely cold. He's also stocked coffee and some canned stuff in the back. He intends to come back."

Cade's fists clenched. Was the bastard preparing the cabin to bring Marly here? Had he somehow convinced himself he could take Marly from Cade, and the family that loved her? The man was clearly obsessed with her, in a way that ruled out any possibility of sanity.

"Let's get out of here. Leave everything the way you found it. Pull out, we'll move along the edge of the rise." Cade eased from the cabin, moving back into the night, heading for his horse.

The light was doused inside the cabin, the door relocked as they rushed back into the night. Cade wanted everything cleaned, out of sight. To catch the bastard, he would have to make him think he was still well hidden, undetected by the family or the ranch hands.

"Clear the horses' tracks from the area," Cade ordered them as he gathered the horse's reins and led them from the cabin yard. "Make it as natural as possible."

He pulled the horses back until they stood in the high pasture grass that made the remote area perfect for grazing.

"What do we do?" Cade could hear the fear in Sam's voice. It was thick, punctuated by harsh breaths and the heavy beat of his own heart.

God. Someone was stalking Marly. And if those pictures were anything to go by, then it had been going on for a while. The truly terrifying part was the range of those pictures. The older ones had begun out of focus, from a distance. As the months had progressed, they had gotten closer. Cade clenched his fists as he watched the cowboys rushing to clean the area of hoof prints, or any sign of visitation. Cade wanted the bastard caught. He wanted to know who it was, and what he wanted, and there was only one way to do that. They had to catch him before he learned that Cade knew he was there. Let the bastard know they were onto him, then he would run, getting more deceptive, more dangerous to Marly.

Could it be Jack Jennings? Cade left the horses with one of the cowboys and moved silently along the canyon that led off the side of the cabin. Stepping on stone and grass, careful not to leave footprints, he worked the flashlight over the ground. The last report they had of Annie's ex-husband, he was working out East, and Annie was safe in California, though the last time he talked to her, she was certain Jack wasn't where he was supposed to be. She swore he had found her again. But the investigator was even more certain, in the form of pictures that Jack was still in the New York area.

There they were. Tire prints. Large ones. A four by four by the looks of it. Cade's eyes narrowed. Dillon wasn't sure what had happened the other night, but he remembered a black four by four, and a large man trying to drag Marly to the truck. Jack Jennings was a large man. Nearly as tall and broad as Cade himself.

"Shit," Cade breathed roughly as he stared around the canyon, thinking of the cabin area. Where could he place guards, get them in and out without being seen until they could take the intruder down?

There was no place. The rise above the cabin might work, but it would be hard for the men to get down without being heard, which would put them at risk. Anyone bold enough to risk the pictures he had taken of Marly on the ranch, would be more than dangerous. And there was also the ammunition found in the back of the cabin. The guy was well prepared for anything.

Working his way back out of the canyon, he rejoined Sam outside the cabin yard.

"Four by four in the little canyon, well hidden," he said softly. "Ammo in the cabin, but no weapons. He has them with him."

"What do we do, Cade?" Sam hissed. "We can't let her leave the ranch now. There's no way we can protect her at school."

Cade shook his head, trying to figure out quickly the best way to solve this problem. Marly would fight them if she thought they were trying to shelter her. She hated that, and wouldn't stand for it. He didn't want to have to fight her, and whoever was stalking her.

"We need to leave some men up here. Catch the bastard when he comes back," Cade told him imperatively. "You know the area better than I do. Where do we put them?"

Sam breathed in deeply, looking around the area. The line cabin was well sheltered from the fierce storms that hit the mountains. Dug into the face of the hill behind it, with only the rough wood front visible to the eye. No other way to get out, which would help. But no other way to get in, either.

"What about the canyon? Catch him as he gets out of the truck?" Sam asked. "There are several small rock houses in there where a few of the boys could hide."

"What about the horses?" Cade asked. "There's no way to hide the damned horses in there."

"Hell, turn them loose. The cattle have been grazing all over this place for a month now. A few more horses shouldn't spook him. After they take the bastard, they can drive him out in his own truck," Sam suggested, his voice rough with fury.

There had been pictures of Marly, standing on her balcony, dressed in one of the shirts she slept in. Cade narrowed his eyes, judging the area the picture would be taken from.

"Let's get back." Cade headed quickly for his horse. "Bret, you and Michael let your horses loose here in the pasture. Get in one of those rock houses and keep an eye on that canyon. When he brings that truck in, take him."

"Yes sir, Mr. Cade." Bret nodded quickly, rushing to join Michael to follow orders.

"You two be careful, Bret," Cade told him roughly. "Don't do anything foolish. If you can't take him, let him go and we'll get him later. I'll send you relief out here in the morning. You have your cell phone?" Cade mounted his horse, swinging quickly into the saddle and turning the horse for home.

"Me and Mike both." Bret nodded. "We have everything we need. You guys head out, I'll check in, in a few hours."

Bret was already removing the saddle from his horse, checking his flashlight, his gun. Cade watched him for long moments, knowing well the competence of the man taking charge of the watch. Bret wasn't reckless, but he wasn't one to back out either. And the Augusts were as close to family as he had since the death of his own parents. He wouldn't let Cade down if he could help it.

Cade nodded, checked behind him for Sam then set the horse off at a run, hearing the steady beat of hoofs behind him.

The time for caution was over. He was going to have to trust in his own experience, and the horses instincts now. His first priority was to get home as quickly as possible.

Those last pictures had been taken from the rise behind the ranch house. It was the only way to achieve that angle, or to get such a clear shot into the pool area. Whoever the bastard was he had plenty of weapons, which meant a bullet could be aimed at her next time. Fear thrummed through his body, setting his blood to a rhythm as harsh and pounding as that of the hooves striking the ground.

Cade had to get back to Marly. The overwhelming need nearly stopped the breath in his chest as he urged his horse to a faster pace, feeling the wind blowing through his hair, the urgency flowing through his body. He had to protect her. He had to keep her safe. And to do that, he had to find the mad man stalking her.

Chapter Seventeen

Cade and Sam slipped silently into the dark house, their rifles ready, their eyes narrowed as they attempted to pierce the darkness. There wasn't a sound that could be heard. Cade glanced at Sam, seeing the tense readiness for action in his body. If anyone had managed to get into the house, he felt he would know it. The bond he and Brock shared would have warned him.

It was eerie though, stepping into a home that had never known darkness. As far back as Cade could remember, the hall light at least was left on after dark, all night. The inky blackness wrapped around them now. There was no creak of floorboards; the only sound Cade could hear was the beat of his own heart.

"Settle down." Brock's whisper was infused with caution. "Marly and I are the only ones in here."

"Then why are all the stinkin' lights out?" Sam growled. "I can barely see my hand in front of my face."

"Beats the bullet getting a clear aim to your heart," Brock hissed back. "Quit being such a baby."

"Baby —"

"Enough." Cade wanted to rap both their heads together. Now was not the time for another of their infernal arguments.

Brock had stepped from the shadows of the curved staircase that led upstairs. He walked out, a dark silhouette moving dangerously through the darkness. He was more controlled, quieter and less intense than his twin.

"Where's Marly?" Cade's voice was strained and concerned.

"Still sleeping on the couch. I left her there." Brock nodded to the opened door of the study. "All things considered, maybe we shouldn't let her sleep in her room for a while."

"Why?" Cade's eyes narrowed on Brock's expressionless face as he neared them silently.

"Come upstairs, I'll show you why. I saw it right after you left." Brock moved quickly up the steps as they followed. "After Marly went to sleep, the cattle started acting funny in the pasture out back. So, I locked everything up, shut out all the lights and started watching. I didn't see anything until I got to Marly's room."

He opened the door to Marly's bedroom, careful to stay against the wall as he entered rather than moving into the center of the room. Edging along silently, he came up beside the glass balcony doors.

"Look out there, and tell me what you see." He nodded into the night.

Ducking to use the cover of the balcony railing, Cade slid over to the other side of the doors. Leaning over slowly, he stared outside. The night was moonless, a thick cover of clouds making the land darker than usual and filled with shadows. At first Cade didn't see anything. He knew the area the stalker was most likely taking the pictures from, so he centered his attention there. It only took a few minutes to see what Brock had seen.

A flare of light in the darkness, the strike of a lighter or a match as tobacco was lit. As Cade watched closer, he was able to pick out a shape moving against the boulders on the furthest point as a shaft of moonlight lit up the inky darkness.

"He's watching her room," Cade said softly. "That's why he wasn't at the cabin."

"He could be using infrared glasses too," Brock said softly. "I watched him for a while through my own. He can see everything going on from the house, and would know the minute anyone set out for that rise, in any direction."

"Are you sure he's using them?" Cade asked carefully.

Brock breathed roughly. "Not sure, but I wouldn't doubt it. None of our men have seen him, and if he didn't know what the hell was going on down here, he would have been caught by now."

"We'll trap him. He has to leave sometime. We'll let more of the cattle out into the pasture there, and give the impression we're working it tomorrow. That should run him off again until dark," Sam murmured. "He would come back soon. The man's obsessed."

Cade watched the area, considering Sam's plan. It had merit, but it required waiting, and taking a chance that they missed him entirely. He was there now, watching the house, waiting to see Marly. Undressing. Cade gritted his teeth, wondering how many times the bastard had watched her dress, or undress. His fists clenched with the need for violence.

"This room is easily watched from that rise," Brock told them as they continued to stare at the high rising hill. "Cade, yours is harder. But if the bastard is intent on grabbing her, he's gonna be damned hard to catch this way. We're cowboys, not Green Beret's."

Cade swiped the hat from his head, running his fingers through his hair worriedly. Brock was right, they weren't soldiers and had no idea how to be. But a man didn't have to be a soldier to track a rabid animal. And the one on that rise could be nothing else.

"We tell Marly about this, it's going to terrify her," he said softly, moving carefully from the window. "Let's get downstairs, I need to check on her. There's no way to watch that son of a bitch from here for long. He could sneak away and we'd never know it."

They moved from the bedroom, using the same route they had entered, careful to stay away from the window just in case the infrared binoculars were being used.

"Cade, remember that pair of investigators the Stewarts used a year or so ago when that kidnapper tried to take their daughter?" Sam asked as they made their way down the stairs. "They caught four guys, and rescued the girl on the last attempt. Maybe we need to check into that. Brock's right, we're cowboys, not hot shot bodyguards or military types."

Cade breathed out roughly. His heart was pounding sluggishly in his chest, fear moving through him. They entered the study quietly, and Cade saw immediately that Brock had closed the shades on the balcony doors.

Marly was sleeping where he had left her, her hair fanning and falling around her, her face composed and innocent in sleep. He breathed out deeply, relief nearly overwhelming him. Brock and Sam were quiet behind him, but Cade had nearly forgotten they were there anyway.

She was lying on her back, her face turned towards him, her lips parted as she breathed deeply. Cade went to his knees beside her, his finger touching a curl that teased her cheek and moved it back gently. She whispered his name, turning toward him, reaching for him even when unaware of his presence.

Cade lowered his head, his heart clenching with pain. How in the hell was he going to protect her from this?

"Get two of the boys in here. Brock, you come with me. Sam, you stay. Get Marly the hell out of here if you don't hear from us soon." He rose to his feet, moving quickly from the room.

"What the hell are you going to do, Cade?" Sam whispered fiercely. "Dammit, you aren't going out there?"

Cade went to the door, motioning two of the half dozen cowboys he had left waiting on the porch, the others came to attention when they saw his face. The night wasn't over.

"You two stay here with, Sam—"

"Dammit, I'm not staying anywhere," Sam bit out. "If you and Brock go, then I go."

"What about Marly?" Cade turned to him furiously. "If something happens to us, who will take care of Marly, Sam? Who will get her out of here and make sure she's safe?"

Sam grimaced in indecision.

"Cade's right, Sam." Brock checked the pistol he was carrying on his thigh, then grabbed his rifle from where he had propped it against the wall.

"Then you stay," Sam bit out.

"I've done my babysitting for the night," Brock informed him harshly, but Cade knew it had nothing to do with sitting with Marly. Sam didn't have the hard core of violence Cade and Brock carried. "Your turn at it, bro."

"Stop trying to protect me," Sam bit out, watching the other two with a furious glare. "Dammit, what happened to the 'we're not Green Berets' bit? This is stupid. Marly needs us all."

"And we need Marly, Sam, or have you forgot that?" Cade bit out. "Whoever that bastard is out there, he's not playing with a full deck. Do you want to risk her this way?"

Cade watched Sam grimace. Pure fury lit his face and his gaze, but he knew there was no other way.

"Dammit, be careful," he growled. "And remember, you two bite it, and this ranch will go to hell. Be damned if I'll try to run it alone."

For a few moments, Cades eyes widened. Hell, Marly was more important than the ranch, but still—he was going to have make certain he was damned careful. This ranch was Marly's livelihood.

"Let's go." Cade headed out the door with Brock following close behind.

Cade waited until he heard the lock snap into place, then he turned to the other four cowboys.

145

"Brock, take two with you and head up the west slope. I'll take the other two and head up the east. Hopefully, we can catch him between us."

Terse nods greeted his orders. Staying low and moving carefully around the house, they kept a close eye on the area pinpointed as the stalker's location. It was nothing more than shadow, the entire area. Impossible to make out, or to catch movement this far below the bench where he hid.

The moon was tucked carefully behind clouds, its rays blocked from the land below. It left the area in a blanket of deep night, usually not a concern. Unless there was a mad man with a gun hiding within it.

Cade and the two cowboys following him stuck to the shadows as they made their way through the back pasture. The trees that had been allowed to grow there provided them with a bit of cover, meager though it was. The cloudless night helped all it could.

"Spread out," Cade ordered the men following him as they started up the rise. "And be careful, for God's sake."

The rise was a tall hill, not really a mountain, but steep and tall just the same. It sloped up nearly a half mile, with a flat bench near the top. On that bench, hidden behind the concealment of large boulders, sat the stalker. Cade gritted his teeth in fury as he began a parallel path up to that bench. The son of a bitch was watching her, taking pictures of her, and only God knew what he had planned.

The shadows were long and deep on the hill, the trees sheltering as he moved along them carefully. He fought to move his body soundlessly through the underbrush and dried twigs. It wasn't easy, though, to clear a path as he went. Damned if he knew how the Indians used to do it. One thing was damned sure, they didn't try to do it in boots.

Still, he moved slowly, if in silence up the hill. He kept a careful watch on the bench above him, wondering, waiting.

Cade well admitted the stupidity of even trying to catch the crazy bastard, but he was pissed. Those pictures of Marly had sent his rage level out the roof. He wanted to kill the man who dared to violate her in such a way.

Moving stealthily, Cade neared the bench, his eyes narrowed in the darkness, searching for any sign of movement that would indicate the stalker's location. There was nothing. The wildlife in the surrounding trees and brush were silent. Not even a birdcall, or the click of a cricket.

Stepping carefully, he moved along a small stand of trees perpendicular to the bench, straining to catch a glimpse of movement. Anything. There was nothing. Moving carefully, Cade turned to try another angle when wood flew from the tree behind him. Almost instantaneously, the sharp retort of a rifle followed.

Cade dropped to the ground as he brought his own rifle up, scurrying to find cover among the trees and small boulders that littered the lower end of the bench. The shots kept coming, followed closely by rounds being returned from the cowboys below.

But that didn't keep the bullets from coming his way. Another sheared off rock above his head, causing pebble-sized pieces to fall around him. Aiming haphazardly into the area the shots were coming from, Cade fired off several rounds of his own, then jumped to his feet, heading for a larger tree several feet in front of him.

He was almost there when the bullet hit him. It flung him backwards as it punched into his shoulder, causing him to land heavily on his back. He shook his head with a tight movement, fighting the pain as he raised his gun and fired again.

"Boss, he's moving," one of the cowboys called out.

Cade fired again as he came painfully to his knees, following the swift running shadow disappearing around the rise.

"Dammit, he's getting away," Brock's voice was filled with fury.

Lumbering to his feet, Cade held the rifle in one hand and moved as fast as he could push himself, to follow the assailant. Son of a bitch, he cursed. He couldn't believe the bastard had actually managed to shoot him. But his shoulder and chest felt like a boulder was resting on it, and fire was laid to it. Oh yeah, the bastard had definitely managed to shoot him. The pain of it was like an animal gnawing on raw flesh.

Breathing harshly, adrenaline and rage surging through his body, Cade grew closer to the assailant, his legs pushing him further, faster, despite the wrenching agony in his shoulder. When he was only mere feet from him, Cade launched his body at the man in a rolling tackle that would have done him proud ten years before, but he swore was killing him the minute he collided with the big body.

There was no time to enjoy his success or moan over the agony. With his arms gripping the long legs, Cade took him down. But one powerful kick from boot-covered feet into his wounded shoulder had him releasing him just as fast as the pain ground into his brain with sickening force. A sharp kick to his ribs didn't help matters.

"Bastard," a voice growled above him. "You touched her. Now you die."

Cade blinked up at the pistol aimed at him.

"Cade!" Brock's voice echoed from the darkness, a gunshot reverberated around the hillside, and the assailant, deciding to use caution rather than fury, ran again.

"Boss, you okay?" One of the cowboys was quickly at his side.

"Dammit, Cade. Are you hit?" A flashlight was quickly turned on, the brilliant light blinding him. "A couple of the boys followed him, but he had a hell of a head start on us."

Brock knelt at his side, his fingers probing at the gunshot wound.

"It went on through," Cade wheezed, still clutching his ribs. "But I swear the son of a bitch must have busted my ribs with that kick."

"Damn. Marly will be pissed over this," Brock swore darkly. "Just you wait, she'll chew you're ass for sure."

Chapter Eighteen

Marly was silent as Dr. Bennett treated Cade in his bedroom. She sat in the large, overstuffed chair by the bed, watching as the bullet wound was cleaned and bandaged, and his ribs poked and probed at.

"No breaks," Bennett grumped. "Maybe a crack or two. Take it damned easy and I still say you should come into the hospital for x-rays."

"No x-rays, Doc." Cade shook his head, his face still pale from the exam. "I'll just rest up here for a while."

Dr. Bennett shook his graying head and Marly's eyes narrowed as she looked from Cade, to Sam and then to Brock.

Dr. Bennett scratched his head, messing his frizzled gray hair further as he stared down at Cade.

"Hell of an accident," he murmured, shaking his head. "I thought you were smarter than that, Cade."

At least he had the grace to look ashamed, Marly thought coolly. As though the lie these three men had conspired in was actually believable.

"Yeah, well—" He met Marly's gaze and she almost smiled as she saw the worried expression on his face. "Shit happens, ya know?"

Dr. Bennett merely grunted.

"I thought something smelled," the good doctor muttered beneath his breath, but Marly caught the words, as did Cade.

Once again, his gaze came back to hers, cool and probing, as though she couldn't see the lie in those stormy depths.

"Thanks for patching me up, Doc." Cade cleared his throat as he broke Marly's stare. "I knew I could depend on you."

"Just wait till you get the bill. Pulling me out of bed after midnight is extra time, young man. I need my sleep," the doctor grumbled as he closed the old fashioned black bag he carried as he moved for the door. "I'm going home now. Try to stay away from rabid animals in the future."

"I'll walk you down, Doc." Brock moved behind the older man, and Marly noticed he still hadn't removed the gun belt he wore, or the lethal pistol encased in it.

"Thank you there, young man. No telling how many of those critters are lurking outside the front door." The doctor's voice was definitely mocking this time. He didn't believe them any more than Marly did.

Marly looked back at Cade, then at Sam. She stared at the younger brother coolly, arching her eyebrow curiously as he began to shift nervously beneath her regard.

"Are you feeling any better, Marly?" Cade's tired voice drew her attention from his brother and back to him.

"A bit," she answered him carefully. "The headache's gone now."

"Good." He closed his eyes, then opened them again. The injection the doctor had given him earlier must be knocking him out. "I've been worried about you."

"I could tell." She tilted her head, watching him as his eyes grew dark with weariness.

She watched as he sighed deeply.

"You're angry." He shifted uncomfortably on the bed, wincing at the pain in his shoulder and ribs. "It was an accident Marly."

Marly glanced at Sam as he shifted nervously while Cade spoke. He stood with his rear braced against the dresser, watching Cade and Marly silently.

Lora Leigh

"Was it?" she asked him as she continued to watch Sam.

Sam avoided her gaze, and Marly's eyes narrowed. Sam was too open for the lies they were trying to pull over on her. Marly's only question was why they were lying.

"Stop trying to intimidate Sam, Marly," Cade sighed.

"Stop trying to lie to me, Cade." She leaned back in the chair once again, crossing her legs as she adjusted her robe. "What happened out there?"

He looked at her, his eyes heavy-lidded.

"Wolf."

"My ass," she snorted.

"You have a fine ass, darlin'. So pretty and tight it's enough to make a man come just thinking about it." Marly sighed in exasperation as Cade's voice slurred.

It was more than obvious she would get nothing out of him tonight.

"Sam, go help Brock." Cade glanced over at his brother, and Marly saw the edge of concern in his expression.

"Sure thing, Cade." Sam nodded, then looked over at Marly.

"Marly, keep me warm." Cade patted the bedside him. "Come on honey, I need you tonight."

Sam blinked in surprise. Then he shook his head as he smiled and walked from the room.

"Please, Marly," Cade whispered when she stood, turning on the table light and turning off the bright overhead light. "Sleep with me."

Marly trembled at the sound of his voice, the husky bass, like a deep, sensual rumble. It stroked over her body like a physical caress.

"You should rest." She stood at the side of the bed, watching his eyes darken, like dark heavy clouds amassing for a storm.

"I need to hold you, Marly," he whispered. "Help me undress, then get in here with me."

He indicated the socks and jeans he wore. Marly looked at his flat, hard stomach, then swallowed deeply at the erection beneath his jeans. She licked her lips, her gaze returning to his face. She flushed as she saw his awareness of where her eyes had been.

"Come on, Marly." With one hand he released his belt, then the buttons on the fly of his jeans. "Help me get them off."

Marly moved slowly, her breathing almost a whimper as she exhaled. Her hands gripped the waist of his jeans, then she pulled them slowly from his body, dragging his underwear carefully with them.

"God, Marly," he groaned weakly as her fingers trailed down his thighs. "Damn you. I'm too drugged up to do it right, and you're just making it worse."

"Poor baby," she whispered as she dropped his jeans on the floor then allowed her robe to join them.

She was naked now, her hair flowing around her body, teasing her back in a way that made her feel sexy and alive. Her breasts were swollen, her nipples hard and peaked. She needed him. Needed him desperately. And there was no way in hell he could take her tonight. The pain was easing due to whatever Doc had injected him with, but he knew he was in no shape for what he wanted to do to his Marly.

"Come here." He indicated his side as she drew the blankets over him.

She moved into the bed, hesitant and unsure as he drew her close to his side.

"I'm sorry, Marly, about the other day," he whispered against her hair. "I was like an animal. Hell, I still am. I'm so hot for you, it's killing me."

"You could have had me," she told him sadly. "At any time."

Cade sighed roughly. "You don't know me, Marly. You're so damned young and tender, and I'm rough, baby. Rougher than you know."

"You think I haven't heard about your affairs, Cade? I told you I have. Everything," she bit out, anger coursing through her at the thought of it. "I shave myself there because I heard about Lisa Gilmore, and how you made her and every woman you sleep with shave there. I heard about the hours upon hours you rode your women, and the different ways you took them. Trust me, Cade. They were more than eager to let me know about it, especially after I got older."

She felt him tensing beside her as she spoke. Rising up, she stared him straight in the eye.

"Do you think I wasn't more than aware of the significance of where your finger went the other day? Do you think I don't know what you wanted? What you will want if I come to your bed? I've known for years, Cade."

His hand tangled in her hair as she watched his face flush, his eyes becoming heavy lidded. Slowly he drew her down, until her lips almost touched his.

"I'll fuck you there. Is that what you want, Marly? And it won't stop there. There will be no going back to school, no girlish nights out, no flirting with other men, nothing but me fucking you day after day, night after night. Do you understand that?"

Her stomach clenched, her thighs weakening at the thought of it.

"I don't accept no for an answer when I want something sexually, baby," he whispered tightly. "I told you I was rough, and I meant it. I won't deliberately hurt you, but I'm not a virgin's lover. I'll shred your innocence, not just your virginity."

"You think you didn't do that on the floor of that stall, Cade?" She was breathing harshly as his breath caressed her lips. "Did you consider that romantic?"

"As romantic as I get," he growled. "Candlelight and your mouth sucking me like you're starved is my ultimate idea of romance. That or my mouth on you, licking every drop of honey I can find from between your smooth little thighs."

Marly gasped, heat curling through her body as his words stroked her. She could feel her body preparing itself, heating and growing wet at the need flowing through her.

"You're in no shape—"

"Damn doctor and his shots," he muttered drowsily. "If I weren't ready to knock out, Marly, I'd show you what I want."

Marly shivered at the sensual threat in his voice. Lying against his side, feeling his body hot and tense, knowing how hard he was, was the worse torture she could think of. Only part of the dream, her mind whispered, she needed it all.

"It can wait." She was breathing harshly, her body humming with desire. Between her thighs, she could feel the growing moisture on her bare flesh.

"Are you wet for me, Marly?" His arms bent beneath her neck, his fingers sinking into her hair.

"Don't, Cade," she whispered weakly. "I need you too badly."

"Like I've needed you this past week. So hard I was nearly bursting my jeans, and you were flaunting that pretty little ass all over the house anyway?" His voice was tortured.

"I was willing. And able," she reminded him tartly.

"Damned if I ain't willing as hell right now. Able..." he sighed roughly. "Dammit. I'm going to be asleep in five minutes flat."

Marly smiled at the disgust in his tone, despite the heat radiating in her body.

"Go to sleep then. We're both tired. Maybe tomorrow you'll tell me what really happened tonight."

His big body tensed.

"That wolf is dangerous, Marly," he whispered, his voice so dark and haunted she shivered. "Stay close to the house, and don't go out alone anymore."

"A wolf wouldn't come into the ranch yard, Cade," she reminded him.

"A rabid wolf will show up anywhere," he muttered. "Just do as I say. Just for now."

Marly frowned. There was more to it than a wolf, and she knew it. But she knew Cade was not yet willing to tell her whatever was actually going on.

"You hear me, Marly?" His voice was slow, almost slurred as sleep caught up on him.

"I hear you, Cade," she told him softly. "Go to sleep, we'll talk about it tomorrow."

* * * * *

He was sore, aroused, and pissed. Cade stood at the French doors of his study and listened to Sam and Brock arguing behind him.

"You didn't have to call them," Brock bit out furiously, not for the first time. "We can handle this ourselves."

"Oh yeah, you handled it real well last night," Sam assured him sarcastically. "Cade got shot, and you twisted your ankle, and the bastard got clean away without even knowing who he was."

"It was dark—" Brock began.

"It was a damned stupid move and you know it," Sam bit out furiously. "We're not trained for something like this. We need help."

Anger. It pulsed and throbbed between the three of them, a remnant, not just of the danger the night before, but of the past. There was no longer the illusion of control. It had slipped dangerously through their fingers. They had to find their way back into the structured stability they had built for themselves.

"He's right." Cade turned from the doors and faced his brothers now. "We need to concentrate on protecting Marly. That means someone trained at tracking bastards like this is needed. We can't fight this alone."

He watched Brock snarl an obscenity.

"When will they be here?" he asked Sam.

"Tomorrow," Sam told him in relief. "I talked to their boss this morning. Their names are—"

"Rick and Tara Glaston," Brock growled.

Cade glanced at Brock, knowing his fury was directed at the situation, not the bodyguards.

"I want this kept from Marly," Cade warned them both quietly. "Sam, you meet them before they get to the ranch, I don't care where. They're friends, and they're just visiting. I don't want Marly to know what the hell's going on."

Sam rolled his eyes.

"Cade, we can't keep this from her," he warned him quietly. "Marly's not stupid."

"I'll take care of Marly, and I'm very well aware of the fact that she's not stupid. I want her protected from this."

"You think she doesn't know we're lying to her about that damned wolf?" Sam bit out. "Get serious here."

"You heard me." He moved slowly back to his desk, lowering himself to it slowly.

"What about her bedroom?" Brock asked. "He has a clear view into her room from several different angles. And Marly keeps those damned shades open on her balcony doors."

"Not anymore." Cade leaned back in his chair tiredly. "She'll be sleeping with me. She'll be staying with me. She's mine now."

Silence thickened in the room. Cade knew that the other two men were well aware of the implications to his statement. He ran his fingers through his hair and sighed wearily.

"Uh, Cade," Sam ventured.

Cade shot him a warning look.

"You two were so hot to convince me how much I want her. Well you were right. I did, and I still do. Starting today, Marly will find out just how much."

It wasn't a decision he was entirely comfortable with. To be honest, becoming Marly's lover scared the hell out of him. He was terrified to take her, walking a precipice he wasn't certain he could maintain. He loved her, loved her enough to try to give her what she needed first, and to pray to God nothing pushed him over that thin edge that separated the man and the monster.

He watched as Brock and Sam exchanged a speaking look. They too understood, and Cade was furiously aware of the fact that they had most likely been looking forward to this for a while.

"She's mine. No games," he warned them both quietly. "She can't handle them, and I won't force it on her. I'll give her what she needs for as long as I can. Then, it will be Marly's choice."

Marly's choice. He wanted to bite his tongue, because truth be told, he may not have the strength to give her a choice at all. Marly had heard tales of his sexuality, but not the more explicit, damning stories that only hinted at the truth of a lifestyle that he shared with his brothers.

They had made a pact years ago, had sworn by it, and truth be told, found great pleasure in it. It was exhilarating, seeing a woman he had claimed being touched by the brothers he loved. Sharing in the ultimate intimacy of bringing a woman to peak together, often despite her hesitancy in accepting it. Cade had never questioned that aspect of their sex lives, until now. He had protected Marly from it all her life, and he knew she would never accept the act of affirming his bond with his brothers in that way. She would never lie before the three of them, accepting the pleasure they could bring to her body.

She saw love in the black and white haze of sexual need and possessiveness. Not that Cade wasn't possessive. He would kill a man, outside of his brothers, if they dared touch her. But the thought of watching her, dazed and filled with lust, the sole recipient of, love, not just for her, but each other, was nearly more than he could bear. It was also something he knew he would be forever denied with Marly.

"Marly's not as timid as you think she is, Cade," Brock offered quietly, his voice low and charged with excitement.

Cade shook his head. "No, Brock. I won't do it to her. I can't stand the thought of her horror if I tried. She won't be with us long now, let me have her while I can."

The other two men lowered their heads. They knew Cade's love for Marly went much deeper than did their own. She was loved, desired and needed by all three of them. But she was Cade's heart.

"Where is she now?" Sam finally asked.

"Asleep for now. She was awake most of the night after I passed out from that damned shot Bennett gave me. She finally went to sleep after I woke up." Curled in his bed, her hair tangled around her body like living silk. He had to fight to control the urge to go to her now.

"So what do we do from here?" Sam asked him slowly.

"We keep Marly safe and let your commandos do their job," Cade told him firmly. "We'll all three stick as close to the house as possible, and make certain the bastard doesn't get anywhere near her."

Cade could feel his fear for her crawling through his body. He leaned his head back against the chair, closing his eyes and fighting the need to take her and run. To get her the hell away from the ranch and the danger he could feel was closing in on her.

"Cade, go easy on her," Sam said carefully, his concern for Marly now that Cade had made his decision to take her to his bed uppermost in his mind.

"Too late, Sam." He shook his head wearily. "You know me, man." He opened his eyes, staring at him with an edge of anger. "She's too damned innocent for this. For me. But it's what she wanted, and what you helped push at me. Now both of you can live with it."

He rose from his chair, steeling himself and beating back his own concern.

"Get out of here now. Check with the boys we left up on that damned hill and make sure they're okay. I want to know the minute they see anything. Keep the chopper ready, and stay on standby. I want this bastard the minute he pokes his head out of whatever hole he's hiding in."

"He hasn't come back to the cabin. Bret's still there, and he hasn't seen anything yet." Brock shook his head. "Somehow, the bastard knows we're onto him."

"Call Bret. Tell him to gather those fucking pictures up and get the hell back here. Better yet, you and Sam head out in the chopper and pick him up. You get the pictures yourselves. I don't want to risk anyone unnecessarily. He knows we know about him. It will make him more dangerous." Cade stood to his feet, walking around the desk. "The house is still locked up, make sure you lock the front door as you leave."

There was no mistaking the intent in his voice, and Cade knew it. He had been pushed too far, tempted too long, and now his fear for Marly was the breaking point. There was one way, and one way only to tie her to him, to be certain she stayed at his side where he could protect her.

"Cade," Sam said hesitantly. "Be careful of her."

He stopped; staring at his brother for a long, tense moment.

"I've always been careful of her, Sam, because I loved her. It's the one and only reason I never touched her after she came of age. It's too late for warnings now."

He strode quickly from the room, his body driving him to Marly, his desire for her reaching the breaking point. He needed her. He would take her. And he would take her now.

Chapter Nineteen

ᔓ

He was aroused nearly past bearing, and Cade knew it. He also knew himself and his desires. Many could be controlled, but there were many that couldn't be. He was extremely dominant sexually. He required, no, he needed submission no matter the demand he made. He was also highly sexual to the point that he would often ride his lovers for hours at a time. His first ejaculation would only build his need for another.

He stepped into his bedroom, closing the door behind him and locking it securely. Marly was still asleep, which was just as well for now. He would arouse her before awakening her, keeping her relaxed, ensuring she didn't become frightened before he took her. He didn't want to hurt her, but he had never taken a virgin before, and the thought of taking Marly's innocence made his palms sweat with fear.

She had kicked the blankets off her body, displaying her slender body for his eager gaze. Her breasts were full and hard, her nipples tight in the air-conditioned coolness of the room. Her hand was lying against her flat stomach, her slender thighs parted marginally, allowing him to glimpse the pale perfection of her bare pussy.

His mouth watered, his hands tightening to fists at the sight of her. His cock throbbed, demanding release. Slowly he undressed, watching her carefully, eagerly. He had denied himself for two years now, knowing deep inside how desperately he wanted her. Joe had been right in his accusation that there was nothing Cade wanted more than to fuck her. And Cade rarely denied himself when he needed something this badly.

Naked, his body hard, demanding action, he strode quickly to the bed. Ignoring the now minor ache of his ribs, and the wound at his shoulder, he lay down beside her, drawing her carefully against his body. Today, Marly would become his lover.

* * * * *

The dream was back, vivid and hot, torturing her with need. Marly's lips opened beneath Cade's harsh growl, her mouth accepting the smooth thrust of his tongue as he kissed her. His lips ate at her as he kissed her, making her arch against him, her skin to sensitize, her body to heat with longing. Her hands went to his shoulders, feeling the smooth, hard muscles beneath his skin, her nails flexing against it. She groaned harshly, fighting to get closer, to make the kiss deeper, rougher. She wanted him as she had heard he was. A demon, kisses hot and addicting, his touch demanding.

"As sweet as candy," she heard him groan as he finally gave her what she wanted.

His lips ground down on hers as he raised over her, his tongue a conquering warrior as it captured hers. He bit at her lips, licked them, sucked her tongue into his own mouth as his hands went crazy on her.

His palms cupped her breasts, his fingers tweaking at her nipples, plumping them, driving her crazy with the hot flashes of sensation that arrowed between her thighs, making her arch closer to the thigh that suddenly wedged itself between hers.

"Yes," his voice was a hiss of approval as she moaned at the caresses.

His lips left her lips to travel to her neck, his teeth scraping at her flesh as his lips and tongue had her crying out at the sensations he produced there. Marly's eyes opened slowly, realizing it was no dream lover biting at her skin, licking the small wound gently. It was Cade, unlike she had ever known him to be.

His big body was braced over her, a large muscular thigh pressed tightly between her legs as she rode it languorously. She could feel the moisture of her desire seeping from her body and coating his flesh as well.

"Cade?" Her nails bit into his shoulders as his lips moved to her breast, his tongue stroking one nipple with quick, hot flicks of his tongue.

"I can't wait any longer, Marly," He gasped against her nipple, his teeth clenching on it briefly as she cried out.

Her heart was thumping out of control. Her thighs tightened around his, her hips arching against him as pulse after pulse of need tormented her inner body. His lips were playing at her breasts, sipping from them, suckling them tightly into the fiery depths of his mouth.

Marly could only arch closer, pressing the painful tips of her flesh into his mouth. Her head tossed on the pillow as sensations assaulted her body, one after another, too quick to grasp or make sense of.

"Cade?" She called his name out with a vein of fear. She needed to catch her breath, to make sense of the painful clenching between her thighs and the fire racing through her system like nothing she had known before.

"It's okay, Marly," he whispered against her stomach as he moved lower. "I won't hurt you, baby. I swear I won't hurt you. But don't fight me. Don't fight me or it may be more than either of us can handle."

"He likes it rough, is what my sister says." The words haunted her now as his hands clasped her hips, his teeth biting at the smooth skin of her stomach. *"She says he goes crazy if she resists something he wants. Makes her take him and makes her love it. He loves it when she fights him. She says it makes him harder, makes him ride her forever. Like an animal."*

Fear skated beneath the hot need he was drawing from her body. He wasn't giving her time to assimilate the sensations. To control her body.

She screamed out his name when his mouth suddenly covered her clit. He drew it quickly into his mouth, his tongue flickering over it with light, quick strokes that threw her instantly into orgasm. And he didn't stop. Despite the near painful sensitivity that attacked the hot knot of nerves, he kept the flickering assault on her, holding her hips between his hands as he suckled at her in time to the caress.

She pushed at his head, thrashing against the bed as she fought to escape the building inferno he was commanding. He growled, the sound vibrating against her clit as he locked her hips in place, his mouth never once releasing her from the torment.

"No!" She screamed out against the shattering intensity of sensation.

"She says never tell him no, because he'll make you take it. It makes him so horny he goes crazy."

The words hit her mind as the assault increased, and Marly felt her blood pounding at her clit, his mouth working her, destroying her. He was intent, focused and out of control. When the second orgasm hit her, her wail echoed around her, then she screamed again as his mouth dived for the small slitted entrance to her body.

His tongue pushed into her vagina as he held her hips arched to his mouth. Growling sounds of pleasure pulsed against her as his tongue drew the slick heat from her, his mouth sucking at it harshly. She twisted in his grip, lust ripping through her until it terrified her. Not yet. Not again. She was flying too high; she would shatter beneath his mouth if he made her —

His thrusting tongue flung her into another pulsing dimension of sensation. She could feel the slick essence of her climax flowing from her body, into his mouth. It coated the bare flesh of her cunt, and her inner thighs, made his lips and cheeks slide against her hotly, no barrier between his ravenous desire and her flesh.

Then he was rising above her, pulling her thighs apart. Her eyes met his, and she cried out weakly. His pupils were nearly black, his face flushed and damp from her cum.

"Now," he growled.

She felt the thick head of his cock lodge at her entrance.

"Tell me no," he whispered roughly, his teeth bared, his expression so carnal it was sin.

"Cade." Her head twisted weakly against the sheets, perspiration coating her skin, glistening on his as he lodged the head of his erection in her tight entrance.

She felt the entrance to her vagina stretch impossibly, and her eyes widened as his went to the point where he nearly possessed her.

"You're stretched so tight around me." His voice was guttural as his fingers went to where the lips of her cunt flared around his erection. "Tell me to fuck you."

His eyes darkened further as he commanded her.

Marly was breathing harshly, blinking up at him as he stared down at her.

"Cade." Her voice was a protest.

"I warned you," he whispered harshly. "I warned you, Marly. Now tell me. Tell me to fuck you. Say 'fuck me Cade. Hard.' Say it now, Marly."

His voice was so thick and rough it didn't even sound like him. Then his hands went to her breasts, his fingers gripping her nipples erotically as he rocked against her.

"Say it," he demanded. "Now, Marly."

"Fuck me, Cade. Hard." Her head fell back as the breath left her body.

His cock plunged inside her, tearing past her hymen, sinking furiously to the hilt as the words left her mouth. Marly couldn't breath for the pleasure. Her inner muscles gripped his pulsing flesh, stretching impossibly to accept him, protesting the intrusion with a bite of pain that nearly had her climaxing on the spot.

Cade arched over her, bracing his arms at her shoulders as he bent his head to her. His tongue speared into her mouth as his hips began a harsh thrusting tempo that had her gasping for breath, for release. He was killing her. The powerful pistoning strokes slammed into her body over and over again, drawing her closer, ever closer to death. The orgasm would kill her. No woman could bear such pleasure. She couldn't stand it. Not yet.

She began to fight him. Her nails bit into his shoulders as she bucked against him, tearing her mouth from him, unable to control herself, her body, or the pleasure/fear racking her.

He ripped her hands from his flesh, pounding her harder as he slammed them to the mattress, holding them there. His mouth went to her neck as he fucked her forcefully, yet kept her from release, driving her higher, harder.

"No. No, Cade!" she screamed out as he controlled her thrashing body.

"Don't fight me, Marly," his groan was a tormented plea. "Please, baby, don't fight me now."

His words barely registered as she felt her inner flesh clutching at him, heating, melting, a painful pleasure unlike anything she had known building in her body as she fought for breath. And she fought him, fought the pleasure and the rising vortex taking over her body.

"Don't fucking fight me." He raised to his knees, his face a mask of tormented desire as he slammed his hips harder against her, driving his cock so deep inside her she felt as though it were lodged in her stomach rather than her vagina. "Damn you, don't fight me."

He held her thighs apart, ignoring her struggles, her gasping pleas as sweat dripped from his body, and her vagina pulsed around the driving cock possessing it.

It was happening. She was going to die. Marly fought it. Her nails bit into his arms, raking his flesh as she fought to get away from it, as she writhed beneath the pounding cock. When it struck, she couldn't scream. She couldn't move, she could only gasp, her vision darkening as the explosion tore through her body. She heard Cade cry out, but only the driving flesh between her thighs commanded her attention. The involuntary tightening of her flesh around his thrusting erection, the sharp, painful orgasm that wouldn't stop.

She was going to pass out. Cade pushed himself toward his own ejaculation as he felt the spasms of her body, the continual gush of her orgasm along his heated flesh. The multiple orgasms ripping through her body were too much for her. She was dazed, uncomprehending as he tried to hold her to him. She shuddered against him, pulse after pulse of her rich cream washing over him. Finally, with one last harsh push into the heated, tight depths of her slick flesh he felt his sperm erupt from his body, blasting her with his hot, thick release.

She gasped, pulsed again, then again, and went limp.

Cade was breathing roughly as he collapsed over her. His cock was slowly losing its desperate hardness, as her vagina trembled around it. He withdrew slowly, grimacing in pleasure at the feel of her slick flesh sliding over him. Marly was limp beneath him, her breathing shuddering in and out of her body as she lay unconscious beneath him.

"Shit," he whispered, wiping the sweat from his brow as his body shook from his own release.

It had never been that good. Never, in all the years of sexual exploits had an orgasm ripped through his own body like that. Suddenly weary, the scratches on his arms and shoulders from Marly's nails throbbing like badges of courage, he grinned tiredly and lay down beside her. Pulling her into his arms, he jerked the blankets over them and fought to catch his own breath.

He felt exhilarated. The blood ran through his veins, energizing him rather than tiring him. His cock was limber for now, sated with the hard ejaculation it had experienced. But he couldn't wait to touch her again. Cade knew that at a moment's notice he would be thick and throbbing again, ready to fuck her until she was screaming for more. Damn, he couldn't wait until she learned how to control the intensity of the desire, and scream for more.

He closed his eyes, pushing back such thoughts. She would sleep for a while, and when she awoke, he seriously doubted she would be ready for more. She would be hesitant, he would have to convince her to take him again, to risk the hot rush of pleasure that destroyed her control. He looked forward to it. He could hardly wait.

* * * * *

Marly awoke slowly, peeking through her lashes and seeing the bare spot in the bed beside her. She breathed in shaky relief. He was gone. She licked her swollen lips slowly, feeling the sensitivity there, as she did in the rest of her body. She ached, between her thighs, her breasts. She closed her eyes again, swallowing tightly. She hadn't expected the sensation, the intensity of the pleasure that bordered on pain. She hadn't expected it, and she wasn't certain she could handle it again.

"I have your bath ready." Cade's voice was smooth black velvet, drawing a gasp from her lips.

She clutched the blankets to her breasts and turned her head slowly. He was propped against the doorframe of the bathroom, dressed in low-slung jeans, his erection bulging beneath the material. His eyes were dark, heavy-lidded and watching her carefully.

She licked her lips again, then nearly gasped as his gaze flared intently, tracking the move.

"I'll bathe later," she whispered.

He shook his head slowly.

"You're sore, Marly. And frightened now. I promise you, I have no intentions of taking you again for a while. I just want to help you." He came toward her, making her heart beat quickly at the slow, rolling walk. He was too damned sexy.

"I want to sleep some more." She didn't want to be naked in front of him. She didn't want to tempt him.

"No you don't." He drew the blankets away from her, ignoring her grip as he pulled them from her hands. "Come on now. Don't fight me. Not right now, baby."

His voice deepened, the muscle at his jaw working furiously as he stared down at her nakedness. Staring up at him in distress, Marly allowed him to draw her from the bed, barely hiding her gasp as her thighs protested every movement. She remembered the hard hands holding her, the driving thrusts inside her, and trembled at the memory. Too much. It had been too much pleasure, too many sensations piling inside her body with no ease, no time to assimilate them.

"I don't want to bathe right now," she protested as he picked her up in his arms and began to carry her to his bathroom. "I can bathe in my room, Cade."

"This is your room now." He set her down in front of the large sunken tub, swirling with steamy water.

Her eyes flew to his at his startling statement as he gathered her hair, twisting it expertly atop her head and anchoring it there with a thick clasp.

"No—" She shook her head in protest.

Cade's lips quirked sensually at her instinctive reaction, and she watched the arousal that flared in his eyes. She shivered in reaction, her nipples hardening as his eyes flickered over them.

"Yes, Marly. My woman sleeps in my room, in my bed and bathes in my bath. It's that simple," he explained firmly.

"The others didn't." She shook her head, confusion running rife through her body.

"The others weren't my women, Marly," he told her gently. "I fucked them. They relieved an ache. That was it. I warned you what you were asking for. You can't say I didn't prepare you."

The tender understanding in his voice brought tears to her eyes that she refused to shed. Her body throbbed for him, but she was terrified of the sensations he could build within it.

"Come on. Into the bath, then dinner. No more play for now, I promise. I know you hurt, Marly." He reached out, his fingers caressing her cheek with a gentle touch.

He helped her into the bath, pushing her back until she was reclining against the back of the tub. The deliciously warm water washed over her sore body, and lapped at her swollen breasts. Her nipples were so hard they ached.

"You still want me." He smiled down at her as his fingers caressed over one hard little point in a soft movement.

Marly closed her eyes on a whimper. She was so sensitive. Her body primed and ready, but her fears surrounding her.

"Sit and soak for a while." He retreated from her, bringing a soft sigh of relief from her lips. "I used an extra dose of salts, and there's relaxing oil in there as well. You'll feel better when you get out."

"I'm frightened, Cade." She couldn't stop the words. The fears.

He sighed roughly as he knelt beside the tub, leaning on the rim thoughtfully as he watched her.

"I know you are. I knew you would be." He grimaced. "The fear will go away in time, Marly. That's all I can tell you. I won't let you go now. I can't. There's nothing we can do but get through this learning stage together, the best way we can."

"I can't take it again." She shuddered, remembering the violent pleasure that racked her body. "It's too much."

"It's not near enough," he denied softly. "And you will take it baby, as soon as you've rested. Whenever I think you're ready. And it never gets easier, but it does become less frightening. That's all I can tell you."

He caressed her cheek with his fingers, then leaned close and kissed her cheek with a light, reassuring touch.

"Your clothes will be laid out on the bed when you get out. Dress and come down to dinner. I'll be waiting on you."

There seemed a wealth of meaning in those last words, but Marly wasn't able to decipher the message. She just prayed he didn't mean what she was scared he did. She sighed roughly, sank to her shoulders in the water, and began to reconsider Cade as a lover.

Chapter Twenty

附

The clothes Cade had laid out would have been one of Marly's choices if she was still intent on seducing him. Black silk thongs, a short black, stretching silk sheath that dipped low in the back, and skimmed the tops of her breasts in the front and made Marly feel like a million bucks. Smoky black thigh-highs and her favorite black heels completed the outfit. She looked like a dark angel when she finished, with her hair falling in long, riotous curls down the middle of her back.

She smoothed the dress over her hips, standing in front of the full-length mirror that had somehow made it from her room to Cade's. She sighed; her clothes filled his closet as well, and his dresser. He had been busy while she slept. She wasn't certain if she cared much for the high handedness he was displaying.

He was taking complete control of her now, and she didn't much like it. It didn't matter that he had warned her he would, she wasn't a child to be ordered, nor was she so submissive she would willingly give him total control in everything. She shivered, remembering the control he had exerted over her in bed. She couldn't fight that, and she knew it. For the first time since beginning her campaign to seduce him, she doubted herself. She wasn't experienced enough to handle Cade, and she knew it.

"Stop worrying so much, Marly." He had slipped into the bedroom quietly, and now stood watching her with that intent dark stare that made her stomach tighten spasmodically.

She swallowed deeply as he came toward her. He was dressed in jeans again, a smoky gray cotton shirt, and boots. And he was aroused. She closed her eyes as he came up behind her, pulling her hair away from her neck to deposit a kiss there. She shivered at the caress.

"You're beautiful." His gaze met hers in the mirror, and Marly barely contained a groan of pure sensation as his look traveled over her body. "Absolutely beautiful."

His hands moved slowly down her bare arms, making her breathing escalate.

She couldn't speak. She wanted to. She wanted to protest the sudden heat flaring in her stomach, the erection she could feel pressed against her back as he leaned close to her.

"Dinner's ready. Marie cooked for us and left everything on the stove to serve ourselves before leaving. The boys are out for the evening and we'll have the house to ourselves." He watched her as he spoke, and Marly knew he was assessing her silence, her expression, everything.

"Where did they go?" Her breathing hitched in her throat when his lips began to caress her neck again and his hands gripped her hips, pulling her closer against him.

"Hm, who knows about those two?" Marly watched as his eyes closed, his mouth moving to the bend of neck and shoulder.

"Cade." Her neck arched despite her own best intentions as his teeth nipped the skin there, sending heat rolling through her body.

"Shh, it's just a kiss." But he was breathing hard, and the hands at her hips were pressing her firmly into his thighs. "I promise, no play for a while."

But his control was shaky at best, Marly thought. He wanted her again; she could see it in the wild swirl of color in his eyes as he glanced at her in the mirror.

"Come on." He finally sighed roughly, moving away from her. "Dinner. Then maybe a movie. We haven't watched a show together in forever, Marly."

Marly felt dazed, confused. His voice smoothed out once again as he took her hand and led her from the bedroom. He was almost like the old Cade, gentle and non-threatening. Marly was well aware of the irony of the situation. She had wanted nothing more than his passion until she had it. Now, she still wanted it, but the extremity of it terrified her. Perhaps she should have paid attention to the warnings her friends had given her years before.

Cade escorted her from the room, his hand riding low on her back as they walked downstairs. The lights were low in the house tonight, the silence so pervasive that the hollow click of her heels on the hardwood floor of the hallway was almost eerie.

"Are you going to ever speak to me again, Marly?" Cade finally asked her softly as he led her into the kitchen, and pulled her chair out at the table.

"I'm sorry." She cleared her throat, fighting the huskiness in her voice.

"Here." He poured her a glass of wine, setting it softly in front of her, then moved back to the stove.

Dinner was fresh grilled steak and shrimp, potatoes and greens with soft rolls on the side. The wine was smooth and slid easily down her throat, loosening the tension in her body as she sipped at it. As her glass emptied, Cade refilled it, all the while watching her as the silence wrapped around them.

"Finished?" he finally asked her as she pushed her half eaten meal away and sipped from the glass once again.

"Yes." Her fingers played nervously with the stem of her glass.

Cade sighed, standing to his feet and carrying the plates to the sink as Marly sipped from her wine once again. She rarely drank, usually not caring much for the state it left her in. When her inhibitions loosened, she thought too much, wanted too much. But the nervous tension in her body was just as bad. She hated feeling this way, hated the hesitancy she now felt at wanting Cade. She loved him so much she ached from it, but he terrified her now.

"Come on, Marly." He pulled her slowly from the chair, watching as she hastily retrieved her wine glass.

"Where are we going?" Damn that smoky sound in her voice, she thought. She didn't want to sound sexy right now.

"To watch television." She could hear the amusement in his voice.

"You're laughing at me," she whispered as he pushed her ahead of him, careful to keep his hand at her back in case she needed to be steadied.

"You're nearly buzzing on two glasses of wine," he said, and she could hear the smile in his voice. "I can assume this means there were no wild parties at school. You still aren't used to alcohol."

Marly frowned. He sounded tolerant. She hated it when he sounded tolerant and patient, as though she were still a teenager.

"I don't like parties, you know that." She shrugged as he led her into the family room and pulled her down on the couch beside him.

"I know you don't, baby." He pulled her against him as he flipped the television on and began scanning through the channels.

Marly took another drink of the wine, closing her eyes as she felt the alcohol slowly easing her terrible tension. When she opened them again, glancing at the television, she was surprised to see the latest action movie she had heard advertised. Thank God, he hadn't chosen to watch one of the racier channels she knew the satellite carried.

"Stop being scared of me, Marly." He lifted the empty glass from her hand and set it on the table beside the couch.

"I'm not scared." She was terrified.

"Are you feeling better after the bath?" He changed the subject abruptly.

"Yes, thank you." Her fingers laced together nervously.

"I didn't mean to be so hard on you, Marly." His hand smoothed her hair, his attention seemingly on the movie before them. "I lost control."

Marly shrugged, not certain what to say.

She felt him sigh deeply, and knew when he turned his head he was watching her closely. He held her against his side, his large body sheltering, his arm wrapped around her shoulders so his fingers could play with the curls at the side of her head.

"Marly, look at me." She shivered at the dark, rough quality of his voice.

She tipped her head back, staring up at him quietly.

"You said you heard about me and what I like sexually?" he asked her softly.

Marly nodded, thankful for the calming effects of the wine.

"Then you know I wouldn't hurt you, don't you?" he asked her gently, his other hand framing her face warmly as he watched her.

"Yes." She licked her lips, a bit of her earlier nerves stealing over her. "You didn't hurt me, Cade."

"If you heard what I liked, then you know what it does to me when you fight me. When I know the pleasure is killing you and you deny me. Don't do that, Marly. For both our sakes, because I don't like scaring you." He was watching her intently, staring down at her as he breathed roughly. "I can control myself until you do that."

"It's too much." She trembled against him. "I can't do it again, Cade. I can't."

She needed him to understand. She hated being frightened. She had never been frightened since Cade had removed the threat of Joe striking her again. He and Sam and Brock had done everything to make certain her life contained no fears. And now she was terrified.

"Trust me, Marly." He kissed her forehead gently. "Trust me to guide you through it."

She shook her head, then stilled as his eyes darkened. He smiled slowly, sexily.

"I can feel how much you want me, Marly," he assured her. "I can see it in those hard little nipples poking through your dress, and I bet your panties are wet, even now."

Marly shook at the sound of his voice.

"This movie is supposed to be good," she stuttered out in a desperate attempt to draw his attention away from her. "I've been wanting to watch it, Cade."

His gaze narrowed. Finally he sighed, moving his hand from her face and turning his attention back to the movie.

"By all means, let's watch it then," he said in resignation. "We can talk later."

They watched the movie as tension swirled around them, keeping their senses heightened. Finally, Cade moved from her, walking to the built-in bar at the side of the room. He poured himself a drink, mixed another for Marly, then returned to his seat. Marly had shifted back a little, her legs tucked beside her on the couch as her head lay against the back of the couch.

"Here." Cade handed her the glass, watching as she tasted it, then sipped comfortably.

The mix of soda, gin and whisky would go down smooth, and he hoped it would help to calm her nerves. She was riding on nerves and arousal, fighting both with her inexperienced fears. He had to calm those fears. If he didn't, he knew she would never come willingly to his arms again. And he was dying for her. He remembered the tight, hot clasp of her vagina as though it had been seconds rather than hours ago that he had thrust into it. The slick, wet heat, the torturous grip on the sensitized flesh of his erection was more pleasure than he had ever known with another woman.

The movie was finally over. As the credits rolled he checked her glass, thankful it was empty. Taking it, he set it with her wine glass on the table beside him. Narrowing his eyes, he watched as the next movie came on. He wasn't going to make it through the night, he thought miserably. He was so hard, so horny he could barely stand it.

"Why did you call me a whore in the barn, Cade?" Her voice was thoughtful, her question shocking. Cade's cock jerked at the remembrance of her hot mouth wrapped around it.

He turned to her, angling his body into the corner of the couch so he could watch her expression.

"Frustration. Wanting you so badly it was tearing me apart with guilt, Marly." He shook his head at his own ignorance that day. "You pushed me too far, and I reacted out of anger."

"Why did you stop fighting it?" She raised her eyes to his, her head tilting as she studied him. "You gave in too easy."

He watched her, a shadow of pain and anger in his eyes.

"There's so much you don't know," he said, his voice so gentle, yet so filled with bitterness it brought tears to her eyes. "So many things I can't tell you, Marly. I wanted to protect you. That was all. Just protect you."

"From what, Cade?" Confusion whirled inside her brain. "What would be so bad that you have to protect me from it?"

He laid his head back on the couch, staring at the ceiling in silence as she watched him. He was so strong, so broad. He exuded quiet confidence and power. He made her feel soft, feminine, aroused.

"I love you," he whispered, resignation filling his voice. "You don't know how much."

Marly's heart sped up, pounding furiously in her breast.

"How do you love me?" She had to know. Had to know it was the same.

"I love you so much, I want to give you everything I am, Marly. Every part of me. Even the monster I've fought to keep hidden." He looked down at her, somber, sad. "Does that frighten you, baby?"

She licked her lips nervously. She could tell it was supposed to.

"No." She shook her head warily. "I want all of you, Cade. Everything."

"The stories you heard about me sexually," he said darkly. "How bad did they get?"

Marly swallowed, fighting past the sudden tightening in her throat as the buzz of distant conversations filtered through her head.

"Bad," she finally whispered, then bit her lip as his eyes darkened.

"Tell me how bad, Marly. The worse thing you've ever heard. How bad was it? What was it?"

She had to fight for her breath.

"You, Brock and Cade." She could barely push the words past her lips.

His hand tangled in her hair as he shifted, facing her now on the couch, his eyes staring down at her. There was no shock in his expression. Marly saw acceptance, and she felt the tremble that suddenly wracked his body. "You don't do that."

He broke eye contact, his gaze going to her shoulder as his hands slowly smoothed over her arms. Bleak. His eyes went so dark, shadows and pain churning in the stormy depths until she thought she would scream out at the torment reflected there

"Something happened to us, Marly. A long time ago." He laid his finger on her lips as she began to ask what. "Please, God, don't ask me, just listen to me. What happened doesn't matter. Brock and Sam won't tell you either. Suffice to say, it was bad enough that it scarred us. Made us different, Marly." His eyes begged her to understand the impossible.

"Different? That goes beyond different, Cade," she whispered, feeling the calloused tip of his finger against her lips.

He took a deep, harsh breath.

"I love you," he said again. "But the day will come, Marly, when I will need this. Do you understand that?"

"And if I can't?" Marly felt her heart breaking at the expression in his eyes.

So much need, so much pain.

"Then I will try to accept that," he sighed, regret filling his expression. "It will be hard, Marly. But I'll try."

"Can't you tell me why?" She touched his cheek, hurting for him, wanting to ease the tortured expression from his face.

"I can't tell you why, baby. But I won't lie about my needs. Just as I refuse to let you. And I don't think you're as outraged as you should be, Marly." The painful intensity changed to arousal as he watched her.

Marly's face flushed. She refused to delve into what she was feeling. But she knew the thought of the three men she loved most loving her physically wasn't as abhorrent as it should be.

Cade's eyes narrowed. His hands went to the buttons on his jeans and he began loosening them slowly. Her eyes widened, her lips parting in a gasp of shock as his cock came free from its confinement.

"You said you wouldn't." She licked her lips at the hard flesh that rose from the material.

"I said not for a while. I said I wouldn't hurt you," he denied. "But the look on your face is about to kill me, Marly. Why aren't you shocked baby? Why aren't you screaming?"

"Screaming?" She avoided the other questions; she couldn't face them just now. "I'm not screaming because you aren't making me scream, Cade," she reminded him suggestively. "Make me scream."

He moved, crowding her back along the couch until she was lying on her back, staring up at him with wide eyes.

"I like submission, Marly," he whispered hoarsely. "Whenever I want you, however I want you. I want you screaming for it, begging for it. I want your mouth wrapped around my cock, I want it buried deep inside your hot little body. I want to eat you like candy. I want it whenever I say I want it. Fight me in any area of our life that you want to, but not sexually. The rest, we'll work out. But don't deny me. I couldn't stand it if you denied me."

He pushed her dress to her waist, groaning at the wet mark he glimpsed on the crotch of her panties. Marly watched his eyes lower, his face flushing. Lust pulsed in the air, in her bloodstream, in the hard cock rising from his pants.

"Touch yourself for me," he whispered. "Push your fingers into your panties and touch yourself. Make yourself cum for me."

Marly gasped as his hand gripped hers, pushing her fingers to her panties. He watched in agony as the slender hand disappeared beneath the material. Her fingers curved, then she cried out as they sank into her vagina. Cade groaned, watching in fascination as the material moved back, then followed as her fingers dipped. He could see the pale flesh from the side of the panties, her fingers disappearing into the glistening slit.

"Make yourself cum," he whispered again. "Let me watch you masturbate, Marly, and we'll go to bed and go to sleep. I promise not to take you. Just give me this."

One hand stroked his own flesh as the other moved the material covering her to the side. He watched her finger sink into her vagina, the bare lips of her cunt parting around the flesh as small slurping sounds emanated from the slick channel. He licked his lips, knowing how good she would taste.

"Yeah, there you go," he whispered, leaning close, pushing her thighs further apart. "Just slow and easy, baby."

He watched her fingers move as she pleasured herself, hearing her gasping moans, watching her hips and thighs flex. It wouldn't take her long. She didn't yet understand the build up, the intense, sexual heat of waiting. He would teach her that later. First, he wanted her comfortable. He wanted her trust.

Her fingers pulled back, the drenching moisture clinging to them as they moved to her clit. Cade didn't protest, but he moved his fingers slowly, pushing one into the tight grip of her body as hers played with the knot of nerves he was dying to taste.

She cried out then, shuddering. He pushed another finger inside her, watching her stretch around his fingers as he thrust shallowly inside her. He wanted her to come fast, knowing the build up scared her. He watched her fingers move faster on her clit, and knew it would be over long before he was satisfied. He allowed her this time, though. Encouraging her, his fingers thrusting inside her much slower than he wanted, he allowed her to throw herself over the edge at her own pace.

She was gasping, groaning as her orgasm drenched his fingers, the muscles of her vagina clenching them. He grimaced with his own need, knowing the hours stretching ahead of him would be miserable. Finally, she collapsed back on the cushions, breathing roughly.

Cade withdrew his fingers, ignoring his need to taste the soft cream she had spilled onto them as the hand at his cock stroked faster, finally bringing a small measure of release with his ejaculation.

"Son of a bitch, you'll kill me." He leaned back against the couch, buttoning his jeans with an edge of anger after cleaning his hands with the napkins he had used for their drink glasses.

"Come on, bed time." She was soft and drowsy as he lifted her into his arms. Curling against him, her eyes drooping as sleep began to steal over her.

Cade carried her to his room, undressed her and tucked her gently under the blankets before leaving the room. There was no way in hell he could sleep with her, he thought. His cock was like an unruly beast and it wanted nothing more than to plunder the tender vagina that gripped it so tight and hot. Besides, Brock and Sam were due back within the hour with their "guests", the paid trackers that he prayed would remove the threat suddenly haunting them all.

Chapter Twenty-one

ഇൗ

Dressed in one of Cade's shirts, and a pair of his socks, reasonably certain he would be out at work, Marly stumbled into the kitchen and made a beeline for the coffee the next morning. Her back was to the table, her eyesight bleary as she poured the hot liquid into a cup and sipped at it with a sigh of pleasure. Caffeine, pure and strong, slid slowly through her system, overriding the film of dazed unreality that came from the drinks she had consumed the night before.

The soreness of her body was nearly gone, but her nervousness wasn't. She was more than thankful Cade was gone—

"Stay just like that." His voice sounded behind her as a strong hand was laid on her upper back.

Marly moved her hands from the coffee cup, trembling as she felt another hand lift the shirt, and move to push between her thighs. She was wet; the excretion of her self release earlier was still present.

"Cade." Her eyes closed as two fingers slid slowly inside her.

"Don't fucking move. Don't say no, don't say anything." The shirt was lifted higher, her legs parted further and she felt his legs move between them. Then the broad, hot head of his cock was pushing past the soft folds of her silken labia.

Cade's groan was harsh as her cry shattered the morning. His hands gripped her hips and he plunged inside her, burying his length in the moist heat of her vagina.

"Sam. Brock," Marly gasped out in fear that they would be caught. Worried because it didn't bother her as much as it should now. That the thought of what Cade needed wasn't terrifying her.

"Fuck 'em," he growled. "They know the facts of life."

His hands went to her breasts, his fingers tweaking her nipples as he began to move with slow, torturous movements inside her.

"Oh, God. Cade." Her head lowered to the counter as she felt the lightning begin to zip through her body.

"Oh, Marly. You're so tight," he whispered at her ear. "So hot and tight I can barely stand it."

He plunged inside her, retreated, slid in slow and easy, retreated then plunged deeply once again. The alternate strokes had her gasping, the building pressure in her body had her fighting the sensations threatening to drown her.

"Don't, Marly," Cade whispered at her ear. "Baby, please don't fight it this time. Just let it go. Relax, sweetheart. I swear I'll take care of you."

She bucked in his grip, her ragged breaths became soft cries as intense pleasure began to flood her body. Then she gasped as he lifted her, pulling free of her gripping flesh as he turned her, lifting her to the counter and pushing between her thighs to plunge home again.

His lips came down on hers almost gently, far softer than she expected as his tongue pushed past hers to twine slowly, erotically with her own. He moved against her gently, drawing out on alternate soft, easy strokes, and harsh groaning plunges that had her ready to scream with the pleasure.

"Get ready," he growled against her lips, his teeth nipping at her as she sipped at his retreating lips. "Get ready, Marly."

He held her firm, driving his cock inside her, the sound of gripping friction, the slurp of suction filling the room as hot, hungry moans erupted from them both. Marly's legs wrapped around his waist as she cried out, her head flung back, her hair cascading over the counter as she felt her climax rushing upon her. She could do nothing but trust Cade to hold her steady as the fire whipped through her body, plunging her headlong into sensation.

When she exploded, she was only a second ahead of Cade. She felt the hot wash of his semen pulsing inside her as she screamed out her orgasm, heard his gasping groan of completion as he held her tightly to him. She shook and trembled in his arms, wondering if she would be able to retain consciousness this time.

"It's okay, baby," he whispered at her ear as she spasmed again, then again, each time her distress rising. "Don't be scared, just let it have you. I'll hold you Marly."

It pulsed over her, making her blood sing through her veins and her heart race in time to the desperate release quaking through her body.

"There you go." He nuzzled her neck as the first violent tremors began to ease from her body. "There you go, baby. See, it's just fine."

He petted and soothed her as she slowly eased from the terrifying grip of release. Pulling back slowly, he drew his cock from her flesh, but he didn't release her from his arms. He laid his forehead gently atop hers and smiled slowly as he watched her gasp for breath.

A harsh knock at the door between the kitchen and dining room had them both jumping in surprise.

"If you two are done, I need my fucking coffee," Sam griped from behind the portal. "Dammit, we have bedrooms for this."

Marly flushed furiously as her eyes widened in shocked embarrassment. Her gaze went to Cade as he moved back from her slowly.

"Stop blushing, he'll live through it." He lifted her from the counter, then restored his jeans to proper order.

"Do you think he came in?" She didn't like the sharp bite of pleasure that idea brought.

"Most likely." Cade shrugged over her embarrassment. "At least he had the good sense to leave the room. I know other people who don't." He flashed her a wicked look, reminding her of the night she had caught him in the study and damned near de-manned him with her brush.

"She was a slut," Marly sniffed, hiding her face as Sam entered the kitchen.

"Dammit, you two aren't minks," he muttered grumpily as he stalked to the coffeepot. "And the fucking counter wasn't made for that shit."

He slammed a cup to the counter in question and poured his coffee. Marly's eyes rounded in surprise at his ill mood.

"I'll be out in the barn when you wake up, Sam," Cade told him, his smile slow and easy as he dropped a quick kiss on Marly's lips. "Hurry up, we have work to do."

He lifted his hat from the hook on the wall and made his exit with a slow rolling rock that made Marly's mouth water.

"Stop eating him with your eyes," Sam griped as he flung himself in a chair and watched her broodingly.

"What's with you?" Marly fought her blush and her embarrassment at being caught, at knowing a truth she didn't want to face just yet. "You're never this grouchy."

His expression became shuttered.

"He's not using rubbers," Sam bit out. "I'm slow, but I'm not stupid."

Marly shrugged, knowing her face was beet red at his observation.

"I'm on the pill." She shrugged. "And I know for a fact that Cade's careful. He bitches at you two too much not to be."

Sam's eyes narrowed on her.

"Cade know about the pill?" he asked her curiously.

Marly rolled her eyes. "What business is this of yours?"

"None." He frowned darkly, turning his attention back to his coffee.

Marly rose from the chair, retrieved her cup and after pouring out the cooling coffee, re-poured more. She took her cup and went to the back door, opening it and stepping out on the porch. Dawn was just a few hours past, and the mists of morning still lay on the ground. Spring was nearly over, and she knew summer was moving quickly forward.

She sighed deeply. She was going to have to make a decision about school quickly. If she were going back, she would have to leave in just a few days. The lasts months before summer break were usually pretty intense.

"I le won't let you leave now." Sam stepped behind her, somehow in tune to her as he always was.

It frightened her now, how she knew these men so well. How they knew her as they did. She was confused, how she should feel versus what she did feel, and it was rioting through her mind like a crowd out of control.

She sighed deeply, staring out at the dew damp morning with a frown.

"He's not what I expected," she whispered, knowing Sam would understand. Knowing he wouldn't question her. He would wait, as he always did, for what she wanted.

"And I know he warned you he wouldn't be, Marly," he told her softly. "You pushed him, we all did, and maybe we were wrong in that. "

She hunched her shoulders against his reminder.

"Cade's not an easy man, none of us are. I know him, and I know what he's like. He hasn't had a woman since the night you caught him in the study with one of his floozies, and he has a lot of time to make up for."

Marly frowned as a metallic glint flashed in the distance, catching her attention.

"Maybe I really am too inexperienced for him." A sharp cracking sound heralded her words.

Hard hands gripped her, throwing her back as Sam grunted painfully. They landed on the kitchen floor amid

Marly's hair and spilled coffee. Angrily, she turned to blast him, then screamed out in fear at the bloodstain blooming over his chest.

"Sam!" She screamed, her shocked gaze going to his dazed one.

He blinked up at her, his hand pressing to his chest weakly, then coming away, covered in blood as he stared in horrified fascination.

"Son of a bitch," he gasped his surprise at the blood coating the hand he had pressed to his chest. "God. Damn, Marly."

"Cade." She jumped to her feet, her desperate scream followed by the sound of rushing feet, both through the house and on the porch. "Cade. Oh, God. Oh, God. Sam." She jerked a dishtowel from the counter, pressing it to his chest as Cade threw himself into the house, slamming the door behind him.

"Son of a bitch. He's shooting fucking wild." Cade yelled, rushing to Sam when he saw his brother lying prone on the floor.

He slid to the floor as Marly pressed the towel to the bloody wound. Reaching out to touch his brother, he jerked his hands back, fists clenching as his eyes widened in horror.

"Sam?" Marly heard the fear, the pain in that single word.

"Damn, Cade, this shit hurts," Sam gasped, staring up at him. "Fucking hurts."

Cade shook his head, his eyes going to Marly as she watched his expression fill with fury, with gut wrenching pain. She cried out at the sight, wondering why he hadn't cried out himself.

Suddenly Brock rushed into the room, followed by strangers, raised voices and flashing weapons. The room erupted into chaos, jerking Cade back to reality. His eyes cleared, and Marly watched as all emotion, pain, fear and need was wiped away.

"Brock, call the sheriff," a female voice ordered as she knelt at Marly's side. "Cade, get her out of the way. Rick, you have a sight on that son of a bitch yet?"

The woman ripped Sam's shirt straight down the middle, parting the edges as she pressed the towel against his chest.

"Bastard's on the run." Marly looked up at the big male figure looking through the lens of a rifle's telescope. "I can't get a bead, son of a bitch is fucking gone."

He rushed to the door, throwing it open as he tried for another angle from the porch.

"Bullet didn't hit anything serious, but it's a nasty damned wound," the woman barked out. "He needs medical attention fucking now. Get an ambulance out here, Brock."

Cade dragged Marly back as Brock yelled into the phone. The voices were raised and demanding, as cowboys began to pour into the house, rifles and pistols waving, their faces hard masks of determination.

"Cade, what's going on?" Fear shook her body as he pulled her close, moving her along the floor to a corner of the room, out of the way.

"Stay here, Marly. Don't fucking move," he bit out, staring down into her face, his expression savage. "Do you understand me? Do not fucking move from here."

She nodded shakily, her eyes widening at the fury she could see in his face.

"Do not move." He jerked one of the jackets hanging on a peg above them free. Wrapping it around her quickly, he stood to his feet, picking up the rifle he had dropped to the floor then rushing from the house.

"Steady there, Sam." The woman working over Sam was cool and collected, her pretty face concerned as she kept a steady pressure on the wound. Her eyes rose and collided with Marly's. "He's going to be okay."

Marly nodded, clutching Cade's jacket to her as she watched the commotion going on around her, confused and frightened as her body shook from the cold that seemed to wrap around it.

"You okay?" The woman asked her quickly.

Marly nodded again, ignoring the nausea building in her stomach.

"You must be Marly." The woman smiled.

"Stop with the fucking social pleasantries," Sam bitched harshly. "Where the hell is the doctor?"

"Oh, stop your whining," the woman told him firmly. "It just hurts. You'll be fine as soon as we get you to the hospital."

Marly looked at Sam's chest, then raised her gaze back to the woman. Whoever she was, she was worried, Marly could tell.

"Ambulance's ETA is an hour at least," Brock called out. "Bret, get the fucking chopper ready, we'll fly his ass in."

"Son of a bitch. I hate that fucking chopper," Sam groaned.

"Get it going. I'll get him ready for transport. Let the sheriff know what we're doing. Rick, call Monty and tell him to get Lisa and Anna there on the double. I want security on his room."

Nothing made sense now. Marly huddled against the wall, watching as everyone scurried around the kitchen, listening as Sam bitched and complained about the chopper, but hearing the fear in his voice. Her hands fisted in the jacket. She felt twelve again; terrified and uncertain, unable to figure out what the hell was going on or what she was supposed to do.

Cade ordered her to stay put. He had never used that tone of voice, or looked so frightened for her as he had when he pushed her into the corner and made her swear not to move. She stayed. She hated herself for it, hated the fear and the lack of understanding, the inability to help. But she stayed, just like he told her to do.

Chapter Twenty-two

ဢ

She had sat there for hours. Marly watched the hands of the wall clock tick from seven o' clock until nine o' clock. The chopper had left long ago with a bitching Sam, a worried Bret, and highly competent woman forcefully ordering them all. The man, Rick, had stayed behind and she could hear him and Cade on the other side of the door talking quietly.

Cade had forgotten she was there. Tucked carefully in the corner between the pantry and the door she listened in horror to their conversation.

"He was her step-father. He's insane," Cade told the man quietly. "Marly's mother brought her here when she was twelve, and started running, after he tried to molest Marly."

"Well, he's a slick one." The deep voice of the stranger told Cade with a slow drawl. "Background check on him shows time in the Marines. It must have been well spent. We also have a report of several years spent with some of the homeland terrorists out in Utah. He's a badass, Cade. I won't try to sugar coat it for you. You're lucky he didn't kill you the night you went after him."

Marly's breath shuddered from her chest as she fought to control the sobs racking her body now.

"Marly's all that matters, Rick," Cade told him carefully. "I want her protected above all else. The bastard must have thought Sam was me when he shot. The pictures we found out in that cabin shows he knows my relationship with Marly, or at least suspects it."

Marly clasped her arms around her chest, closing her eyes in pain as she listened.

"He's definitely obsessed with her. The pictures show that for a certainty," Rick assured Cade. "He knows you found the cabin by now, and his little hidey place up on the hill. He'll be harder to find now. Your best bet would have been to call us in first, Cade."

"Yeah well, I wasn't thinking real clear after seeing those damned pictures," he bit out roughly. "Son of a bitch, Rick. Marly's had things hard enough. She doesn't need this."

"Her bedroom is out of bounds. It's too accessible by too many directions. Keep her in your room."

"That's why she's there now," Cade grunted, and Marly felt a wound strike her soul that she wasn't certain she could recover from. Shame struck her, making her body rock with the agonizing pain inflicted on her heart.

"No one needs these bastards running around," Rick sighed. "Where is Marly, by the way? I haven't seen her since the shooting started."

There was a moment of complete silence before she heard Cade's muttered obscenity. She couldn't stem her tears, so she just lowered her head, burying it in the jacket she had wrapped around her body.

"Marly." There was a wealth of pain in his voice when he stepped around the door. "God, baby. I'm sorry."

His voice was tormented, rough with worry. She shook her head, refusing to raise it as she heard him kneel in front of her. His hand touched her hair, the other one lifting her chin. There was worry and fear in his eyes as he watched her now.

"You lied to me, Cade," she whispered, her breath hitching with her suppressed sobs. "About the wolf, about why you suddenly wanted me. All of it. You lied to me."

Her chest ached with her pain, with the sense of betrayal running through her. And she was right. She knew she was right by the look on his face.

"God!" Her fists clenched as she fought the demoralizing knowledge that he hadn't taken her because he couldn't resist her, or because he loved her, needed her. He had taken her to keep her close, to ensure her obedience and protection.

Sobs ripped from her chest as the pain lashed her soul.

"Marly please. Baby. It's not like that." But it was, she knew it was. She had seen the truth in his eyes.

Moving painfully, her muscles cramped from the hours spent on the floor she raised to her feet, ignoring Cade as he now towered over her.

"He said he wouldn't let me go," she whispered, remembering those terrifying hours before her mother had returned home and caught her step-father touching her.

She remembered with blinding shame the things she had refused to think about for years. The ways he had touched her, making her cry with pain as he groaned in pleasure. She remembered how he held her down, hurting her, his lips always moving over her, his hands harsh and hurting.

She clamped a hand over her mouth as she fought the heaving of her stomach. She wanted to scream, but it hurt too badly to even try.

"Marly." Cade's voice was tortured now as he tried to pull her to him.

"Don't touch me," she cried out, flinching away from him, unable to bear the touch of his hands now. She had been a fool. Such a fool to think he could love her. "It was all a lie. All of it. God, what a fool I made of myself."

No wonder there had been no gentleness, no sense of caring in his touch when he fucked her. And he had fucked her. He hadn't made love to her, he hadn't possessed her, he had used a bodily function to control her.

Her hand flew out, connecting solidly with his face. Shock and fury flared in his expression, though he stood silently.

"You lied to me." She was shaking harshly, her teeth nearly chattering from the overwhelming pain and anger. "It was all a lie. 'Tell me to fuck you, Marly'," she sneered his words back at him. "Well you fucked me Cade, good and proper." She didn't care about the audience she had attracted. The unknown Rick, or Brock's brooding concern as he watched from the kitchen doorway. "You fucked me good and proper."

She turned away from him, her head held high as she saw the confusion in the stranger's dark face, and Brock's sympathy. She couldn't stand it. She could feel her soul breaking apart, tearing loose from the moorings that had always held it. For eight long years she had believed her dreams would come true. That Cade would love her, that he would need her.

Such a fool's dream. She shook her head and walked tiredly away from them all. She didn't run. There was nothing to run from, nothing to run to. Her whole world was collapsing around her and she didn't know which way to turn now.

"Marly." Brock touched her arm as she went to pass him. She pulled back, staring up at him, and rather than seeing the brother who had comforted her through the past eight years, she just saw another lie. Pity and sympathy rather than the love she had needed.

She clenched her teeth tightly to still the ragged sobs tearing from her chest. Shaking her head and holding her hand up in rejection, she moved slowly past him.

"Dammit, Marly," Cade called out behind her, but his voice lacked it's usual determination. He didn't care. He should be glad she finally knew.

She mounted the stairs slowly, step by step pulling herself up them. One arm wrapped around her stomach, the other on the banister as she made herself expend the energy to keep moving. She wanted to lie down and wail out her misery, but the misery refused to exit her body.

She entered her own room, locking the door behind her. The heavy curtains were drawn over her balcony doors. She stood in front of them, staring at the dark brocade and wondering if the son of a bitch would put her out of her misery if she opened them. She shook her head. No, Jack didn't want her dead. She knew that. He wanted what he had been denied when she was twelve years old.

The tears had stopped, the desperate sobs no longer ripped through her. Looking down at the large silk shirt she wore she began to unbutton it slowly. It dropped to the floor, and the heavy men's sock she wore on her feet followed. Moving to her closet, she found the only articles left were the gowns that Cade kept supplied. He had been too kind to refuse her the shirts, she thought, so he kept the gowns on hand just in case she grew out of the need to sleep in his clothes.

She grimaced, remembering the comfort those shirts once brought her. She pulled a linen gown and its matching robe from a hanger, then went to the shower. She could feel Cade on her flesh; smell the rich scent of his cologne and his release into her body. Her stomach knotted in renewed agony. God, she hadn't known anything could hurt so badly.

She stood beneath the pounding spray of the shower, letting it wash over her face as the tears fell once again. She huddled against the wall, so miserable she didn't know if she could face another day. Sam was nearly dead. Because of her. It was all her fault.

A whimper escaped her lips, then harsh, grinding sobs. The broken sounds she could not release earlier came now.

"Oh, God," she cried out, sinking to the floor of the shower, rocking miserably, dying inside. "Oh, God, help me."

Cade stood outside her shower, braced against the wall, his head grinding into the plaster as her wail shattered the steamy confines of the room. Her cries were destroying him, yet there was nothing he could do to halt them. He needed to know she was okay though, at least physically. He knew he had destroyed something precious and dear the minute he realized she had heard his conversation with Rick. He had done more than ravage her innocence. He had shredded her heart.

He lowered his head, his heart breaking with her cries. He had sworn she would never know fear again. That she would never cry again. And yet here she was, broken, sobbing in pain and fear, because of him. And there wasn't a damned thing he could do.

Shaking his head he moved from the bathroom, his hands pushed deep into the pockets of his jeans as he felt self-disgust crawl through his body. He had seen her shame, her realization that he hadn't taken her to his bed because of an overwhelming love for her. God help him, he did love her, he did desire her unlike any woman he had known in his life, but he knew it wasn't the love Marly needed. She needed a white knight, and God knew his armor had been tarnished years before.

He sat down on his bed, his hands dangling between his thighs as the sounds of her cries drifted into his room. What would he do now, he wondered. What would Marly try to do? She had always been delicate, fragile. She had been protected all her life, and had no idea how to handle the sudden destruction of everything she believed.

They shouldn't have spoiled her so badly, he thought. He should have been firmer with her while she was growing up, establishing himself as an authority figure rather than one she would adore. But her adoration had brightened his life. Her laughter and freedom with him had dispelled many of the dark, lonely days he had gone through. But that didn't make it right. He had never told her no, and when faced with the one thing he couldn't give her, Marly had decided to get stubborn. Spoiled.

He heard the shower turn off long minutes later. He waited, watching the opened connecting door with brooding eyes. Finally, she moved into the room, covered from head to toe with one of her gowns. He frowned.

"I need my clothes," she whispered.

"You can't sleep in there, Marly." He shook his head tiredly. "I know you're hurt and confused, but I won't let you risk your life."

"I know to keep the shades drawn and the lights low." She moved to his closet.

Seconds later she exited the large, walk-in room with an armload of clothes and went into her bedroom. Cade stayed silent as she hauled her clothes from his room and deposited them back into her own closet, her own drawers.

"Move them all you want, Marly. But when bedtime comes, it's my bed you'll be sleeping in." He rose from the bed, gripping her arm roughly as she moved past him once again. "Do you understand me? You started this, dammit. Now you can fucking see it through."

"You don't really want me," she cried out, trying to jerk from his grip. "It was just to protect me."

"Oh, I do want you," he growled softly, his head lowering until he was in her face, snarling down at her. "I want you so bad my cock throbs with it. And you know it."

"No." She shook her head violently. "I won't do this, Cade. You don't love me—"

"I love you dammit." He shook her harshly. "I've always loved you Marly, just not the way you've built in that fairy tale you live in."

"Stop." She shook her head, crying out at the anger in his voice.

"No, I won't stop. You're going to listen to me,"

"I don't want to hear anymore," she screamed out furiously, her blue eyes blazing up at him wrathfully. "You fucked me so you would have a reason to watch me, that was it. That was all. I heard you. Your cock may have got hard for me, Cade, but its because you never loved me enough either way. I wasn't your niece and I wasn't woman enough to take your heart either. Either way, I was fucked."

She jerked away from him then, the fury in her eyes surprising him, the white flash of such anger towards him that it shocked him clear to his bones.

"I'll stay until your goons find Jack, then I'm going back to school."

"Like hell," Cade bit out. "Do you think for one minute I'll let you leave before finding out if you carry my child or not, Marly? Do you forget what happens when you fuck?"

She turned back to him, mocking amusement crossing her pale face.

"Sorry, Cade, I've been on the pill since I decided to seduce you. I wasn't as stupid as you obviously think I was. There won't be a child. Not with you. Not ever."

She slammed the door behind her, and for the first time in eight years, he heard the key turn in the lock.

"Fuck," he bit out, running his fingers through his hair.

He clenched his teeth, setting his hands on his hips as he considered his options. There weren't many, he admitted. But he had made his mind up when he took Marly to his bed. He would marry her. She was his, and he'd be damned if he would let her go. He may not love her like she wanted, and he may have upped his schedule in fucking her due to Jack's threat to her, but he wasn't about to backtrack now. And by God, he wasn't about to let her do it either.

She wanted him. She wouldn't be able to deny him for long once he started touching her. And once he did, she would learn what it meant to be his lover. To belong to him. To be part of his family. She wasn't outraged over Sam and Brock, she was curious. He knew that now. She would see where curiosity led.

His eyes narrowed on the door. He had the key. She wouldn't sleep there. He wasn't about to let her. She belonged in his bed, in his arms, screaming beneath the pleasure he would be certain she received. Playtime was over.

Chapter Twenty-three

ဆ

She was dressed in jeans and a soft cashmere sweater that barely met the waistband. The gold chain was missing around her waist, but the little gold ring was visible beneath the fabric of the sweater. Cade watched her broodingly as she entered the family room and moved to the built in bar late that evening. She mixed a soda and gin, then a splash of Jim Beam. She sipped it often until she had the taste where she wanted it.

The jeans curved her rear, and skimmed over her knock out legs. On her feet she wore running shoes, her hair was tied back with a soft cream scarf that matched the sweater. She carried a dark red love bite on the back of that creamy neck. Cade's cock hardened further at the sight of his mark.

"Marly, I think it's time you meet our guests," he spoke softly, but his voice carried a ring of steel.

She turned to him, her eyes shadowed, her face carrying a mask of expertly applied makeup. He had never seen her in makeup and he didn't like it now.

"Rick and Tara Glaston, this is Marly McCall. Marly, Rick and Tara. They're from Security Unnamed —"

"You two were the ones who rescued the little girl a few years ago." Marly smiled brightly as she moved forward to shake their hands. "I've heard a lot about you."

"Miss McCall." Rick was watching her with soft brown eyes, sympathy spilling over in his rough voice. Cade hated him.

"Marly, please." Her pleasant smile never once reached her eyes, and Cade could see the fine trembling in her slender hand as she shook first Rick's hand, then Tara's. "How's Sam doing?" she finally asked Tara.

"Bitching every breath," Tara breathed out, her smile bright in her slender, pretty face.

Tara Glaston was several inches taller than Marly, with short silky red hair, and big green eyes. A scattering of freckles fell over her nose, and she seemed friendly and vivacious.

"That's Sam for you." Marly moved back from the group, avoiding the couch like the plague and sitting instead in one of the large chairs on the other side of the room.

She took a healthy sip of her drink as Cade frowned over at her.

"Have you eaten anything yet?" he questioned her cautiously, knowing she hadn't shown up for dinner.

"Of course." She shrugged. "I was starved, and Marie's roast is the best."

Thankfully, the former housekeeper had agreed to return to fix the evening meals after Marly's return home. She was needed more than ever with Rick and Tara now staying in the house as well. Cade's culinary abilities weren't the best.

Cade frowned deeper, though, as he watched Marly now. At least her appetite wasn't suffering. And neither was her thirst. She was drinking like the stuff was pure water.

She leaned back in her chair, crossing her legs as she turned her attention to the news on the television as Brock and Rick began to discuss finding Jack. Cade listened with only half an ear, his attention centered on Marly. She was wired, running on nerves and it made him nervous. Her hand shook as she drank, and her expression was distant, reserved. He had never seen Marly either distant or reserved.

"I want Marly and Cade to stay indoors." Cade watched Marly stiffen at Rick's advice. "He knows they're having sex, and it's pushed him over the edge. He'll make his move soon. Until then, let's be certain we can control as much of the situation as possible."

Marly's eyes narrowed, her teeth clenching so harshly Cade could see her jaw knotting as her face flamed in embarrassment.

"He'll soon learn better, then," she bit out as she tipped her glass back and swallowed more of the drink.

Rick glanced over at Cade as though wondering how to handle the situation. Cade shrugged. Hell, he didn't know how to handle her; she had never acted this way. He half expected her to outright refuse any suggestion he made anyway. Rick shook his head as he grimaced in resignation. Evidently, he'd had to handle stubborn women before. So why then was Cade the one who received the disgusted look?

"Look, I know this situation is delicate right now." Rick leaned forward, his expression so fucking soft and caring Cade wanted to knock the hell out of him. "But we have to be careful, Marly. Jennings isn't sane. Right now, your best defense is to let him keep believing it."

Her hand shook, causing her to grip her glass tighter. Cade could see the wild emotions darkening her eyes as she glanced at him.

"No movement in your room, Marly. You don't leave the house without Cade beside you."

Marly was breathing with quick, hard breaths. She drained the half full glass then rose shakily to her feet to pour another.

"I don't think so." Cade moved in front of her, gripping her hand before she could pick up the first bottle.

"Please." She kept her head lowered, and his chest tightened at the fear and pain in her voice.

"Drinking won't help, baby." She flinched at his soft endearment.

She shook her head, and he could tell her control was hanging by a thread. He couldn't stop the move that had him pulling her into his arms, bending over her as her head lay on his chest, in a gesture of protection.

Lora Leigh

"I won't let him hurt you," he whispered out, agonized. "Not again, Marly."

Her nails dug into his chest, and for a moment, just for a moment Cade thought she would loosen up enough to allow him to comfort her. But she pushed away from him instead, her head lowered as she sat back down. She seemed to curl into herself, to retreat from everyone.

Rick glanced at Cade with a concerned frown.

"Marly, I know this is hard," Tara said softly. "Bastards like this don't deserve to live, and nice people like you sure as hell don't deserve the pain. But it's here, and if you want to live, then you have to help us."

"I didn't say I wouldn't cooperate." She raised her head, staring the woman in the eye defensively. "But I want to sleep in another room."

"And I understand why." She wasn't the least sympathetic to Cade's cause. "But your life is more important than your pride, or his."

Marly flashed Cade a hateful look. He almost flinched from the searing look. Never had Marly looked at him like that, challenging, furious. His eyes narrowed on her. He smiled at her, slow and sure, his gaze heavy lidded. He watched her flush with a flare of satisfaction. Yeah, fight baby, he thought. Fight all you want, but when the score's tallied, we'll see who wins and who begs.

"Fine." Marly didn't sound fine with it, though. Her lips were pressed tightly together, her eyes flashing in anger and determination. He liked that flash. He crossed his hands over his chest and watched her with a quirked smile.

"Okay then, boys and girls. If my hunch is right, we won't have to wait long on him to make his move." Rick clapped his hands together in a gesture of finality. "I suggest we all get a good night's sleep, and get started tomorrow drawing the little prick out."

Marly's head turned suddenly.

"What do you mean? Drawing him out?" she asked him suspiciously.

"Well now, baby, what do you think he means?" Cade leaned against the bar as though relaxed and ready. "Sex with me is what draws him out, so we'll see if we can't tempt him a little bit."

Marly was on her feet in a flash, shock rounding her eyes as anger pulsed in her body. Son of a bitch, if she wasn't the prettiest damn thing he had ever laid his eyes on. Her face flushed, her body tight, tense, her breasts heaving with anger. Like a volcano, boiling and ready to blow, she teetered on the edge.

"I hope to hell you aren't suggesting what I think you are," she exclaimed loudly.

Cade widened his eyes, smiling in pleasure.

"Well, honey, this afternoon my windows were replaced with bullet proof glass. And you know how much I love leaving the curtains open to stare into the starry skies at night."

Her face paled, her eyes glittered. It was all Cade could do to hide his shock at the unwilling excitement he saw in her eyes. She was shocked, furious, holding onto her pride and her sense of morality, but he knew that hot little glitter in her eyes for what it was.

"Bastard," she growled. "There's no way in hell I'll let you touch me with the damned curtains closed, let alone opened so some pervert can watch it."

Fury, blistering and hot vibrated through her body. Her fists clenched, her muscles visibly trembled.

Cade shrugged.

"Tara brought a pretty black wig with her. We can let her—" He barely ducked in time to escape the flying glass she launched his way.

"Bastard. Fucking creep!" she screamed furiously, her body shaking with rage as she turned on Tara. "Do it, by God. You're more than welcome to his lying ass."

She stalked from the room, her body rigid, her face flaming. Cade could only watch her in surprise and arousal. Son of a bitch, that was the most beautiful sight he had ever seen in his life.

"Mr. August, I suggest you refrain from using me in your battles." Ms. Glaston came to her feet now, staring him down imperiously. "I don't throw glasses, I throw punches, and trust me, they do damage."

Cade sighed. He honestly hadn't meant any harm. This time.

"I was merely going to tell her about your damned plan for you and Rick to do it instead," he bit out in frustration. "Are all women so damned jumpy or what?"

"Are all men so damned stupid, or is it just you?" Tara snapped. "I'm going to bed myself. I've had about as much as this ignorance out of him as I can stand. Reminds me of why I stopped guarding damned men to begin with."

She stomped from the room as Rick covered his mouth, fighting to hide his grin.

"She always so damned jumpy?" Cade plopped into a chair, staring at the doorway with a confused frown.

"Pretty much." Rick grinned.

"She must be hell to be married to," Brock broke in at this point with a dark look.

"Don't know, I never asked her ex about it," Rick shrugged, watching Brock with a frown.

"What are you, if not her husband?" Brock asked. "You sure as hell don't look like her brother."

"Brother-in-law. Ex to be exact," Rick snickered. "And trust me, boy, she has a damned fine figure, but that's one woman you don't want to tangle with. She has PMS every day of the damned week."

Chapter Twenty-four

ഔ

Cade slammed the bedroom door him as he stalked into the room. Arousal and anger vied for supremacy within him, though his shaft throbbed harder than his fury burned at the moment. This was what he had wanted to protect Marly from. This furious build up of need, the demand that he dominate her, take her, make her affirm his control over her body. And he would. He had tried to do it her way. God knew he had fought the baser instinct that he knew drove him, but he couldn't fight them any longer. And Marly. Sweet precious Marly was about to learn more about her lover than she had ever dreamed possible.

"Undress." He kept his voice calm, his body still. He understood this. He could handle himself knowing what was to come. The craziness of fighting it made him unravel.

Amazement crossed her expression.

"I will not," she bit out, frowning at him furiously.

Cade smile. A slow curve of his lips as he anticipated the night to come.

"I warned you not to deny me, Marly." He unbuttoned his shirt, pulling it from the waistband of his jeans as he watched her eyes widen. "I had hoped we would be able to put this off until you were more comfortable with me, but I see we can't."

He loosened his belt, then pulled off his leather boots. Picking up his boots he set them neatly in his closet, then pulled off the shirt and laid it in a chair beside the door.

"Are you insane?" she squeaked, blinking. "This is no longer a sex game, Cade. Are you into rape too? Strange, I never heard about that one."

Her bravado was commendable. He liked that about her. She rarely ever backed down, and even though he could see the flare of apprehension in her eyes, she wasn't balking. At least, not at his anger.

"It never was a game, Marly, that's what I tried to make you understand." He locked the bedroom door, then the connecting door. "I tried to warn you, and even after you disregarded those warnings, I've tried to take it easy on you. But you've pushed me too far."

"I pushed you too far?" Her slender finger was like a harsh exclamation point as she pointed first to herself, then to him. "Are you forgetting who is in the wrong here? You lied to me, Cade."

"I tried to protect you, just as I've always done," he corrected her gently. "Perhaps in the wrong way, but I tried all the same. Now, are you going to take those clothes off, or do I have to tear them off you?"

She blinked, shaking her head.

"I said no."

His cock jerked, throbbed as lust kicked him hard in the stomach. She was saying no, and if he thought for one damned minute she wasn't well aware of what saying that one little word meant, then he would have stopped. But she knew. He knew. He could see it in her eyes, in the way her nipples peaked beneath her sweater. She would deny it until hell froze over, but Marly knew what she was doing. It was her choice.

"Take the fucking clothes off, Marly," he growled harshly. "I don't want to have to ruin them."

Her eyes widened in apprehension. It was a tone of voice he used only when he meant business. One she had never refused in the eight years she had lived under his roof. And it excited her. He could see the excitement in her eyes. Damn her, if he didn't know better he would swear she had planned this. But her fingers shook when she pulled the sweater over her head, then removed her jeans, all the while watching him carefully. Before going to her, he walked to his window, jerking the curtains opened with a rough flick of his wrist.

The double windows were large, giving a clear view to anyone watching of the well-lit room, and Marly's nearly naked body. She flinched, but stood her ground.

She was exquisite. He stalked her slowly, moving around her as she watched him nervously. Her breasts were rising and falling quickly, the hard little nipples puckered and flushed.

As he moved behind her, he smacked her butt smartly. Crying out, Marly jumped away from him.

"What the hell was that for?" She frowned, keeping her back to him, edging away from him as he moved closer.

"You left your panties on. Take them off." He kept his voice harsh, his expression closed.

"I'm tired of this—"

"Now!" He didn't raise his voice. He didn't have to. He knew how to use it effectively.

He watched her swallow tightly, then her hands went to the band of her thong panties.

"I warned you, didn't I, Marly?" He asked her softly as she stepped out of the silk. "I told you not to say 'no'. I told you my appetites could be more than you could handle. Didn't I tell you that?"

Her lashes raised, her eyes darkening in both fear and arousal.

"Yes," she said hesitantly.

"You've told me 'no', several times now," he said, keeping his voice calm, cool. "You have to learn not to tell me no, because it makes me crazy. And I don't want to hurt you. If you ever don't want to do something I want, do not say no. Tell me you're frightened. Tell me what's wrong. But never say no. I know what I'm doing, and I know if something is hurting you. There's no reason for you to deny me anything, Marly."

He watched her face flush with anger.

"That's not fair," she bit out. "I have a mind of my own — " She stopped when he arched his brow.

Each movement carefully controlled, Cade went to the chair by the bed, aware that any movement from there could be seen from the window.

"Come here." He motioned her forward with his hand.

She glanced nervously at the window.

"Don't worry about Jennings. Worry about me, Marly," he ordered her softly.

Her eyes flew to his, widening at the dark promise in his voice.

"Come over here, now. This is the last time I ask you nicely." He patted his thigh.

Licking her lips nervously, she walked over to him.

She stopped directly in front of him, trembling. He liked watching her stomach tighten in arousal and nerves. The way her nipples hardened, pointing out to him with needy supplication. Even more, he loved the glaze of moisture that built on the bare lips between her thighs.

His hand reached out, his finger running through it slowly as she breathed in hard.

"You're wet." He brought his finger to his mouth, sucking the cream from it in pleasure. "You want me, Marly."

He watched her breathe harshly. Finally, he had his control back.

"You're scaring me," she whispered.

"A little fear is good for you." He moved, pulling the drawer to the bedside table out. There, nestled in silk was a new dildo he had purchased for her, several plugs and other assorted devices, and several tubes of lubricants. Marly gasped.

"Lay across the bed, with your hips raised," he ordered her softly. "Head down to the mattress."

"Cade." She couldn't take her eyes from the articles in the drawer.

"The plug you bought was too small, Marly," he explained softly. "When I take your ass, I want you open and ready. I don't want to hurt you. So we're going to get you ready for it."

"Close the curtains." She shook her head tightly. "Please don't let him see this."

If he thought for one minute she wasn't aroused, wasn't ready for whatever he wanted to give her, then he would close the curtains. But Cade saw the building moisture between her thighs, and he knew she was turned on. Knew her body pulsed with excitement.

"Every time you tell me no, someone will see your punishment. Usually Brock and Sam. I'm letting you off easy this time, baby. Now lay across the bed before you make me mad."

Her eyes flared with arousal. The deep blue color darkened, deepened until he could see the need pulsing in her.

"You wouldn't," she whispered faintly.

"I would," he growled harshly. "Now do as I say before I have to prove it and bring Brock up here alone."

She did as he ordered. Turning, she got on her knees at the edge of the mattress, her head on the comforter, her hips raised high. The pearly globes of her rear had his breathing accelerating. Rising from the chair, he approached her from the side. He wanted Jennings to see this clearly, if he was watching.

He pulled the tender cheeks apart as he lifted a tube of lubrication. Marly was shaking, but the moisture from her cunt had already coated the crack. She was more aroused than she had ever been.

Slowly, he lubricated the little hole, his fingers stretching her, ignoring her moans now, the little shifts of her hips and the muscles flared around his fingers, then relaxed, stretching easily. When he could safely thrust two fingers into her with no resistance, he picked up the thick butt plug and lubricated it heavily.

"This will pinch at first, you're not used to anything this large," he explained as he laid the head of it at her opened anus. "I want you to breathe deeply, push out and try to relax. Okay, Marly?"

"Cade." Her voice was filled with hesitancy.

"Answer me. Okay?" Like a whip, his voice became sharp and hard.

"Okay," she answered quickly.

"I'll know if I'm hurting you, Marly. Trust me to do this." He began to push it slowly into her.

She moaned as her hole widened for the toy, breathing deeply as he ordered, pushing against the invasion. Then the sound became louder, higher as the thickest portion began to enter her.

"This is nearly as thick as my cock. It will get you ready," he told her, his own breathing harsh now. "When it's removed, Marly, my cock will slide easily into you, without pain." He pressed the base in, hearing her cry of pained pleasure as it finally lodged behind the tight ring of muscles that would hold it.

He looked down as the flat wide bottom that held it securely outside her body. His thighs clenched at the thought of how tight she was holding the plug, her muscles gripping it, hot and tight. He brought his hand down on the cheek of her ass with another small smack. She cried out, but didn't try to move. Again, he treated the other cheek to the same treatment. She was gasping, but still on her knees.

"You like that." His hand cupped her cunt, feeling her juice, thick and hot against it. She was soaked.

He smacked her again, bringing another cry from her throat. He repeated the small punishment several times, watching the cheeks of her ass flush. When he stopped, Marly was moaning loudly with each slap, her cheeks clenching over the plug buried deep in her flesh, her cream now coating her thighs.

"Stand up." He moved away from her then, going to the chair as he removed his jeans. Marly faced him as he kicked the material from his legs, his cock swinging free and standing stiffly away from his body.

He sat back down in the chair and motioned her forward. She moved timidly, obviously not used to walking with the plug stretching her so tightly.

"You will use it everyday," he ordered her tightly. "Before I come in each evening you'll insert it. If you don't, Marly, then I'll insert it, and I'll let Brock and Sam help. Is that what you want?"

She shook her head fiercely, her face flaming.

"Good," he whispered. "Now, spread your legs. I want to fuck you with your new dildo before you suck my cock for me."

He lifted the thick shaft from the drawer, watching her eyes widen at the size of it.

"Oh yes, it will fit," he promised her, seeing the protest in her eyes. "Now, spread your legs. Brace your hands on my shoulders if you have to, but don't move."

Cade shifted forward as he lubricated the head of the dildo. Excitement flared inside him, fire pulsed in his cock. She was his, and tonight he would prove it to her.

Marly was shaking as she stared down at Cade, barely able to stay steady, awash in the most incredible sensations of her life. The plug had her stretched to capacity, burning her, making her so wild to have Cade she couldn't stand it. But it wasn't him she was about to get, it was the thick dildo he was slowly preparing, his eyes locked with hers as he spread the lubrication on it.

"Spread your legs wider. We want Jennings to get a clear view," he told her softly.

Marly flushed, her heart speeding with fear as the idea of her stepfather watching. Then she couldn't think anymore. Her hand clutched at his shoulders as she felt the head of the rubber cock being inserted in her vagina.

"Tight," Cade growled as he slowly pushed it further, small shallow, twisting thrusts that lodged it deeper and deeper inside her. It stretched her impossibly, made the plug in her rear shift gently almost throwing her head long into a climax.

"Yeah, take it all, baby." She felt his hand at her lips as he pushed the dildo deep inside her, making her back arch and her cry to echo around the room.

He pulled it back, then pushed it in again, fucking her with slow easy strokes that had her forgetting all about who was watching, or who could hear her. All she cared about was the fire burning in her body and the need turning her into a creature of arousal, of lust.

"Cade. Cade. I can't stand it." She tossed her head, her inner body clutching at the slick device as he thrust it over and over inside her body, making her crazy. She could feel each movement, each fold of skin as it stretched over the flared head and thick shaft, clutching it, gripping hot and tight as she fought for release.

"No, not this time." His fingers plucked gently at her nipple as he pulled back, then pushed in again. "You can't climax on the dildo, baby. I'm just getting you ready for my cock. And you know how I like to fuck you."

Marly screamed as the dildo speared home again in a long, hard thrust that had her teetering on climax. Then he pulled it back easy, delaying her as she cried out, nearly begging for it again.

"Suck my cock." He jerked the dildo from her body, allowing it to fall carelessly to the floor. "Bend over and suck it, Marly. Remember, you're being watched."

She filled her mouth with his erection, not caring who saw or how angry they got. The hot flesh filled her mouth as Cade's fingers went to her hair, clenching in the curls as he moaned against the suckling motions as she drew on him.

She drew over the thick length slowly, wanting to please him, wanting him groaning in his need for her. She felt his cock throb between her lips and beneath her hands that clutched the base of it. His hips lifted to her, thrusting himself inside her mouth as he fought his own release.

Her tongue flickered against the head, laving it, then her mouth sucked in deep, her lips stretched over the width, loving the taste of him, the sound of his harsh groans, the way his hips lifted to her.

"Enough." He pushed her back. "Lay on the bed. Spread your legs real wide for me, Marly. I'll make you come before I pull that plug out and sink into your tight little ass."

Marly whimpered. She moved to the bed, doing as he told her, lying back on the bed, her legs spread wide. She watched as Cade moved over her, his hard cock angry looking, thick and full as he braced his weight on his elbows. He didn't prepare her. He just adjusted his position then slammed himself to the hilt inside her. That was all it took. As he set up a hard, driving rhythm Marly's climax shattered over her. She heard herself screaming his name, felt her body explode into white-hot fragments of pleasure that left her gasping, her chest heaving with the effort to draw in enough air to survive as he built her up again.

He pushed in, thrusting inside her again and again. His face was drawn into lines of agonized pleasure as he raided the tight, ultra-sensitive channel. Marly could feel the snug fit of her vagina around his erection. The device filling her rear making the pleasure so extreme, so impossible to resist that within minutes she was shattering again, bucking against his body, hearing his triumphant male cry and feeling the harsh blasts of his release into the receptive portal he plundered.

Marly was exhausted, her body dripping with perspiration, the echoes of pleasure unlike anything she had ever known vibrating through her as she felt Cade gently turning her body, placing her hips over the pillows he had lain beside her.

"I've dreamed of this, Marly," he whispered as he slowly drew the plug from her rear, making her body shudder with renewed pleasure.

It was too much. She moaned on a protest as she felt the cool, slick application of the lubrication there once again.

"I've waited a long time, baby," he growled, moving behind her now, one hand pulling the cheeks of her rear apart. "Too long for this."

He sank in slowly, easily. Marly's cries were more guttural now. She was distantly shocked at the sounds as she felt him slide to the hilt inside her. Finally, agonizingly, burningly aware of the tight fullness, the rush of blood as she lifted her hips, she took all of him.

Cade lay over her, his weight braced on his elbows at her shoulders as his lips ran a line of kisses over her shoulder.

"You're so tight," he whispered hotly. "So damned tight and hot I won't make it long."

As he started to thrust slowly, one hand moved beneath her body, his long fingers seeking the slick flesh of her vagina, then two fingers were plunging inside her in time to the heated thrusts burning her alive from behind. She tightened around him, making him groan harshly. She bucked against him, driving him deeper, whimpering as she felt a crescendo of pleasure unlike anything she had known before. She was drowning in it, burning alive as he began to move faster, harder. His fingers filled her, his cock destroyed her. Her vision grew hazy as fire spread along her body, drawing her taut, frightening her with its extremity.

"Don't fight it, Marly," he panted at her ear as her head began to toss in fear. "I'm here, baby. I'll hold you. Just let it have you, Marly. Let it have you."

She didn't have a choice. Marly wanted to scream, but as the orgasm raced through her body, she couldn't find the breath to emit that desperate cry. Then Cade's fingers were plunging one last time, and she toppled over the precipice. She stiffened, tightened on his thrusting erection, his long fingers, further, relishing the drawn out moan of surrender, as she felt harsh, hot jets of his sperm releasing into her body.

Chapter Twenty-five

ꙅꙅ

"My kingdom for a beer." Sam was pitiful, confined to his hospital bed, staring in bleak reflection at the wall opposite his bed.

"You don't have a kingdom," Marly informed him as she stared at him from the bottom of his bed.

He gave her a narrowed look promising retribution.

"Fine, then. Cade's kingdom for a beer. My fucking Harley for a beer. Some one get me some damned alcohol."

"What kind of drugs are you on?" Marly frowned down at him, wondering at his morose state of being.

"None of your business." His mouth turned down, his blue eyes staring moodily up at Marly. "Did you bring me a beer, Sweetness? Please say you did."

Marly tilted her head, then checked the doorway, ignoring his hopeful look.

"You brought me a beer?" Pleasure infused his voice.

"No, I didn't bring you a damned beer," she bit out, turning back to him and reaching into her large purse. "I did better than that. I made Cade stop at BK. That's even better."

His eyes lit up at the familiar bag, and he eased himself into a sitting position as Marly set the bag on the bedside table and wheeled it closer. Then she pulled out a large cola, poured it into his ice pitcher and set it beside him.

Sam dug into the bag, emitting pleasured whimpers as the smell of the Whopper with the works wafted across his senses. Within seconds he was biting into the huge burger, growling like a starving bear as he ate.

Marly sat down in the chair beside his bed, a smile crossing her face at his enjoyment. Sam was nothing more than a little boy in a man's body. He wasn't dominant like Cade, or intense like Brock. He enjoyed the simple things, and found laughter where he could. If there was one person she knew cared about her, it was Sam.

"Oh man, Marly, I knew you loved me the best." He smacked his lips as he swallowed, then bit into another bite as he plucked several fries from the box and stuffed them in behind it.

Marly propped her chin on her fist as she watched him eat. Gusto. That described Sam. He did everything with gusto. Whether it was a ball game, a fight or a feast, he went after it with everything he had. She fought her blush as she wondered if he had approached sex with the women he had shared with his brothers in the same way.

"Do you have any idea how lousy their hospital food is?" he mumbled around the burger. Then he grinned. "Sorry hon. Forgot."

Marly shook her head. How could he forget all the times she stayed in the hospital? It was usually him Cade hit for being in on whatever put her there. She frowned. She wanted to hit Cade. The man should be outlawed for being a nuisance.

"I'm glad to see you're doing okay." Marly felt tears gather in her eyes as she watched him. "I'm sorry about this, Sam. It's all my fault."

Sam frowned. "How?" he asked her around another mouthful of food.

"I know who did it, and why." She wasn't going to allow him to lie to her. Not Sam. She couldn't handle it. "I know everything now, Sam."

Sam sighed, plopping the last bite of burger and fries in his mouth and chewing thoughtfully as he stared at the ceiling. Several long drinks of soda later, he finally brought his gaze back to hers.

"None of us could have predicted what he would do." He shrugged carefully. "I don't blame you, Marly. None of this is your fault."

"Did you know Cade was sleeping with me to keep me protected?" She had to know the truth. She had to know who was in on it.

Surprise lit his eyes, then amusement. "Oh yeah. I forgot. Cade's dick gets hard for every damsel in distress he meets. Get serious, Marly."

Marly lowered her head, relief rushing through her.

"I heard him talking to Rick Glaston. Rick told Cade to keep me in his room, and Cade said that was why I was there to begin with," she told him softly, the pain of it still present in her voice.

Sam frowned. He sniffed thoughtfully, then pursed his mouth in consideration.

"And you believed it?" Sam asked her, narrowing his eyes on her.

Marly shrugged. "He said it, Sam."

He belched softly, then leaned back, his eyes never leaving hers.

"He hurt you, huh?" He frowned at the thought of that.

"Yeah." Marly lowered her head, her fingers picking at a loose thread in the knees of her well-worn jeans. "He did."

"So you two had a huge fight, and you're refusing to have sex with him, and he's now on the defense trying to worm his way back into your pants?" Sam laughed at this, shaking his head. "I love it. I couldn't have planned this one better myself."

Marly's eyes narrowed. "You sure that bullet didn't travel to your brain, moron?"

He chuckled again.

"It's perfect. See, Marly. Knothead has no idea just exactly how much he does love you. He's been fighting it for years.

Now, he's gonna have to come off his little island long enough to prove it." He nodded as though it had been his plan all along.

Marly blinked.

"You know, Sam. I'm real glad I'm not blood relation to you in particular, because you are certifiably insane. And I really don't want to pass that gene to my children later."

He looked at her in amazement.

"Hell, Marly, Cade's my brother. Course it'll get passed."

"Not if I never touch him again," she snarled, thinking about last night, the domination, the wild pleasure. The self-confidence of a man who knew what he was doing and what he wanted.

"Whoa!" He blinked now, amazement crossing his face. "You look like you mean that, Munchkin."

Marly rolled her eyes. She hadn't spoken to Cade since the night before. Since her last gasping moan, her last desperate plea deep into the night as he used the large rubber dildo in sync to his own deep thrusts inside her body as he whispered to her. Reaffirming the wild rumors, warning her, daring her to push him into it. Daring her to make the choice by denying him, by whispering the forbidden word, 'no'.

"Son of a bitch, I get laid up here in the hospital and all the good shit starts happening and I can't even be blamed for it," he moaned. "When did you decide to grow teeth anyway?"

"When my lover decided to fuck me to keep me from getting killed instead of because he just couldn't keep his hands off me," she informed him bitterly. When her lover had jerked her out of the fairy tale she would have been content to live in.

Marly didn't like the things she was learning about herself, or the depraved images her lover had put in her head.

"You think so, huh?" He asked her softly. "Interesting."

"You don't act convinced." Marly crossed her arms over her breasts as she watched his psuedo-innocent expression.

His brows arched.

"Brother Sam knows many things, little Munchkin," he chuckled. "But trust me, you're way off base. But give him hell anyway; he needs it. You always were too agreeable with him."

Marly sighed in resignation, watching him with his former morose expression. She had expected Sam to be just a tad bit more sympathetic to her plight here.

"Tell me, Marly, what's the one thing about Cade that you love the most?" he finally asked her gently.

She lowered her head, fighting to control the hurt and the tears.

"Come on. There has to be one thing," he urged softly, his hazel eyes velvet soft as he watched her with affection.

She lifted a shoulder negligently.

"Let me see, we've had a lot of conversations in the past," he mused quietly. "But the one thing that comes to mind, is the fact that Cade is always so determined. No matter what, to see to your happiness, your safety, your smiles and your pleasure. You've always been in awe of that, haven't you Little Sister?"

She looked up at him with a frown. "That has nothing to do with it."

How could he have her pleasure in mind? Her needs uppermost. He wanted to share her. He wanted to watch her writhe under the touch of his brothers' hands. Marly shook off the flare of excitement, attributing it instead to fear and disgust. She wouldn't enjoy such a thing, she couldn't.

"Doesn't it, Marly?" he asked her patiently. "Come on, Marly. Cade wouldn't make love with you if he loved you like a sister or a niece. He wouldn't be so concerned with all those things in any other instance unless he loved you like a woman. Cade just doesn't realize it yet."

Marly shook her head. "You're wrong, Sam," she denied painfully. "I wish you weren't, but you are. It's not love, as much as I wish it were."

Sam sighed roughly. "Come here, Munchkin, if you have to cry, at least let me pet you while you do it."

Marly shook her head. She couldn't go into his arms. She couldn't. Did he get hard when he held her? Did his mind fill with sexual thoughts, sexual needs? Her hands shook as she remembered her own flare of desire the other morning, the hot flush of arousal at his touch. The information Cade had given her only made it worse. Could she handle it now, without wondering—

"Marly?" He tilted his head, his blue eyes quizzical and faintly hurt. "You won't let me hold you?"

She couldn't hurt Sam. She couldn't let her fears do this to her. They wouldn't force her. She knew they wouldn't. But could she keep herself from wanting?"Now, here's what you're gonna do," he advised her quietly at he patted her shoulder. "You're gonna give him hell for being a knothead. And he deserves it. But be careful, Marly, because he can be hurt, too. And you are the only person guar-an-damn-teed to be able to hurt, Cade."

"I couldn't hurt, Cade," she whispered. "Even now, when it hurts so bad, Sam. I can't hurt him."

"That's because you love him. And I know Cade didn't deliberately hurt you. He's just a little fried in the brain from all that rough and ready kitchen sex you two have been having. Dangerous for the mental faculties there, Marly-girl," he told her half-seriously. "Not to mention my mental well-being. I'm young and impressionable, ya know?"

"Yeah, sure you are. I heard about you too, Big Boy," she muttered. "Dillon Carlyle has nothing on your little exploits."

At least he had the grace to blush.

"Get the hell out of that bed, Marly." She jerked in surprise at Cade's furious voice as he spoke from the bottom of the bed.

She frowned. "Don't you get tired of skulking around?" she asked him irritably, but didn't move from Sam's arms.

"Last warning." She was amazed to see his face flushed, his eyes dark with fury. "Get the hell out of that bed and let's go."

"Damn, Cade, I can't even have sympathy now." Sam was more than put out with Cade's attitude as well if his rough voice was anything to go by. "What the hell is your problem anyway?"

Cade's eyes flashed with dark fire.

"Eager to start already, Marly?" he asked her coolly, his look suggestive as he flung his threat in her face.

Marly tensed with her own anger, and felt Sam do the same. It wasn't jealousy. It was need. She could see the lust riding Cade, the inner fury at himself, not at her. But it hurt all the same.

"Damned good thing I'm laid up, Cade," Sam bit out. "Cause we'd fight for that one."

He hugged Marly tightly for a second, then lifted his arm from her shoulder.

"Remember what I told you, sweet thing." He winked slowly, but there was no amusement in his smile. "I'll be home in a few days, I promise."

"Thanks, Sam." She kissed his cheek softly, then rose from beside him, moving quickly past Cade. "Maybe when you come home, asshole will be in a better mood. Or I'll be gone."

She heard Cade curse behind her, but continued until she was outside the door, and standing silently in the hall, staring in silent determination at Rick and Brock as they blocked her way. She sighed deeply, fighting for patience and tolerance as she faced them.

"One of these days," she mused. "Some big dumb man is gonna stand in my way at the wrong time."

"Long as there ain't no crazies stalking in the shadows at the time, then I'm with you, honey." Rick's lips quirked in amusement as he watched her.

Breathing out as she raised her eyes heavenward, she sat down in a hard plastic chair and resigned herself to waiting, if a bit impatiently, for Mr. Ass to decide to leave.

* * * * *

Cade wanted to hit someone. Preferably Sam. But how do you hit a man that took a bullet for you? He escorted Marly into the waiting limo, watching as she moved to the far corner of the seat. He sighed wearily, entering and closing the door behind him.

He allowed his head to fall back and rest along the seat, closing his eyes tiredly. Marly was, once again, not speaking to him. She sat in stubborn silence, staring outside the tinted window, her arms crossed over her breasts. Her long hair was tied back, falling over her shoulder, shielding most of her face, and her expression. She was beautiful in her anger, but he was getting tired of seeing her so damned mad. He couldn't make her understand, no matter how hard he tried. Hell, he didn't understand his feelings sometimes himself. All he knew was that he needed her. Needed her unlike anything he had ever needed in his life.

"What do you want, Marly?" He was tired of fighting with her. He wanted to hold her; he wanted her close to him. Just in his arms if nothing else. He hated frightening her. He hated pushing her. He wanted her, needed her.

"I don't want anything, Cade." Her voice was calm, cool. She didn't look at him, didn't acknowledge his presence in any way other than to simply answer him.

"I'm tired of saying I'm sorry," he sighed. "I'm who I am, Marly. I warned you of this."

"A liar?" She turned to look at him with haunted eyes. "I never thought you would lie to me, Cade. Until now."

"I didn't lie to you." He raked his fingers though his hair impatiently. "I couldn't have resisted much longer, Marly. You know that as well as I do. But the threat against you terrified me. It just sped things up." Frustration and aggravation lined his voice.

"This isn't even about that anymore, Cade," she told him hoarsely.

Cade knew what it was about. She was worried, concerned. But she wasn't running.

"Is it about the sex?" he bit out. "Dammit, you enjoyed it. I know you did."

He knew women could be confusing, but this defied anything he had faced before.

"And that's all that matters, isn't it, Cade?" Her voice sounded understanding, so why did he feel she wasn't the least bit understanding?

"What else matters?" he questioned her roughly. "Dammit, you said you heard the rumors a long time ago. You suspected what it would be like Marly, you can't deny that. Do you think I don't love you? That I don't want you? I told you, this wasn't the fairy tale you needed."

"How do you know what I need, Cade?" she bit out furiously. "You've never tried to give as well as to take. Maybe that's what I need."

Cade shook his head, fighting to understand her.

"What do you need, Marly? Tell me. At least give me a chance to give it to you."

She frowned for a moment, watching him, her eyes dark and considering as whatever female form of logic twisted in her head. He groaned silently. Dammit, when did she get so complicated?

"Tell me, Cade. Just how desperate are you to kiss up?" His cock perked up for sure, but Cade had a feeling that wasn't what she meant.

"I'm getting pretty desperate here," he sighed, frowning. "Will it involve pain?"

"It will likely be the most painful thing you've ever experienced," she told him softly. "Think you can handle it?"

He narrowed his eyes on her. "Will I be able to walk later?" He winced, hearing his own desperation. Dammit.

"Only if you really want to." She shrugged. "It's all according to you, I guess."

His lips pursed as he wondered if she could really hurt him. Yeah, he sighed, she was mad enough to.

"Fine. Go ahead." He winced, wondering what he was letting himself in for.

Marly's eyes narrowed. "Move into the middle of the seat," she ordered him softly.

Watching her carefully, Cade did as she told him.

"You aren't allowed to touch me. If you touch me, then you prove you have no intentions of making up, and all you want to do is fuck." She scooted a bit closer to him.

The fresh scent of her body reached him, making his body harden. Then his eyes widened as she moved to straddle his thighs slowly. Automatically his hands rose to clasp her hips, but with an arched brow she reminded him of the conditions.

"You're going to torture me." He watched her as she allowed her thighs to clasp him, settling against the bulge of his erection softly.

"Torture?" she asked him gently. "Last night you were begging me to touch you. I'm just going to touch you, Cade."

She bent close, her lips settling softly against his neck. Cade's eyes closed as her tongue licked at his skin in short, flickering strokes. The caress was like a blaze of fire that had his body drawing taut.

"I love to touch you, Cade," she whispered. "But you never give me the chance."

"I do," he groaned, feeling his body racked with need as her lips caressed his skin slowly. She tasted him, stroked him, her inexperienced touch driving him insane.

"No, you don't," she told him softly. "You take control, and force the response you want. I don't want to be forced, Cade. I want to be loved."

Her hands were against his chest, burning through the silk of his shirt.

"Do you know why I always liked sleeping in your shirts, Cade?" she asked him as her nails bit through the material.

"Why?" he growled as he felt her teeth against his skin. She was killing him. He had never felt anything so damned hot as Marly moving slowly against his body, destroying his control.

"Because they were yours. They had been next to your body, and they smelled of you. So masculine and warm. They made me feel safe." She nipped his ear as she whispered her secret.

His breathing was shuddering from his body, and he had to literally sit on his hands to keep from touching her. He could feel his heart pounding, the blood rushing through his body and it amazed him. He had never felt this, a pleasure deeper, stronger than anything he had ever known, and from something as simple as Marly's lips on his neck.

"I liked you wearing the shirts," he groaned. "I always did, Marly."

His hips arched against her as she rubbed her cheek against his. Her skin was so damned soft he couldn't stand it. He wanted to touch her so much it was killing him.

"Why did you like me wearing the shirts, Cade?" she asked him, her breasts rising and falling with her own quickened breathing, pressing them against his chest.

He stared at her, seeing her eyes go dark with arousal, and considered her question.

"At first, just because you liked doing it." He finally shrugged uncomfortably.

"And later?" She breathed against the corner of his mouth.

Cade groaned. "So I knew something of mine was touching you. Anything. God, Marly, please let me touch you."

"No. You promised, Cade." Her teeth nipped at his lower lip in punishment. "Just feel me against you for a change. Let me feel you. You've never given me a chance to feel you."

Her fingers went to the buttons of his shirt, and Cade knew it was going to kill him. Hell no, he wouldn't be able to walk later, he thought. His cock would explode and kill him.

He watched her slender fingers as they loosened the buttons, then parted the edges of the fabric with slow, torturous movements. His head fell back against the couch, he couldn't stand to watch. Then pleasure struck his body like a flare of heat as she pressed his nipples between her sharp little nails. He arched his hips against her, growling at the searing sensation.

His eyes opened as one hand lifted, wrapping around his neck to draw his head down.

"I want to kiss you." Need, naked and harsh was reflected on her flushed face. "Not like you kiss me, Cade. I want it soft and easy, like it means something."

"Dammit, Marly. It always meant something." He shook his head in confusion. How could she believe otherwise? "You act like I raped you."

"You raped my senses. You took the choice of control from me, just as you took the choice of participation, Cade,"

230

she accused him. "You controlled it all. Even your own pleasure. Now I want to control it."

"Marly, honey, I don't know if I can do this," he whispered regretfully. "God help me I want to, but you're killing me."

"I haven't even started. And you promised me, Cade. Touch me, and I'll know that all that matters is getting your way, not pleasing me."

She was a siren; sexy and drunk on her own power, Cade thought desperately. She didn't know the demon she was tempting. Had no idea how strong and fierce his need for her really was.

"Let me kiss you, Cade." And her lips settled, light as a feather, against his own.

Chapter Twenty-six

Cade's heart kicked in his chest. The muscles of his stomach knotted, and his hands curled into fists as he fought to take the kiss away from her. Her lips were too light upon his, teasing him gently, making him mad for her. Her tongue reached out, the lightest caress in the world sweeping over his, and leaving him gasping like a teenager begging for more. He sought a deeper touch, but she retreated, staring down at him, her eyes dark and wild as her hands framed his face.

Then her lips came back, her tongue sneaking past his lips in a kiss that destroyed him. He groaned harshly, fighting the need to throw her to the seat and pound into her.

"You're so rough and tough." She smiled against his lips. "It's killing you, isn't it."

Was it? He had never known anything so damned sensual in his life as Marly's soft caresses. Was it killing him, or was the need for more destroying him?

"Don't stop," he growled roughly. "Please, Marly—"

He saw the pleasure flare in her eyes, deep and intense.

Her lips burrowed into his again, and he moved against her, her questing little tongue touching his as he tilted his head to deepen the pleasure. She was breathing hard now, nearly as hard as he was. Her hands were at his neck, her little nails scraping his skin as her breasts pushed into his chest and her jean covered mound ground against his erection as he thrust against her.

"Let me hold you," he panted, his head rising as she stared down at him, heavy lidded and intense. "Please, just let me hold you."

He was going to rip the leather off the seat with the force of his fingers digging into them if she didn't let him touch her.

"No. I want to touch you. If you touch me, you'll take over, Cade," she whispered. "That's your problem, you always have to take over."

Her head lowered, then her questing little mouth tasted the skin of his chest. Cade's head fell back along the seat, his eyes closing in torment.

"I only know one way, Marly," he groaned.

"Then it's time to learn Marly's way." Her voice was smoky and aroused as her teeth nipped at the skin of his chest.

Pleasure raced through his body as her lips moved lower. She was going to kill him. Slowly, torturously, she was out to kill him. His cock was throbbing like a pulsing wound, demanding relief. The confinement of his jeans was killing him. He could think of nothing more tormenting than the way the nails of her fingers barely scraped his skin. Unless it was the slow licks, soft kisses and delicate nips she took from his chest.

"You're tormenting a man already possessed, Marly," he growled, breathing harshly.

"Tormenting him?" She asked absently as her tongue licked beneath the edges of his shirt. "You're free to ask me to stop at anytime, Cade."

Ask her to stop? He was within a breath of pleading for more.

His hips arched from the seat, driving his erection into the vee of her thighs. Little minx. She lifted her body away from him, a soft laugh feathering over his skin.

Cade had never experienced anything like it. He was burning alive, his senses overloading with the small, delicate pleasures she was bestowing upon him. He wanted to throw her to the seat and ravage her. But a part of him wanted her beneath him, his lips showing her the torturous sensations she was giving him.

"I always wanted to make love to you, Cade." Her breath, hot and sensual whispered over his flesh. "And have you love me as well. But you throw me into the maelstrom, rather than easing us both into it."

He barely heard her words, but he felt them against his flesh. He moaned raggedly as she ground herself against his cock, choking back a harsh demand that she release him from the bonds she had placed on him. A bond he couldn't break. If he touched her, she would stop. God in Heaven, as tormenting as it was, he couldn't let her stop.

"You enjoyed it." It was the only thing he could gasp aloud.

"How would I know if I enjoyed it, or if only my body did?" she asked him gently, raising her head to stare into his eyes.

What was it he was seeing within those darkened depths, Cade wondered. Definitely passion, definitely need. But there was a pleasure and erotic heat he had never seen before, in any woman.

"You're not making sense." His fingers dug into the seat once again as her lips returned to his neck, the suckling pressure on it driving his blood pressure higher.

She shrugged languidly, smiling against his skin as she traveled lower, Cade slid his body lower to keep his hard flesh in contact with the vee of her thighs. But no matter how hard he tried, she still ended lower, her lips and hands now on the clenching planes of his stomach. And she loved the taste of him if the sounds coming from her throat were any indication.

"Perhaps it will make sense later then." She rose from her bent position and began to unbutton her blouse.

Cade fought to drag air into his lungs as her fingers, trembling and unsure, released the buttons of her blouse. Then she was peeling it from her shoulders and tossing it into the corner of the seat. His mouth watered as she cupped the white lace covered mounds of her breasts. Then she released the clip holding them together and removed that barrier as well.

"Son of a bitch, you're trying to kill me." He couldn't take his eyes off the hard tipped, plump flesh, or the way her fingers slowly toyed with her nipples, making them harder, longer.

The soft pink flesh darkened, the mounds rising and falling harshly with her breathing as her hand framed and caressed them. His cock jerked, screaming for release. His heart thundered, and somewhere deep inside, Cade felt a part of his soul unravel.

Marly couldn't believe he was actually allowing her to touch him the way she had always longed to. That his gray eyes were nearly dark with pleasure, his hard body taut and reaching for her. She had always dreamed of him touching her as well when she did this, but she knew Cade would take over. She needed this chance, this stolen time to show him how she needed him, how she loved him.

She faced him, watching his gaze as it centered on her hands, the way his tongue ran over his lips longingly. She pinched her nipples lightly, hearing the small groan that escaped his lips, and the pleasure from it racked her body.

"Let me—" his voice was dark and deep, rumbling from his chest.

"Let you what? Use your hands?" she taunted him. "No, Cade. This is my time. My way."

"God, Marly." He licked his lips again, his eyes darkening further.

Marly felt her own stomach clench in pleasure at the look on his face. His cheeks were lightly flushed, his eyes heavy-lidded and dark, his lips full and moist and parted for her.

She eased closer, lodging the nipple of one breast between his lips. He groaned, latching onto it instantly to suck it into his mouth.

Marly moved back, feeling her breast pop free of his mouth as his lips tried to follow.

"God. Damn, Marly," he cried out, his eyes never leaving the moistened flesh he had held in his mouth.

Marly frowned as he stared at her like a man starved. She shook her head, smiling at him when he raised his eyes to hers.

"Marly's way," she whispered, bending her head to a hardened male nipple on his chest.

Her tongue touched it slowly, wrapping around the point as he arched, groaning like a demented creature.

"Son of a bitch." His breath wheezed from his throat as his head fell back against the seat.

As her lips caressed the tight point, her fingers went to the other, stroking and soothing, then scraping lightly as she alternately licked and sucked at the tip she held in her mouth.

Then she rose to face him again, her own breathing out of control. His chest was tight and hard, muscular and warm. It rose and fell harshly as he raised his head slowly. Once again, Marly slid her nipple past his lips.

Fire lanced her body as his tongue touched it. He suckled lightly, but his body was as tense as a drawn bow as he did so. He wanted to devour her, to eat her body with all the desperation running inside him. But he did as she asked, laving and suckling, his teeth biting gently. But he added a new dimension to it. One that had her crying out in her own need within seconds.

He sipped at her, suckled her, licked her with slow lazy movements and harsh growls of passion. His hands didn't touch her, but his mouth, teeth and tongue made up for it. Nuzzling, stroking, suckling slow and easy, then fast and hard until Marly was gripping his shoulders, arching closer and screaming out in pleasure.

"You taste like nectar," he whispered against her skin, then suckled her deep again. "Sweet and exotic." He licked her roughly, then soft and easy.

Marly bucked against the hard flesh driving between her thighs, cursing the barrier of jeans and panties between them.

Suddenly, he wasn't touching her anymore. His head fell back against the seat, and he moaned like a mad man.

"I will not make you cum," he growled. "I will not, Marly. I will not let you cum while you have me fucking bound up like this."

Marly was breathing harshly now, her breasts aching, her stomach clenching with need.

"Huh? How? You weren't touching me." She blinked down at him.

She knew the pleasure had been exquisite, unlike anything she had known, but she wasn't going to climax.

He raised his head, staring at her in surprise.

He suddenly groaned again, his head falling back as he ground it into the back of the seat.

"Doesn't matter. I fucking refuse to get you off, and not even have my hands involved." But his hips pushed against her again, making them both whimper in need.

"You can do it like that?" Marly had never imagined such a thing. She knew the pleasure was so erotic, so hot it made her scream out in need, but she didn't imagine she could climax with it.

Cade's eyes flared with heat, darkening as his face flushed further.

"Yeah." His look flickered to her breasts. "I could get you off like that. But you have to let me use my hands."

Marly frowned.

"How do you have to use your hands?"

He grinned slow and sensually.

"I won't touch anything but your breasts, I promise."

Marly licked her lips nervously. She didn't want to lose control. She didn't want to lose consciousness.

"Sometimes I forget how tender you are," he whispered, his voice gentle, regretful. "I told you, I'm rough, and sometimes it takes a hell of a blow to show me I'm being too rough. You showed me, Marly. Now let me prove I can be easy."

"What about you?" She was breathing roughly, dying for his touch.

He looked up from her heaving breasts, and her breath caught at the hunger in his gaze.

"What about me?" he asked her instead. "You call it, Marly. We're hours from home. We have plenty of time."

"I don't want to pass out again, Cade." It frightened her, her lack of control, the inability to handle the passion he brought out in her.

Cade swallowed tightly, managing a tense smile.

"I can't promise that, baby," he groaned. "Hell, I want to pass out every time I come inside you. But I swear I'll go easier on you. That's all I can do. I want you that bad, Marly. I want you until I feel like I'm dying."

Her heart jumped in her chest, her vagina clenched in need.

"No rough stuff?" She needed the promise.

"No." He shook his head roughly. "No rough stuff, Marly. I promise."

She licked her lips, fighting for breath, for control.

"Okay," she whispered. "Make love to me, Cade. Love me, just this once."

"Just this once?" He burst out on a groan of arousal, of torture. "Damn, Marly. Forever. I love you forever."

Cade undressed her and himself, slowly. His fingers didn't tremble as hers did, his body wasn't shuddering, but he was hot and barely controlled. His breaths rasped from his chest harshly, and when he stretched her along the seat and raised above her she could feel the taut tension that made him seem harder, more masculine than ever before.

"I love your body, Marly," he whispered as his lips touched hers. "So soft and pretty." His tongue speared into her mouth, tangling with hers as he kissed her soft and deep. And slow. A caress, a melding of heat and need.

Marly arched into him, crying out at the exquisite sensations, the longing in the kiss.

"I could kiss you all day." He moved back from her, his naked body braced above her, the long, thick length of his cock lying on her thigh like a fleshly brand.

Marly's hands ran along his arms, his smooth shoulders. She felt the heat coming off his body in waves, and her body arched to it.

"Such pretty nipples." He licked each one. His mouth took delicate sips, his lips closing on them, his teeth rasping the delicate points.

Marly cried out, arching against him, her thighs clenching in desperation.

"And here." His lips moved down her stomach, to her thighs.

Marly whimpered, allowing him to open her thighs gently.

"And here. I love your sweetness, and how wet you get for me." His tongue stroked gently along the lips between her thighs, curling between them, licking lightly, leaving her arching, begging for more.

Marly's hand speared into his hair, her thighs opening wider until one leg rested on the floor of the limo, her hips arching into the soft, gentle touch.

"I've never touched a woman like this, Marly," he whispered, then dragged his tongue through the slick evidence of what his touch was doing to her.

When his tongue reached her clit, it swirled around it slow and sure. He suckled it into his mouth, flickering lightly with his tongue as he applied a steady pressure on the little nubbin.

"Cade." She arched closer, drowning now rather than spinning out of control.

Marly had never known anything so destructive, so sensually searing as the slow licks and gentle nips he took from her. She couldn't talk, couldn't think, all she could do was hold onto him as he unraveled her. A long, broad finger sank knuckle deep inside her as another slowly lubricated the little tight hole lower.

Marly's breathing escalated, her body suspended as she felt him caress her there. Her breath strangled in her throat as she felt his finger sink in. Her muscles parted with little resistance, then clenched on the digit desperately. Her body was inflamed. His mouth worked her into a lather of lust as his fingers drove her crazy. The slow, deep thrusts into her vagina and her anus were building her into a boiling mass of desperation as she felt her climax winding through her body.

"Now, Marly." He increased the suction, the strokes, the flickering licks until she was screaming, arching.

"Cade," her wail echoed around her as she felt it erupt, her release deep and gasping, flowing over her, around her until she was shuddering in his arms.

"My turn." He rose quickly to his knees, then sank the full length of his shaft deep and hard inside the clenching, gripping depths of her soaked vagina.

"Oh, God!" Her legs wrapped around his thrusting hips, her arms holding onto his shoulders as he began to pound into her with long, hard strokes.

Dazed, pleasure zinging hard and bright through her body, Marly watched Cade's eyes darken, his face tauten as he took her. Over and over again, he thrust inside her to the hilt, then retreated and thrust again, driving her mad. The first climax was still shuddering through her when the second tore her apart. She couldn't scream, her vision darkened as she fought to hold onto sanity, hold onto Cade as he thrust one last time then cried out above her.

She felt the thick, harsh jets of his release inside her quivering flesh as she bucked one last time with her own eruption. Then she collapsed. Her arms fell from his shoulders, her legs from his hips, and she gazed up at him in stunned confusion.

It had been just as hard, just as destructive this way, yet she had held on.

Drawing breath into his lungs in quick, labored breaths, Cade stared down at her. Marly still gripped him, still pulsed around him.

"Again," he growled, moving slower now, stroking rather than taking. "Again Marly, before I die."

Her head fell back, her eyes closing in bliss as he began to take her slow and easy. Cade had never seen anything, or anyone so damned beautiful, so damned sexy and alluring in all his life. No other woman had been so tight, so hot, driving him mad with a need he couldn't put a name to, but knew that only Marly could satisfy.

Chapter Twenty-seven

∽

Sam was home within a few days, though he was still weak and tired, spending much of his time reclining in the family room under the watchful eye of his boob tube, or being stuffed with treats by Marie when she came in to check on him. The former cook still had a soft spot for Sam. He was being indulged and pampered, and Marly saw why Cade had put a stop to Marie's spoiling of them years before. If given the choice, Sam would become a spoiled rich brat in no time at all.

Rick and Tara were out of sight, tracking Jack, Cade had told her the night before. Her face flamed as she thought of the things they had done in front of the window. There had been no thought given in regards to the cowboys watching. Or the stalker. Not that it didn't add a new dimension to the sex. Marly still wasn't certain why her blood ran faster, her breathing faster with the thought of the eyes that could be watching.

It frightened her sometimes, the things he whispered to her and the excitement she felt at the thought of doing them. He was pushing her, and Marly knew it. Pushing the boundaries of what she could accept, and what she was comfortable with. There was more he wanted from her, and Marly was more than wary of the fact that those things were not abhorrent to her.

As she came down from their bedroom, the soft soles of her sneakers quiet on the stairs, she heard Cade and Sam in the living room, their voices a quiet, comforting buzz mixed with that of the television. She was wearing the clothes Cade had lain out for her. A short, gauzy skirt that hinted at full spring in the soft creamy background and light pastels of the hazy flowers. The cream colored strappy shirt she wore barely flirted with the waist of the skirt, and with each shift bared her waist, and the small gold ring and accompanying chain that spanned it. She wore white thongs, and no bra.

"There you are." Cade smiled at her from the doorway to the family room, watching her with approval as she moved toward him.

His eyes were heavy lidded, his look sexual as he watched her.

"You aren't working today?" she asked him softly, glad to see that he had decided to take Rick's advice and stay in the house, rather than moving about outside.

"Yeah, Rick put his foot down." He grimaced. "Make sure you stay inside too, we've found signs that Jennings has attempted to get closer to the house."

Marly breathed in roughly as fear skated through her.

"Where?" she whispered.

"Beneath your bedroom window. I don't think the nightmare last week was just your fears surfacing, Marly." He walked over to her, his hand touching her cheek. "I think Jennings was in your room. That's why the doors were opened when you cried out, waking yourself up. I think you knew he was there."

Marly felt disgust crawl over her skin. The thought of Jack in her room, touching her. She swallowed the bile rising in her throat. It was an invasion she couldn't shake off. A rape of her privacy, and her sense of security that boiled in her soul.

"Did he get back in?" she asked desperately, terrified for Cade now.

Jack Jennings would kill Cade if he could; he had already shown that in his attack against Sam.

"No, Marly, he can't get in now," Cade promised her, his arm going around her shoulders. "Come on into the living room. Tara and Sam are in there watching a movie. We'll join them." He dropped a kiss on her head, tucking her close to his body as he drew her into the darkened room.

The shades were closed, dimming the room intimately. The flickering light of the television washing over Tara's pretty, if aggressive expression, and Sam's lazy countenance.

"Munchkin. You finally rouse?" He smiled from his position, stretched out on one of the couches. "Come over here and give me a hug. Cade and Tara are being mean to me."

"You think everyone's mean to you," Tara laughed as she rose from her seat. "You handle him Marly, my patience is wearing thin."

Marly shook her head. Seeing the boyish expression, the teasing in his eyes as Tara left the room. She walked over to him and bent over for the hug. She wasn't expecting him to hold her head and cover her mouth with his as the other hand pushed beneath her shirt and palmed her breast, tweaking her nipple.

For a moment, she was shocked. Lust flared in her. Her nipple hardened painfully, her lips opening beneath the steady assault. His moan seconds later jerked her back to awareness. She jumped away from him, staring down at him in surprise as he watched her with a wicked, knowing expression.

Her gaze jumped to Cade. He was watching her with narrow-eyed intensity and a hard-on threatening to burst the front of his sweats."Come here." Cade held his hand out to her slowly. "Don't be frightened, Marly."

Don't be frightened? She was fucking terrified. Her body was humming with lust, the flesh between her thighs moist and ready from another man's touch. From Sam's touch. And she wasn't supposed to be frightened?

"Why did you do that?" She ignored Cade, staring down at Sam warily.

"Because I love you too, Marly," he whispered. "Not as deep, not as true as Cade does, but I love you as well."

His cryptic answer had her trembling.

"This isn't acceptable," she told Cade, trembling and aware of the sudden sexual tension in the room.

"Come here, Marly." He merely repeated his command, but rather than waiting on her, he advanced on her until he could take her hand himself and lead her to the couch across from Sam's, on the other side of the television. "Stop worrying so much. Let's just sit here and watch television and try to get through the next few hours. Hopefully, this thing with Jennings will be over soon."

Marly couldn't take her eyes off Sam. Her mind was in turmoil. Cade had seen what had happened. He knew Sam had palmed her breast, that his tongue was in her mouth with that kiss, and he wasn't angry. He wasn't ready to kill his brother, and he wasn't furiously charged with jealousy. He was turned on. Just as Sam was.

"Cade?" He reclined on the large couch, propping his head on the pillows at the end of it, then drew Marly down beside him. She was held against him spoon fashion, staring over at Sam as he watched her.

His eyes were dark, and heavy lidded. The soft material of his sweats was tented dangerously with his erection.

"You're trembling, Marly," Cade whispered at her ear. "Don't be frightened, baby. Nothing will happen that you won't enjoy. Your body knows what it likes, who it wants, and what turns it on. Don't be frightened of that."

She was confused. She didn't know where to look, but she couldn't keep her eyes from the bulge beneath Sam's sweats. He hadn't been hard when she came in. He had gotten hard when he touched her. He was Cade's brother. An indelible part of her life. She loved him and Brock, had spent teenage hours lusting after all three men before she set her heart on Cade. She couldn't believe this was happening. She couldn't let it happen.

Cade's erection was tucked against her buttocks. He too wore sweats, the basic loungewear for the men of the house. They did nothing to hide the hardened virility beneath the material.

"What are you going to do?" Her whisper was a whimper as she felt his hand smoothing the top of her thigh, drawing the small skirt further up as he did so.

"Nothing you won't enjoy, Marly," he promised her, his voice dark and deep. "I know you've fantasized about him. There's things I know about you as well. Just as I bet you money your cunt's hot and wet right now, thinking about Sam touching you."

She couldn't deny it. He was right. That didn't mean she had to do it. It was indecent. It wasn't right.

"I want to see it, Marly," he growled at her ear. "There's so much I want to teach you. So many pleasures I want you to know. Things you could never imagine." She felt the zipper at the back of her skirt slowly slide down.

"Cade, please—" She didn't know if she could do this. She was shaking, burning up, yet trembling as though she were freezing.

"I want you to do something for me," he whispered. "I want you to take your clothes off. Then lie back down beside me and just close your eyes. Just close your eyes Marly, and let me take care of everything. Will you do that for me, baby?"

"Don't do this," she whispered, closing her eyes, shocked at the desire to do just as he asked. "Please, Cade. I'm not ready for this."

"Yes you are." His lips caressed her neck gently. "You are ready, Marly, you just don't realize it. We're nice and safe for the moment, and I want this. I need it. Do this for me, Marly. Stand up, and watch Sam as you undress. Then lay back down and just close your eyes for me."

His hand slid beneath her skirt, palming the cheek of her rear nearest to him as he urged her up. Marly stood shakily to her feet. She toed her shoes off first, her toes curling against the cool hard wood of the floor. Then she allowed her loosened skirt to fall to the floor.

Sam's hand went to the waist of his sweats, pushing them to his thighs, revealing the thick cock that pulsed at the sight of her nearly naked body as he sat up on the couch. Then she removed the shirt, nearly crying out at the sensitivity of her nipples as the cloth raked them. Then more hesitantly, her hands went to her thongs. They were pushed slowly from her body now, her mouth watering as Sam's hand stroked his shaft slowly, his fingers moving up and down his cock with a mesmerizing motion.

"Now lay down beside me, on your back." Cade moved against the back of the wide couch. With near hysteria, Marly wondered if this was why all the furniture was so wide, and so much attention paid to comfort.

She stretched out beside him, staring up at him as she fought for breath. He had undressed as she had. His shaft lay along her thigh, his wide chest rising and falling in excitement.

"Don't open your eyes until I tell you," he ordered her, his tone gentle, but the look in his eyes stern. "Do you understand me? No matter what, don't open your eyes."

Marly swallowed tightly.

"Don't disobey me in this, Marly," he warned her clearly. "If you do, Sam will help me spank you. Do you want that?"

She shook her head, unable to speak.

"Good girl. Now close those pretty eyes." He laid his hand over them; making her blink against them, then she closed her eyes as he ordered.

"Now, I'm going to tell you what we're going to do to that pretty body of yours." She felt his hand smooth from her breast to the moist lips of her cunt.

Marly fought for breath. She heard Sam moving across the room, and the shocking moan of anticipation that escaped her lips proved to her that she was just as depraved, just as shockingly aroused by this as she feared she would be.

"You're so pretty, Marly," Sam whispered, his voice graveled, rough with his arousal.

She felt him bend by the couch, could see him in her mind's eyes, his eyes dark and filled with lust as they went over her body. Her thighs tightened involuntarily, the flesh between them so hot and wet. She knew they couldn't miss it. She knew the slick proof of her own arousal lay thick and wet on flesh between her thighs. She could feel it, slowly weeping from her body.

Then he touched her. Sam's hand. It wrapped around her breast, plumping the flesh as Cade mirrored the movement on the other. In sync, long, calloused male fingers caressed her, tweaked her nipples, had her groaning at the pleasure coursing through her body. She didn't know if she would survive it. They touched only her breasts, and her body already flamed with passion.

"So sweet." Cade's declaration followed with the hot, moist warmth of two mouths enveloping her nipples.

Marly tightened, crying out at the sensations. Twin tongues raked her nipples, mouths suckled at her breasts, hands roamed over her stomach, her thighs, then slowly pulled her legs apart.

"Cade." She called out his name in desperation. She didn't know if she could survive this pleasure.

"Easy, baby," he answered her, his voice thick with lust. "It's okay. I promise. Just let us love you, Marly. We would never hurt you, baby."

Warm, possessive, two pairs of hands roved her body. Sam lifted his head from her breast, one hand caressing it again as he leaned close.

"Let me kiss you, Marly." His voice, so tender, so filled with emotion whispered at her ear. "Please, Marly."

His lips settled over hers. Sharp and hot, sensation after sensation tore through her body. Her lips opened, his tongue entered and he groaned harshly. Marly's body bucked as a hand—Cade or Sam's?—moved between her thighs. The twin stimulations took over her mind, throwing her into a vortex of pleasure there was no escape from.

Sam's lips possessed hers, the hand between her thighs moved slow and easy through the slick dew coated on her bare flesh. From her slit to the little bud of her anus it moved, spreading the thick juices.

Sam's lips lifted from hers as the hand between her thighs moved and another returned.

"So good," Sam growled. "You taste exquisite, Marly."

Her eyes flew open as his finger slid from between his lips. He knelt beside her, his erection raising along his abdomen, long and thick, the head throbbing, pulsing, a small pearl of pre-come dotting it.

"You're looking, Marly." Cade turned her head to him.

There was no time to answer him. His lips covered hers as her thighs were pulled further apart. Sam moved; she felt him at the end of the large couch. She no longer wondered why they had such a large couch now. He lifted the leg nearest him, placing it over his shoulder.

Marly cried into Cade's kiss as she felt Sam's fingers part her slick flesh. Cade's tongue dipped into her mouth, drinking in the sound, causing her hips to arch, involuntarily reaching for the exquisite sensations to be found in the ultimate caress. Sam's lips touched her inner ones like a kiss. She whimpered in need, arching to the tongue reaching out, running between them, dipping into the well of cream that flowed like honey from her body.

Marly shook, trembled. Her hands gripped the pillow rest behind her, clenching hard. Cade's lips moved to her breasts once again, enveloping the tip of the swollen mound, rasping it with his tongue.

"Cade. Cade. I'm dying," she cried out, her thighs widening for Sam so he could continue to stroke, thrust, lap at her flesh.

"Not yet, baby," he growled, denying her claim. "Wait a little while. Then you can explode for us."

"No. It's killing me," she wailed, her voice harsh. Sam's diabolical tongue plunged deep inside her, his mouth emitting sighs of pleasures that vibrated against her flesh.

"Easy, Marly." Cade's head lifted, his eyes staring down at her. The carnality of his expression had her stomach tightening in a surge of echoed lust.

Sam's tongue wasn't letting up. It plunged inside her over and over again, lapping at her, drinking in the flow of desire that poured from her body. Cade's hands roved over her upper body, her breasts, stomach, his lips sipping at hers, his eyes staring into hers, refusing to release her.

"I want to watch you come for him, Marly," he groaned against her lips, his eyes never leaving hers. "I want to watch your eyes daze, your face flush, and see the ecstasy ripple through your expression. I want to see it, Marly. I want to know you're feeling it. Needing it."

Desperate. His expression was desperate. Her body was desperate. She was going insane with need.

"Cade. I'm scared." Sam's tongue was driving her closer, his fingers on her clit making it swell, making it throb, pulse, throwing her closer to death.

"I'm here, Marly." Inexpressibly tender, eager, so aroused and filled with desire, his look flooded her with the approval she saw there. "I'm here, baby. Just hold onto me and let it go."

She could do nothing more. She felt the explosion build. Felt it swell through her, ripple over her. It shattered through her body as she felt a finger, one broad finger breach the small portal of her anus and slide in. It tore through her body, heaving it, sending her scream echoing through the room as it tore through her, destroyed her.

"Yes. Oh hell, Marly." Sam moved as Cade lifted his body over her, his voice ragged.

Then Cade was settling between her thighs, wrapping her legs around his hips and plunging his cock deep inside her. Deep. So deep and hard she shattered again when Sam filled her mouth with his erection. It didn't stop. They were insatiable. Whispered pleas, a chorus of encouragement as they moved inside her, loving her, worshipping her body and the pleasure she gave them.

Her mouth tightened on Sam's cock. Her vagina tightened on Cade's. Her eyes closed, feeling Sam pulse in her mouth, feeling Cade riding the last thrusts to completion as she built again towards the next.

"I'm going to come, Marly," Sam groaned, harsh, guttural as he thrust the thick flesh between her lips. "Move. Move back, baby, or I'll come in your mouth."

She wasn't going anywhere. Her lips tightened on him, her legs tightened around Cade. Both men groaned, cried out, pulsing inside her body to their shattered male cries. Lust pulsed through the room to the tune of their cries. Her own moans joined them, and she began to drown in wave after wave, spurt after spurt until her world became only the men she pleasured. Only the men who pleasured her.

Sam settled on the floor beside her long moments later. Cade collapsed over her, bracing his weight on his elbows as his chest heaved, fighting for air.

"Marly. Baby," he rasped against her cheek. "Thank you."

She sighed against his chest.

"I love you," she whispered back, wishing above all things that she could take the pain from his eyes.

"I love you," he swore, his smile a bit sad as he watched her. "More than you know, Marly, I love you. But we aren't finished, baby. I need you to do one more thing for me."

She blinked up at him, satisfaction still coursing through her body.

"I need you to be with Tara. I need you to accept that as well, Marly. Another woman. I want you to make love with her."

Chapter Twenty-eight

ஓ

Cade reached his limit. Furious, insulted, her heart beating with anger, Marly attempted to reconcile herself, days later, to Cade's declaration. She wouldn't do it. She remembered the way his expression shuttered, the way he stilled at her refusal to give him what he desired. She couldn't do it. She loved him, loved Brock and Sam. She wanted to please them. She could accept, if not understand, this need Cade had. Being with another woman, she would not accept. She couldn't accept it.

"You can't avoid me forever." Tara's voice was amused, understanding.

She stood in the doorway to the kitchen, her eyes watching Marly prepare her snack.

Marly kept her head lowered as she continued to make her snack. A glass of cola sat on the counter, and the plate she was filling with fruit and dip was nearly finished.

"I wasn't aware I was avoiding you." She shrugged casually.

She was avoiding Tara. She had no desire to remember that afternoon, to talk about it, or to think about it. She wanted to keep the memory hazy, until she could deal with it.

"Of course you are, and I understand why." The woman moved into the room, and took a seat at the table as Marly sat down.

Still, Marly refused to look at her.

"It's hard, that first time. It offends your sense of morality, your sense of yourself, revealing things you didn't know before. I understand that. I've been there, Marly. It won't be as hard as you think it will be."

"I don't want to talk about this." Marly shook her head quickly. "I want to eat my snack, then go shower and go to sleep. I don't want to deal with it."

"If you don't deal with it now, how will you deal with it when Sam or Brock brings a lover into the house? You'll be expected to participate then, Marly. To not just accept the pleasure, but to return it. This is what Cade needs to prepare you for."

"And why would you agree to it?" Marly bit out. "What's in it for you?"

Tara's look was straightforward as she shrugged. "You're an attractive woman, Marly. It's something I would enjoy."

"Are you—?"

"A lesbian?" Tara laughed. "Not hardly. But there are joys to be found in it, just as there are joys to be found with a man. Cade knows me from the job we did on the neighboring ranch. He knows I like to play."

Marly's chest clenched with pain. Anger. "And have you 'played' with Cade?" She felt like throwing something in the woman's face.

Tara shook her head. "No. A friend of his, though. He just happened to have shown up at the time."

Marly bit her lip, her appetite now gone as she stared down at the fresh

peaches and juicy pears awaiting her.

Tara snagged a slice of the pear, and Marly's eyes rose in surprise when it was suddenly poised at her lips. Tara's deep green eyes were gentle when she rubbed the slick, dripping slice of fruit at Marly's lips.

"That's how it feels, Marly, and it tastes just as sweet. There's nothing to be frightened of." She pushed the fruit into Marly's mouth.

It was sweet and cool, running over her tongue like a sigh of bliss.

"You're not expected to accept it as you do Cade's touch, Cade's taste. But I know he expects you to enjoy it. To want it. They're tied in a way most siblings aren't. Bonded in a way that may be hard to understand, as they sheltered you from the harsher realities of their lives."

How did this woman, this stranger know so much more about her family than she did? Marly watched Tara, seeing the truth in her eyes, wondering how she could know so much.

"What do you mean?" Marly shook her head. "Cade wouldn't tell you everything. He wouldn't even explain it all to me."

"Everything? I don't know if anyone but those men know everything." Tara sighed roughly. "Did you know how their father abused them? He was a very dominant man, and he allowed his sons to be tutored in dominance by a dear friend of his," she sneered. "And they were forced to like it, Marly. Their very lives hinged on convincing themselves they could endure. That they could accept it. It changed them. Changed their sexuality and their feelings for each other."

"They aren't gay," Marly bit out.

Tara arched a brow curiously.

"Gay is a lifestyle, a choice. Sexuality is something else entirely, Marly. Cade much prefers a woman, dreams of you, lusts after you, but he also enjoyed a special closeness with his brothers when he was younger. A bond that is reaffirmed each time he watches one of them fuck a woman he's chosen. Each time he shares her, it's his way of showing his brothers his love for them, and for you. He wouldn't share you, the woman he loves more than his own life, with any other man except his brothers. But it's your choice. You can accept him, and what he needs from you, or you can walk away. Cade won't make you stay."

Walk away? How was she supposed to walk away from him?

"I don't know how to handle this," she whispered. "I don't like what I see in myself, Tara. It's not the 'me' I've always known. And I won't accept being with another woman. You are not part of this family. It's not acceptable."

"You just haven't accepted it. And he doesn't expect you to accept it overnight," Tara assured her. "He needs this, Marly. The four of you, closer than many couples could imagine being with siblings of either side. He needs it, because it's a part of him. Because it's also a part of you. And Cade knows it is. He won't let you hide from it."

"How do you know them so well?" Marly shook her head in bemusement. "You just came here."

"Because, in a way, I'm the same," she told her gently. "Rick is my brother in law, Marly, not my husband. I share his bed every night, and before my husband died, I shared a bed with both of them. I know what they are, and what they need, because it's the same for Rick and myself."

Marly swallowed tightly.

"He sent you in here, didn't he?" she whispered.

"Cade wants you to come into the family room. Sam, Brock, and Rick are there. A bed has been formed in the middle of the room. When we go in, we'll remove our clothes. You'll then be called to one of the brothers. He'll insert the plug into your rear. You and I will go to the bed, and pleasure one another. When we're finished, Cade, Sam and Brock will bring you into the family, Marly. You'll belong to all of them then."

Marly shook her head desperately.

"It's your choice, Marly," Tara told her gently. "You can come into the family room with me, or you can go to Cade's bedroom. If you do that, then he'll know it's your choice to find your own life after the danger is gone. He won't come to you. He won't take you, unless you do this."

Marly's eyes narrowed in anger. An ultimatum? She did not do ultimatums. Cade was pushing her. Pushing her too hard and too fast, and he should be smart enough to know that. If he didn't, then it was about time she let him in on that little fact.

She rose to her feet. Her hands went flat on the table as she went nose to nose with Tara.

"No man, least of all Cade, will make this choice for me," she bit out. "Not now, not ever, and not until I choose. And I'll be damned if I'll walk away just because he doesn't like it."

Tara frowned.

"Marly," she started warningly.

"Get lost, Tara. You and Rick are supposed to be tracking Jack Jennings, not fucking me. Go do your job, and I'll take care of Cade however I see fit. I don't like his high-handedness, nor do I care for his decision making, and he'll find that little fact out now."

She rose to her full, and she admitted diminutive, height and stalked through the house. Waiting on her in the family room, was he? She thought furiously. Had it all waiting for her. Had it all planned? She would do this. She would do that. She would kick all their asses first. Dammit, she wasn't about to let him dictate to her this way.

She stomped into the room, seeing everything laid out for her, just as Tara had said. Cade, Brock and Sam watched her in surprise as she faced them, her hands on her hips.

"The three of you. Don't even say a word. And you." She turned to Rick with a frown. "Don't you have a damned job to do? I'd like to swim in my damned pool sometime this year. So unless you want to personally move it into the house, maybe you should be out there tracking that bastard instead of waiting to get your jollies by seeing me get fucked."

Rick jumped to his feet, then frowned in surprise as he did so. He glanced at Cade.

"Hey, He-Man." Marly snapped her fingers at him. "It's not going to happen. Not tonight, not ever. You do your job, asshole and leave the rest of it to me."

Rick's lips quirked as he fought his smile. He stared down at her, fighting his smile, but a measure of respect flared in his eyes.

"Yes, ma'am." He nodded tightly. "I'll get right on that."

She turned to the men on the other side of the room as Rick and Tara left. Cade was watching her with a frown, his eyes glittering with dark, suppressed emotion.

"I'm not a robot you can order to perform," she told him harshly as she walked over to him. "I belong to you, and in some part to Sam and Brock as well, and I can accept that. The rest, you can ease me into, or you can kiss my ass and put up with me hounding you. But I will not be forced into a choice I'm not ready for. It's my choice, Cade, and I'll be damned if I'm going to be pushed into anything before I'm ready for it. Now, big boys, you strip. Let's see how you like being ordered around for a change."

"You'll be punished for this, Marly." There was laughter and a spark of desire unlike anything she had ever seen in his eyes.

"Yeah well, you get punished first." She gripped the middle of his shirt and jerked. Buttons went flying a second before he jerked her to him and ground his mouth down on hers.

She went on her toes, fighting to get closer to him, aware that she had inflamed all three men to a point of no return. Their hands were on her as Cade kissed her hard and deep, pulling her clothes from her body, fingers and lips roving over her nakedness, invading tight channels, groaning out at the slick liquid that eased their ways.

She was turned, Cade undressing quickly as Brock pushed her to the floor, his mouth going between her thighs, dining on her sweetness, moaning into her flesh. Sam's mouth attacked her breasts, and Cade knelt beside the small raised bed, pushing his cock into her mouth as she moaned in rising pleasure.

These men, they were hers. Cade held her heart the most, but the others had their little part as well. And they would share her body, her passion, because it was her choice, and because it brought her pleasure.

Orgasm after orgasm ripped over her as the moans in the room rose in volume. One after the other moved between her thighs, the soft, slurping sounds of thrust after thrust of eager tongues rising around them, Marly's cries echoing heatedly. And still it went on.

Finally, Cade lifted her above him, holding onto her weary body as he impaled her on his rising flesh.

"Rest, darlin'. We'll take care of you." He moaned as he pressed her sweat-damp head to his chest.

She felt Brock, or was it Sam behind her. Heat flared through her body as she felt the cool sensation of a thick lubrication as he slowly prepared her for his invasion. Minutes later, the thick head of his erection nudged the soft pucker of her anus. She relaxed for him, loosening her body, hearing his harsh groan as he slid deep inside her. Marly couldn't halt her cry of lust, or of pleasure so exquisite she felt seared.

Then another erection, hard and hot was being pushed past her lips as someone raised her head. Hard hands held her body steady, her eyes closed. She didn't care whose cock invaded her where. She was spiraling out of control, enclosed in a place where only heated moans, hard thrusts, and fiery desire ruled the moment. She arched, she cried around the thrusting flesh between her lips, and orgasm after orgasm tore through her body until finally, mercifully, she felt their last hot ejaculations into her, and collapsed wearily against Cade's chest.

Sleep rather than unconsciousness claimed her now. It no longer frightened her. She didn't have to hide. Not from these men, the ones who loved her best. There was no reason to hide, to escape. She was safe, well pleasured, and so tired she refused to move on her own.

* * * * *

Cade watched as Brock lifted a sleeping Marly tenderly from his body. He rose, sitting up as his brother carried her to the couch, laying her down on it as he breathed out wearily, staring down at her.

He knew what the other two were slowly realizing. Climaxing in Marly's body was more satisfaction than he had ever known, had ever believed possible. Sam was lying on the other couch, fighting to catch his own breath, and Brock finally collapsed at the end of Marly's couch.

"Son of a damned bitch," he breathed out heavily, his eyes meeting Cade's. "If I had known that, she would have never started college to begin with."

Known her passion, her strength of will, her acceptance of them. It was what Cade had feared, that she would be unable to accept total surrender to the three of them.

"She's going to kill us, if we keep up like this," Sam muttered. "Damn, did we ever have a woman that could take each of us, then all of us again?"

They hadn't. They had been forced, the few times it had happened, to space the passion to allow for the women and their lack of ability to endure their passion.

"So what now?" Brock asked, his head resting on the back of the couch. "What do we do when they find Jennings?"

Cade looked at him in some surprise. "I marry her. She's not leaving, Brock. She made the choice, she won't back away from it now."

Brock grinned. "Well hell, she'll keep us busy if nothing else. Maybe we need to hire more cowboys. I don't think I want to ride fences anymore."

Cade chuckled. He moved over to his woman, seeing the flush of satisfaction on her face, her body marred with moisture and their combined releases. She was the most beautiful sight he had ever seen.

"Come on, you two can help me get her bathed and into bed. I don't think she's willing to wake up for it."

He rose, bent and lifted her into his arms. She grumbled tiredly, grimacing at being disturbed then settling against Cade's chest with a sigh. He felt his heart swell. Not his cock, he thought, his heart. She filled him in ways he could not have believed possible.

With Sam and Brock following him quickly, he strode upstairs. He wanted her to rest, and he knew she wouldn't do so as the sweat began to dry on her body. She would bitch about the bath, maybe, but when her head hit the pillows, she would sleep, as she never had. And Cade knew, he would as well.

Chapter Twenty-nine

ဆာ

All her jeans were gone, as were her shorts. There was nothing in her closet, or Cade's, except her dresses. She tore one of the longer, full-skirted sundresses from a hanger and dragged it over her head. Her bras were missing too; thankfully, her breasts were full and firm, and looked good without one. It was the principal of the matter, though.

For the past week, Cade had kept her to himself, both in bed and out of it. He hadn't shared her with Brock and Sam, or made any strange demands on her. His passion was still hot and drove her crazy as he pushed her past peak after peak. It was as though that night in the family room was a dream. At least it was until this morning.

Before leaving their room Cade had laid out the plug, and the lubricating jelly, giving her a hard, speaking glance before leaving. She knew well that he meant for her to use it.

Gritting her teeth in irritation at his highhandedness, even as her vagina wept in excitement, she completed dressing, hastily braided her hair and slipped into a pair of strappy sandals.

"Marly, are you coming down sometime today?" Cade called from downstairs, his voice raised, imperious as he urged her to hurry.

Shaking her head, she adjusted the dress, then hurriedly left the bedroom.

"Cade August, I want my blue jeans back," she bit out as she went as fast as the device up her rear would allow. "I need them."

Then she came to a stuttering halt. Cade stood with his back to the opposite wall, his hand raised above his head as he faced the demon from Marly's past.

Jack Jennings stood there, too real, too dangerous to accept. The threat they had fought through the long days of the past weeks could no longer be avoided. Marly's heart jumped in terror, her throat closing, making her breath heave through her chest.

He was tall, in reasonably good shape, and watching Marly with a flushed, hollow-eyed expression that terrified her. It reminded her of the night her mother had run with her, and how much she had hurt from his touch. As rough as Cade had been with her several times, he had never hurt her, not really. This man, Marly knew, would kill her.

"There's my little girl," Jack Jennings sneered as Marly stared at him in horror. "Bout time you got down here to greet your daddy."

Marly felt her body chill. He looked insane, his brown eyes as maniacal as ever as he watched her now. She could smell the stench of his evil as his body shifted, bringing him closer to her.

"Why are you here?" Marly clutched the banister desperately, feeling fear and fury overwhelming her.

He laughed low, like a monster ready to destroy.

"Why, I've come for what's mine of course," he bit out, reaching out and gripping her arm as he dragged her to his chest. "You should have known I'd be here after that little show your lover put on last week, Marly."

She felt her knees weaken, remembering Cade's deliberate taunting of him.

"How pretty you were, all bent over while he shoved that thing up your ass." He gripped her breast, causing her to cry out hoarsely. "Got you all nice and ready for me, little girl."

"You're crazy," she gasped, her heart wild with terror as he wrapped his arm around her, jerking her close to his body.

"That's not nice, Marly," he whined low against her ear, his hot breath making her stomach heave with fear. "I'll make you pay for that later. When my dick is ramming down your throat, you'll beg to take that back."

She would die first. Marly knew she would die before she could ever bear to let this man take her. If he didn't kill her, then she would kill him.

Marly shook her head desperately, tears filling her eyes as she watched Cade's tormented expression. She had to do something. He had that gun at her head now, knowing Cade wouldn't make a move against him if it meant her life. She met his gaze, saw his fury and denial a second before she moved.

She screamed out, ducking and ramming her hip into Jack's crotch as she turned sideways, falling to the floor and rolling against his legs as he caught to keep hold of her. But it was too late. Cade was on him like a madman, then Rick, Brock and Tara were rushing into the house.

Rick jerked her out of the way, pushing her to Tara as he joined Cade and Brock in restraining the more than surprised Jack Jennings. He was cursing; vowing vengeance, but a fist to his jaw shut him up quickly as Rick grew tired of listening to it.

"Son of a bitch." Cade stared at Marly in amazement.

"I took a class at college." She shrugged uncomfortably, not daring to believe it was really over. "Cade, I really need a drink if you don't care. I don't feel so good."

Adrenaline crashed around her. The edges of the room rolled and grayed, leaving her lightheaded as Cade swung her up in his arms.

"Honey, you can have the whole damned bottle," he promised her, carrying her into the study.

She heard Rick talking to the sheriff on the phone; the cowboys' excited voices as they realized something had happened as well and rushed into the house. Cade propped her carefully on the couch, then rushed to the bar. He mixed her drink, barely daring to take his eyes off her as he did so.

"I can't believe I did that." She shook her head as Tara sat down beside her, watching her in concern.

"It's all over, Marly," she promised as Cade helped Marly hold her drink while she sipped desperately from it. "You're safe now. How does it feel?"

"Like it never happened." She shook her head. "This is going to hit me later, isn't it?"

"Most likely." Tara grinned, rising to mix her own drink now. "I think it will take a while for it to hit any of us. You did what none of us could do, caught the bastard off guard."

"She's good at doing that to everyone." Cade shook his head, his surprise and pleasure still glowing in his eyes. "Bastard got right into the house before we knew it. Twenty-five men looking for him, and Marly took him down. Why doesn't that surprise me?"

"She's an amazing woman," Tara agreed with him as she swallowed a large measure of whisky. "Better keep her, Cade. You won't find another like her."

"Oh, definitely." He stared into Marly's eyes. "Forever. Right, Marly?"

Marly breathed out in surprise at what she read in his face.

"Forever?" she asked him hesitantly, her lips parting in hope and fear.

"Definitely forever, baby." He leaned forward, kissing her parted lips softly. "Marry me, Marly?"

"What?" She whispered as he dragged her dress desperately over her thighs, pulling her to the edge of the couch as the other hand tore at the fastening of his slacks.

She felt her drink leave her hand, only vaguely aware that Tara had rescued it as Cade spread her thighs and after hurriedly testing her readiness, thrust his cock deep and hard into her hot channel. Gripping her hips, he began to fuck her in slow, consuming thrusts that had her crying out for release. Her legs wrapped around his hips, her hips lifting to him as her pushed into her over and over again. Gasping, fighting for breath, she met each thrust of his thick shaft into her body.

"I love you, Marly," he groaned, his voice strangled as he jerked her forward, taking her lips in a kiss that touched her very soul.

His tongue speared into her mouth, tangling with hers as he felt between her thighs and slowly pulled the plug free of her rear. Marly arched, cried out, and climaxed with a shattered cry, before he pulled her to the floor, bent her over the couch and pushed into that tighter, hotter entrance.

Her back bowed, a cry strangling in her throat as she felt him fill her once again. Then he was pushing into her hard and fast, driving them as their senses exploded as swiftly as their bodies, leaving them gasping in the aftermath of a release so vicious it still shuddered through their bodies minutes later.

Cade held her close, tight, his body still a part of hers. The heat and hardness that was always a part of him heated her to her soul. His breathing was rough, matching the jerky rhythm of hers.

"Mine," he whispered at her neck, his lips caressing the damp skin there.

"Mine." She smiled, knowing that finally it was true.

If she worried that the threat against her seemed conquered so easily, then she refused to allow it to mar this moment of happiness that she knew Cade needed so desperately. If she feared the choice she had made had done little to still his demons, then she assured herself that her love would at least ease the way. He loved her. She knew that now, and she prayed that together they would defeat the demons of his past, and problems that could arise in their future.

Epilogue

ɞ

Brock was a man driven. A man who had reached the end of his fragile control. He stalked through the gym, bypassing the curious looks, the worried frowns and headed for the back corner where a male worked out among the heavy weights under the lustful eye of the young woman cooing over his bulging muscles.

Rage surged through his veins, pounding with a rhythm of fury that he found hard pressed to control. When he reached the man, he jerked the weights out of his hands and threw them to the floor. The resulting thunder of the action had the cavernous room going deathly silent.

"Hey, are you crazy?" Mark Tate bit out, then gasped as he was grabbed by the front of his thin muscle shirt and thrown heavily against the wall.

Brock didn't give him time to retaliate. In a quick move, he had his hand wrapped around Mark's throat, leaving only meager room for the man to breathe. Desperate hands gripped at his wrist, but Brock only tightened the hold.

"Divorce her," he growled furiously, a killing rage surging through him as he glanced at the scantily clad 'other woman' that always seemed to shadow Mark. "Sign the papers or I'll make you wish you had. You understand me?"

Mark knew exactly who and what Brock meant. He had been warned. Brock had made certain of that when he learned Sarah had been asking for one.

"My wife," Mark gasped.

Brock tightened his hold, watching dispassionately as the other man paled.

"My woman," Brock amended. "Mine. And I mean to have her."

Mark nodded with a jerky movement. Brock eased the pressure on his throat.

"Whose woman is she, Mark?" he asked him coldly.

"Yours," Mark gasped.

"Sign the papers," he ordered him again. "You have until tomorrow evening to get it done. If you don't, and I find you again, I promise, I'll hurt you."

Mark nodded. A stilted, painful movement against Brock's hand. Slowly, Brock released him.

"Don't make me kill you, Mark." He leaned close to whisper the words. "This time, I promise, I will."

Unnoticed, quiet and hidden, the watcher observed the confrontation. It had been by luck alone that he was there when Brock stalked in, that he was close enough to hear all but the last, whispered words.

It was the woman. It was always a woman. His fists clenched in fury. Hatred, dark and all consuming, surged through him. First Cade, victorious in claiming his Marly, and now Brock, thinking he could do the same. If it were allowed to continue, then Sam would seek his happiness. Sam could not be allowed to believe he could seek his happiness. But if Brock, the oldest twin succeeded, then Sam would believe he could as well.

The watcher contained his smile, as he contained his rage. He would take care of Sarah before she could be claimed. Before she was taken to the ranch, before she was given as a sacrifice to the past, he would take care of her. Enough sacrifices, and the demons of pain could be assuaged. He couldn't allow the demons to quiet. Never to quiet. It was the demons and their whispered voices that led him, planned with him, assured him of the betrayer's downfall. The demons needed blood. And blood they must have. The blood of innocence to pay for the blood of death.

He watched Brock stalk out of the gym, then looked to Mark. Good ole Mark. He sneered remembering how easily he was to manipulate. How easy it was to guide him. Yes, just as with Jack, Mark would work out fine. The demons would never be silenced.

Why an electronic book?

We live in the Information Age—an exciting time in the history of human civilization, in which technology rules supreme and continues to progress in leaps and bounds every minute of every day. For a multitude of reasons, more and more avid literary fans are opting to purchase e-books instead of paper books. The question from those not yet initiated into the world of electronic reading is simply: *Why?*

1. *Price.* An electronic title at Ellora's Cave Publishing and Cerridwen Press runs anywhere from 40% to 75% less than the cover price of the exact same title in paperback format. Why? Basic mathematics and cost. It is less expensive to publish an e-book (no paper and printing, no warehousing and shipping) than it is to publish a paperback, so the savings are passed along to the consumer.

2. *Space.* Running out of room in your house for your books? That is one worry you will never have with electronic books. For a low one-time cost, you can purchase a handheld device specifically designed for e-reading. Many e-readers have large, convenient screens for viewing. Better yet, hundreds of titles can be stored within your new library—on a single microchip. There are a variety of e-readers from different manufacturers. You can also read e-books on your PC or laptop computer. (Please note that Ellora's Cave does not endorse any specific brands.

You can check our websites at www.ellorascave.com or www.cerridwenpress.com for information we make available to new consumers.)

3. *Mobility.* Because your new e-library consists of only a microchip within a small, easily transportable e-reader, your entire cache of books can be taken with you wherever you go.

4. *Personal Viewing Preferences.* Are the words you are currently reading too small? Too large? Too... ANNOYING? Paperback books cannot be modified according to personal preferences, but e-books can.

5. *Instant Gratification.* Is it the middle of the night and all the bookstores near you are closed? Are you tired of waiting days, sometimes weeks, for bookstores to ship the novels you bought? Ellora's Cave Publishing sells instantaneous downloads twenty-four hours a day, seven days a week, every day of the year. Our webstore is never closed. Our e-book delivery system is 100% automated, meaning your order is filled as soon as you pay for it.

Those are a few of the top reasons why electronic books are replacing paperbacks for many avid readers.

As always, Ellora's Cave and Cerridwen Press welcome your questions and comments. We invite you to email us at Comments@ellorascave.com or write to us directly at Ellora's Cave Publishing Inc., 1056 Home Avenue, Akron, OH 44310-3502.

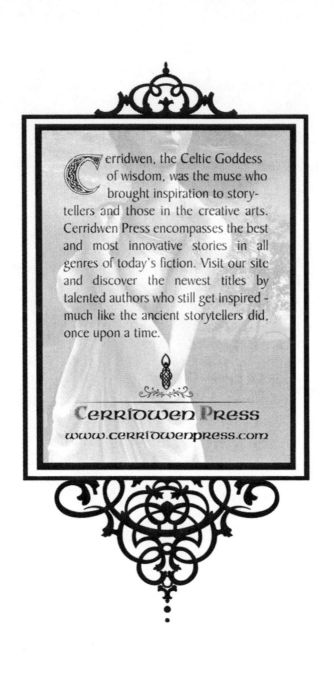

erridwen, the Celtic Goddess of wisdom, was the muse who brought inspiration to storytellers and those in the creative arts. Cerridwen Press encompasses the best and most innovative stories in all genres of today's fiction. Visit our site and discover the newest titles by talented authors who still get inspired - much like the ancient storytellers did, once upon a time.